DAUGHTER OF CHAOS

A DRAGONHEIR NOVEL

BY

SARAH EDGERTON

Lake Charles, LA

Copyright © 2023 Sarah Edgerton

Published by Elizabeth Hawk Publishing

Lake Charles, LA

Edited by Sasha Boyce and Carlene Meredith Cogliati

Cover Art by Beautiful Book Covers by Ivy

Map by Dawn Morton

All rights reserved.

ISBN: 979-8-9886036-0-3

ISBN: 979-8-9886036-1-0

To Michael: Your unwavering love and support were the foundation of this journey.

To Dexter and Penelope: You will always be the magic within me. You inspire me more than any words can express.

To Lea and Meagan: You were the light in the darkness of my self-doubt. Thank you for believing in me.

To Carlene: Thank you for your guidance and willingness to teach me.

The Order of Dragons

Chaos Dragons - Chaos Dragons are the most powerful Dragons to exist. They created the unnamed world and the Elemental Dragons. Their scales are colored in exquisite shades of purple from the deepest violet to the richest amethyst. Their eyes are an intense violet. They can wield all magic.

Chaos Dragongoddess: Nimerah
Chaos Dragongods: Ragnar and Amram

Fire Dragons - Fire Dragons command the flames, breathing forth infernos from within. Their scales are colored in shades of crimson, orange, and gold. Their eyes are like the flames with red and specks of gold intertwined. Their secondary power is shapeshifting.

Fire Dragongod: Vukan

Water Dragons - Water Dragons embody the mysterious waters, conjuring torrents that can both cleanse the senses and engulf their victims. They can manipulate water in any form. Their scales are colored in shades of cerulean, turquoise, and sapphire. Their eyes are dazzlingly blue. Their secondary power is telepathy.

Water Dragongoddess: Anahita

Earth Dragons - Earth Dragons are one with nature. They can connect to the earth itself, shaping mountains, summoning tremors, and upheaving the landscape. Their scales are colored in shades of greens and mossy hues. Their eyes are green like the forest trees. Their secondary power is strength.

Earth Dragongoddess: Dhara

Air Dragons - Air Dragons are ethereal and intelligent. They can harness the power of the wind, creating gusts and whirlwinds that sweep through the air. Their scales are colored in shades of gray and silver. Their eyes are sparkling silver. Their secondary power is empathy.

Air Dragongoddess: Ilmari

Light Dragons - Light Dragons hold power over the light of the world. They can illuminate any space at any moment. Their scales are colored in shades of iridescent white that reflect the sun. Their eyes are bright white. Their secondary power is healing.

Light Dragongod: Endrit

Darkness Dragons - Darkness Dragons embody the essence of night, harnessing shadows and plunging the brightest day into absolute darkness. Their scales are colored in shades of gray and black, making it easy to disappear into the veil of night. Their eyes are an unsettling onyx. Their secondary power is teleportation.

Darkness Dragongoddess: Tamasvi

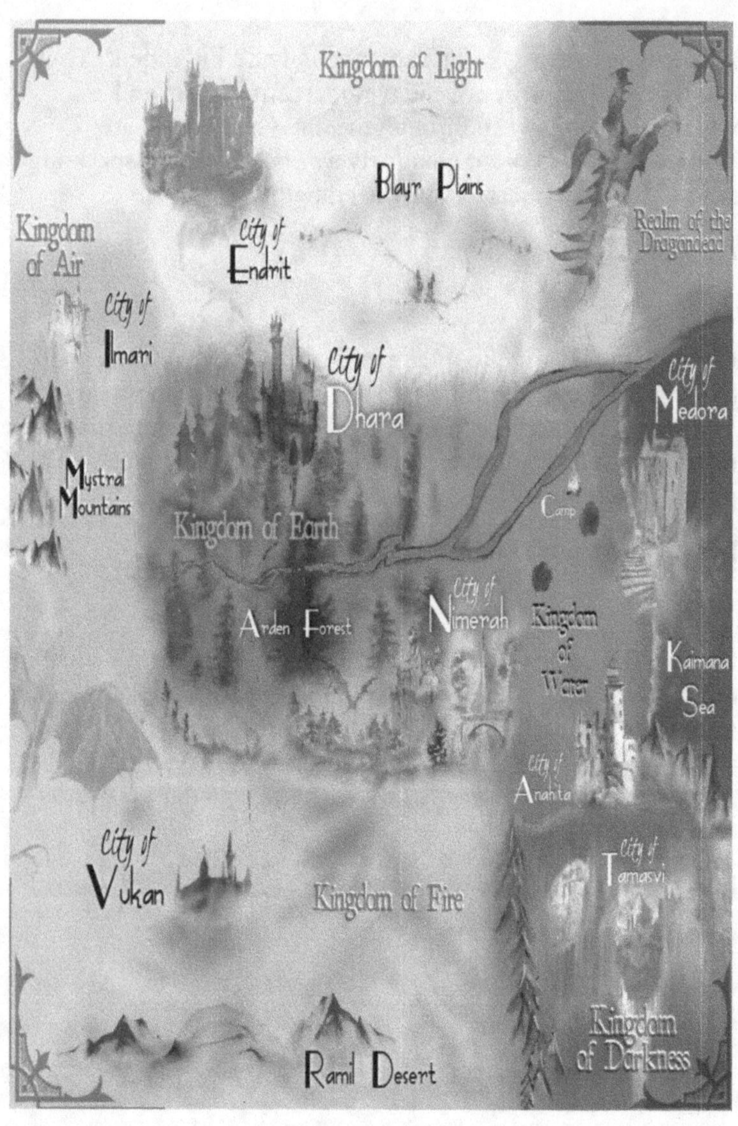

Kingdom of Light
Blayr Plains
Kingdom of Air
City of Endrit
Realm of the Dragonlord
City of Ilmari
City of Dhara
City of Medora
Mystral Mountains
Kingdom of Earth
Camp
Arden Forest
City of Nimerah
Kingdom of Water
Kaimana Sea
City of Ananta
City of Vukan
Kingdom of Fire
City of Tamasvi
Ramil Desert
Kingdom of Darkness

CHAPTER

ONE

I rolled my head back from one side to the other, stretching my neck as a yawn escaped my parched throat. I was tired and thirsty. But it was my own fault being out so late, huddled beside Medora's small church. A light breeze flowed throughout the port town, giving me slight relief from the moist air which was nice, considering how thick my father's black tunic and pants were. I'd worn them to remain hidden, but now I wished I'd gone with something lighter. I checked my surroundings once more and silently prayed to the Dragongoddess Anahita for good luck, even if she probably didn't condone breaking into a church dedicated to her. No matter. I was going to succeed with or without her help.

It was past midnight, and the town was quiet. Most of the townspeople had settled in for the night, but some houses were still lit with candles in the windows. The moon gave just enough light for me to see inside the church from where I crouched beneath the east stain-glass window. I lifted myself up and peered inside. My eyes scanned the altar at the front of the sanctuary, but my targets weren't on it. This wouldn't be as easy as I'd thought. I interlocked my fingers and extended my palms. A couple of slight pops from my knuckles loosened my fingers, and I proceeded.

I gave two short whistles to alert my best friend Dwyn that I was going in. The idea of stealing the Partition's ceremonial basin and dagger had been Nile Ford's, a pompous Dragonborn just two years older than me. Dwyn wanted nothing to do with it at first. She was…How could I put it? Delicate. But it hadn't taken much convincing. Dwyn seemed obsessed with being a Dragonborn. She wanted to see the basin and dagger for herself.

I stood slowly and lifted the windowpane carefully. I didn't think the window would be locked. That Dragonpriest Benigno was naive enough to think no one would attempt to break into the church. From what I was told, most, if not all, Dragonpriests and Dragonpriestesses were naive. They were hand-chosen by the Dragoncouncil, a group of Dragonpriests and priestesses with a representative from each of the six kingdoms. Rumor had it that the lesser priests and priestesses were sent to smaller towns and villages while the rest either lived lavishly in the cities of the kings and queens or within the City of Nimerah. I scoffed at the thought. That logic meant Medora was a lesser town even though it held one of the bigger ports in the kingdom.

The window lifted only slightly but still gave out a loud creak that pierced my ears, causing me to stop and drop to the ground. I waited and listened for footsteps, but none came. So much for using that window. That sound would wake the dead. I got back on my feet, keeping low to the ground, and crept to the backside of the church. If Benigno didn't lock the windows, he probably left the back door unlocked as well. Looking left, then right, I ensured no one was around. I turned the handle, half expecting it to stick.

I was relieved when it didn't.

I shook my head in disbelief as I opened the door slowly. With a wave of my hand overhead, I signaled Dwyn. Eventually, light steps came closer and closer.

"You did it," she whispered. She was a vision in black silk, making me scold myself internally for the clothes I'd chosen. Why hadn't I thought of silk?

"I told you I could."

She combed her hands through her soft black hair—a sign of her being nervous. "You still want to do this? If we're caught, Anahita will surely punish us."

"Correction, she will punish me. I'll claim you had nothing to do with it. I coerced you with my powers of mental manipulation."

Dwyn responded with a smile, but it didn't reach her eyes. They jumped back and forth between me and our surroundings. Yep. She was definitely nervous.

"Even if I was caught, it would still be worth it to see the look on Nile Ford's face," I replied curtly. I was going to show him that I wasn't—how did he put it? A lowly human coward.

Dwyn didn't answer, so I entered the back of the church, and she followed close behind. The Dragonpriest really needed to lock the place up. He was a nice man but too trusting, in my opinion.

I placed one foot tenderly in front of the other and snuck through a short hallway. I passed a door but hesitated and backed up, knocking into Dwyn.

"Could you give me a little more warning next time? That hurt," she said meekly.

Like I said…Delicate. "Sorry. If the ceremonial basin and dagger weren't on the altar when I looked through the window, maybe they are in Benigno's office."

Dwyn agreed. "That would make sense."

I tugged on the door handle, and it, too, was unlocked. I sighed in embarrassment for the Priest. I'd have to nonchalantly mention to him that the church being locked up was a good idea.

The door creaked slightly while I pushed it open, exposing the Dragonpriest's tidy office. Dwyn pulled out a match and lit the candle sitting on a small table beside the door. She was always prepared. I envied that about her.

The glow of the candle illuminated several bookshelves standing against the walls that contained numerous tomes dedicated to the Dragongods and Dragongoddesses; however, most were inscribed with the Dragonhead of Anahita. I ran my fingers across them as I walked by. They were old and musty, with dust lifting from the hardcovers from the brush of my fingertips. The tiny specks floated through the air with every touch.

I paused when my finger landed on the largest one. The War of Three was the thickest tome of Dragonpriest Benigno's entire collection. He probably claimed it was his most prized possession knowing him. I removed the tome from the shelf and turned it over in my hands. It was monstrous in size and weight. I bet it detailed the history of our unnamed world and the six kingdoms beginning with the betrayal of Ragnar to the sacrifice of Nimerah, and then to the formation of the six kingdoms by the Dragongods and Dragongoddesses to ensure no war ever broke out again. They thought they were doing the humans a favor. Instead, what they ended up doing was allowing their precious Dragonborns to take control and become wealthy and powerful while the humans became lesser citizens with no political power. Everything associated with the Dragonborns from that point forward had the word Dragon attached to it. It irritated me that I was to refer to everything that way. Dragon*this* and Dragon*that*. I refused to do it all the time.

I didn't hate all Dragonborns. The King and Queen of the Kingdom of Water seemed nice enough. I was human and lived a pretty comfortable life. But a lot of Dragonborns flaunted their powers, and it bothered me.

I stepped away from the bookshelf and admired the large wooden oak desk decorated with elaborate Dragon carvings. It sat in the center of the room with a plush blue chair behind it. Dwyn sat down in it and laid her eyes on the objects in front of her.

There they were, resting perfectly still on Benigno's desk: a deep sapphire blue basin and matching dagger. The sapphire blue of the basin represented the Dragongoddess Anahita, the Dragongoddess of Water.

A twinkle sparkled in Dwyn's hazel eyes. "They're so beautiful," she said.

"They're something," I muttered.

"Come on, Em. Even you can admit they're breathtaking."

"All right, all right, they're beautiful," I managed to say. Dwyn rolled her eyes.

A statue of the goddess sat perched next to the ceremonial basin; her scales were prominent but just the gray of the stone and not her signature blue. A short stack of texts detailing the history of the Partition sat next to the dagger, along with a detailed agenda for the ceremony. I eyed the list warily. Dwyn grabbed the list gracefully—another jealousy of mine—and read it with interest, her lovely face beaming.

The Partition was bittersweet. In early spring, humans who had turned eighteen would participate in the Partition to determine if any Dragonblood lay dormant within their human blood. The activation ritual would test a human's blood, and if any trace of elemental Dragonblood was found, the human would connect with that element. Scales would appear from the hairline above the temples on one's head and travel behind the ears, down the side of the neck, across the shoulders, and down the arms to the fingertips. The scales would be the color of the Elemental Dragon the new Dragonborn connected with red for Vukan, blue for Anahita, green for Dhara, gray for Ilmari, white for Endrit, and black for Tamasvi. At that point, the human became a Dragonborn, and their mortal lives were no more.

New Dragonborns were immediately sent to live in the kingdom that coordinated with their god or goddess. Luckily, most candidates connected with the Dragon of their present kingdom. If any of my peers were to have dormant Dragonblood, the blood they carried would most likely connect them to the goddess Anahita. They would remain in the Kingdom of Water for their training and most likely, the rest of their lives. However, it wasn't impossible for Dragonblood from another Elemental

Dragongod or Dragongoddess to be awakened. Those Dragonborns would be taken to their rightful kingdom—as the Priest proclaimed—and would then learn how to wield their Dragonmagic.

To me, the Partition was just another day. It didn't signify anything. The history of my family was clear: I was not a Dragonborn in any sense. My mother, father, and all distant relatives had no trace of Dragonblood. Through each Partition, the Edevane family tree continued to be void of any Dragonborn branches. Therefore, the Partition would tell me what I already knew, which was that I would not manifest any magical abilities.

"Okay. We found them. Let's get them and get out," I said. I walked hurriedly to the desk and tossed the bag at my hip onto its surface. Dwyn handed me the dagger exactly when I reached for it.

"Ouch!" I cried out. The dagger had slipped from her hand, slicing my palm.

"Em, I'm so sorry," Dwyn said.

"It's okay," I told her, but I still winced when I raised my palm to inspect the damage. The dagger managed to cut my skin deep enough that blood pooled at the cut.

"Are you sure you're okay?" Dwyn asked, her voice heavy with worry.

"Yes."

Dwyn rummaged through the desk drawers. "I don't see a cloth. I'll go find one. Maybe you should hold your arm over the basin so that it doesn't stain the desk."

She left with some newfound bravery I didn't know she had. I contemplated her suggestion, but I didn't want to ruin the basin. It was beautiful, and I wanted to keep it that way. We'd take it, show Nile, and put it right back minutes before the Partition. Then maybe Nile would leave me alone.

I applied pressure to my wound hoping the bleeding would slow down. But while doing so, blood dripped from my elbow into the dish. I cursed—unladylike, I know—and immediately pulled back my hand. I peered into the basin and then at the Dragongoddess of Water's small statue.

"I guess you think I should clean that up?" I asked sarcastically. Silence answered me, accompanied by the statue's chilling stare. "Settle down. I'll do it when she gets back. Don't be so pushy."

"You must have lost too much blood. You're conversing with a statue," Dwyn teased, and I jumped. She'd made no sound when entering the room.

"Funny." I reached for the cloth she offered me and held it to my wound while she hastily wiped the basin and dagger clean. Once there was no trace of blood, I placed the basin, dagger, and bloodied cloth carefully into my bag and slid it off the desk. We hurried out of the office, and Dwyn shut the door behind me while I headed for the back door. Unlike when we'd entered, this time the knob wouldn't turn. I twisted and pulled with all my might, but the stupid door wouldn't budge.

"That's odd," I mumbled.

"What's odd?" Dwyn asked.

"The door won't open."

"Maybe it's blocked from the outside?"

"That would be our luck." I guessed the goddess Anahita wanted to see me caught. Honestly, I couldn't blame her.

The front of the church was visible to most of the town. If anyone happened to be up late, there was a chance I could be seen. Stealing—eh, borrowing without permission—was one thing. To do it from a church? I shuddered at the thought.

"Ugh! This was such a stupid idea!" I banged my fist on the door.

"Em," Dwyn said softly. "We're going to be fine, right?"

I closed my eyes and placed my forehead on the door, letting the cool wood wash my annoyance away. I needed to stay calm. "Yes, we'll be fine, Dwyn," I said.

I turned on my heels and walked back down the hallway into the sanctuary, although this time I didn't attempt to be stealthy. The clip-clop from the heavy soles of my shoes echoed throughout the hallway until I stopped at the entrance to the sanctuary. It was dark except for the slivers of moonlight shining through the few windows. The breeze had picked up outside because tree branches scraped against the glass.

Gods, this is creepy, I thought.

I moved hastily toward the front door, the moonlight my guide. The quietness of the small church grew eerier—how that was possible, I couldn't say—with every step I took down the aisle. The vacant pews now seemed to stretch on and on. Sounds of the floorboards creaking, the tree branches scratching, and the wind whistling joined together in a frightening song one only hears in nightmares.

Get it together, Em. You're acting like a fool.

But something in the sanctuary shifted midway down the aisle, and I could feel a sense of energy permeating through my body. It was cool and fluid, like a running stream. It began at my fingertips and quickly spread through my entire body. My breathing became ragged, and the beating of my heart quickened. I normally held my fear in check, but the feeling wasn't like any other. I looked at my palms in utter surprise.

Blue scales appeared on my hands and traveled up my arms. Dragonborn scales. I gasped. *What the hell is happening?* I thought. This wasn't right! I wasn't a Dragonborn. I couldn't be. I was only seventeen. It was impossible.

"Em? Why did you stop? Is something wrong?" Dwyn tried to keep her voice calm, but there was worry there. The bravery she'd displayed earlier finally succumbed to her nervous nature.

My breathing hitched, and I fell to the floor, my knees connecting with the hardwood first. I grabbed my throat, frantically trying to understand the sensation I was feeling. It felt like…like…drowning. I stayed there for a moment until I no longer had to gasp for air.

"Emera Edevane! You are not okay!" Dwyn scolded.

"It's…oh...kay…" I told her through shallow breaths. Great. Now I sounded like a panting dog. "It's…oh…kay…I'm…okay." Maybe if I kept saying everything was okay, even I'd believe it.

Dwyn rushed to my side. I pushed myself up from the floor, ignoring the pain from my injured palm. I stumbled but finally stood on my feet. I looked at the front door, willing it to be closer, and staggered toward it, my hands gripping the ends of the pews to keep me upright.

Suddenly, a faint glow of cerulean blue emitted past my body, causing a shadow on the door. I stopped and glanced behind me to see the statue of Anahita now sitting on the altar. Where the color of gray mist had been, its eyes suddenly glowed, casting a shadow beyond me.

Surely that wasn't the statue from the office. It couldn't be, could it? I rubbed my eyes and reopened them. The statue was still there, and its eyes still glowed. I stared for what seemed like hours. Did Dwyn see this too? Was she just as captivated by it?

My fear subsided, and I was mesmerized by the beauty of the statue's eyes. My body calmed, and my senses opened. I became acutely aware of all my surroundings.

Within seconds, a faint, lovely voice in a language I didn't recognize began to fill the church. It was like a beautiful song from the finest harps. It grew louder and louder. *I needed to be near it.* I crept back to the altar, my face angled to inspect the statue's now vibrant eyes.

Dwyn followed me to the altar. "Em? We need to go. This is terrifying."

I stood before the statue with my hand stretched out to get the slightest touch. *I needed to touch it.* The song called to me, and the energy that previously felt like it was suffocating me had now completely transformed into filling a sense of peace within my soul. All I wanted was to touch it. *I needed to touch it.*

My trance-like state snapped when the front doors crashed open, and Dragonpriest Benigno's angry voice filled the air. "What in Anahita's name is going on here?" A second passed. "Emera," he said slowly, the anger fading from his voice. It was probably an unusual sight to behold me staring at a statue with glowing eyes, clutching my bag with an injured hand.

I kept my eyes locked on the statue. "It is…calling to me," I whispered.

"Miss Brizo," the priest said to Dwyn, "I think you should leave immediately."

"I'll be at our usual spot," she called to me.

"Miss Edevane, however, will not," replied the priest.

I wanted to tell him that he had no authority over me and that I would meet her there, but I didn't. I forced myself to tear my gaze away from Anahita and turn around. Dwyn was gone, and the Priest Benigno looked like he'd seen a ghost. He cautiously took a step toward me. "You are injured. Let me take you home." He didn't yell. He didn't scold. He didn't demand to understand my intentions. He just walked toward me and searched my face for any sign of sanity.

The still, tranquil feeling in my body began to dissipate, but all I could do was nod in agreement. I should take care of my hand. I discarded my bag on the first pew, and Priest Benigno hooked his arm within mine. His seafoam eyes were soft behind his round glasses, indicating no signs of anger or hostility. His rather large stomach still hid beneath the blue robe with vibrant, almost silver-like white stitching that he'd worn during our private tutoring the previous afternoon. I studied my scales and compared them to his. His scales had once been the same exquisite blue as mine, but they had faded with age. The slight frown beneath his short white beard didn't escape me, though. He didn't look angry, just puzzled.

I welcomed the saltwater air into my lungs and took a deep breath once we were out of the church. Priest

Benigno and I made our way through the small town of Medora to the docks by the bay. Medora was nestled by the Kaimana Sea at the edge of the Kingdom of Water, right by the border to the Kingdom of Light. The town was populated with homes, businesses, and a thriving fisher's market. The scent of saltwater and a cool breeze permanently drifted throughout the town. It was a home I had grown to cherish regardless of how I felt about fishing. Stupid fishing. I imagined the children playing after lunch and several townspeople carrying cargo from the incoming vessel. The memory eased my heartbeat into a steady rhythm, and I smiled.

"Quickly," he demanded.

I looked ahead but couldn't see anything that he would be fixated on, so I quickened my pace for home. Priest Benigno didn't notice I'd left him behind. Well, he'd said I needed to move quickly. If that is what he wanted, that is what he'd get.

The apothecary I called home sat at the beginning of the docks, close to where shipments from other kingdoms arrived. I was accustomed to meeting new people and learning all about the other kingdoms. I took pride in my knowledge of the world and—arrogantly, I'll admit— deemed myself more cultured than others my age. The mountains within the Kingdom of Air, the vast forests within the Kingdom of Earth, and the expansive caves within the Kingdom of Darkness fed my curiosity. The stories I heard from travelers created dreams of grand adventures traveling all over the six kingdoms, searching for rare herbs and bringing them back to my family. I was destined to be nomadic, the open world my home.

All thoughts of adventure aside, I pushed open the large oak door and stepped heavily into the shop. Both my mother and father were still busy with their mortar and pestles, grinding herbs into fine powders. The cling-clang of stone on stone made my mood lift. I would never tire of the sight. Struan and Cordelia Edevane were the definitions of loving parents.

"You have some explaining to do," my mother warned. She stopped working, wiped her hands on her pale pink dress that was wrinkled and dirty from the long day's work, and dragged her eyes over me head-to-toe. Once she saw the scales, her demeanor abruptly changed.

"I'm sorry. It was stupid," I said with a haughty sigh. There was no use lying to her.

"Could it perhaps have something to do with the Ford boy you've been complaining about?" my father asked. He didn't look up from his work, continuing to crush and twist, crush and twist. His brown tunic also showed signs of labor abuse with white powder all over it. His trousers, also dark brown, looked the same.

"Are those scales?" my mother breathed.

Without thinking, the night's events came pouring out. "I cut my palm on the ceremonial blade for the Partition, and when I tried to stop the bleeding, some of my blood dripped into the ceremonial basin which caused the eyes of Anahita's statue to glow. Then these appeared." I held out my arm so they could examine the scales. A small headache formed, its pounding gradually increasing. I raised both hands and applied pressure, massaging each temple delicately.

"Emera," my father said in a low voice. He stopped working and opened his mouth to say more. But he didn't have time to say anything else because the priest entered. Priest Benigno looked around and walked into each of the rooms, pausing to hear any sounds. When he was satisfied that we were alone, he looked my parents in their eyes and nodded.

CHAPTER

TWO

"What are you talking about?" I asked.

Priest Benigno ignored me. "You must hurry with the final preparations," he said in a hushed tone. I glanced between the priest and my parents.

"How much time do we have?" my father asked.

"Not much," replied Priest Benigno. "The activation process has begun."

"This can't be. It's too early," my mother argued. "You said it wouldn't happen until the Partition when she's eighteen."

Although the Priest hadn't gone over the activation process of the Partition in my studies yet, I still knew the basics of the ritual. A human's palm was cut with a small fine blade of Dragonbone, and the blood was forced to drip into a ceremonial bowl on the altar. The priest or priestess recited the ancient invocation and should the blood transform into any color of an Elemental Dragon, the human was labeled as a new Dragonborn.

"This doesn't make sense. Tell me what is going on, now," I blurted angrily.

Tears stained my mother's cheeks. "Em, please come sit." She took my hand and guided me to a seat at the table.

"Mother, you're worrying me. I'm not a Dragonborn. It's not possible." She looked at me through full, wet lashes. Her eyes glistened, and at that moment, I knew. I knew I was wrong.

"What do we do now?" my father asked Priest Benigno calmly.

"Make sure she is ready to go. Have all of her belongings destroyed following her departure, and make sure…"

"Excuse me," I snapped. I'd had enough of being in the dark. "I am right here. Stop speaking as if I'm not capable of understanding the situation."

"Emera," my father began, "My honeybee." He crossed to the table and took my face in his hands. "Your mother and I have done all that we could to keep you safe from what lies ahead. We love you with all that we are."

"And no matter what is revealed to you, we are your parents," my mother added.

"The time has come for you to leave us," father continued. "You are our world, but the world is yours."

"What does that mean?" I demanded. My patience was wearing thin.

"You are a Dragonborn," chimed in Priest Benigno.

Frustrated, I groaned and turned to the Priest. "I figured that," I said sharply.

"But not just any Dragonborn. You, my dear, are *the* Dragonborn. You're the Dragonheir of Nimerah. The most powerful of the three Chaos Dragons. Do you know what this means? You're a Dragon of Chaos."

"Impossible," I said. "That's not a thing. A Dragonheir is just some made-up story told to human children to make them think some savior will come to their rescue and bring them out from under Dragonborn rule. The Dragonborn have fed that lie for ages."

"We know how unbelievable this sounds," mother said, "but it's the truth. You're a Dragonheir. The only one of Nimerah's bloodline to exist. And now that your powers have made themselves known, you're not safe."

Tears still dampened her eyes, but she was no longer crying. She was trying to be brave. And, knowing my mother, it was for my benefit and not hers.

I looked between them all and a deep laugh left my throat. Did they think I was just some gullible child? "Look, I'm sorry about tonight. I truly am." I faced Priest Benigno. "I didn't mean any harm. It was just a dare. I planned on giving everything back."

Priest Benigno cleared his throat, "This is serious business, Miss Edevane." I opened my mouth to speak, but my father stood and raised his hand to silence me.

"As we said, your mother and I hid this from you your whole life so that you'd be safe."

"Now that your Dragonblood has activated, you are in danger, Emera. We must get you out of Medora," Priest Benigno explained. He turned to my parents, "I must leave. I've stayed here too long. The Dragoncouncil needs to be informed that our plans have been pushed forward."

"You're leaving?" I cried. I noticed my hands were shaking, and I had unknowingly started bouncing my leg nervously.

"Cultists from all over the six kingdoms will be after you. I've been able to remain concealed in Medora, but now I must leave. If they know where I am, they'll connect me to you. Following your training, we will reunite in the Eternal City." The priest turned his attention to my parents. "She must be ready by nightfall tomorrow. I will make sure the deliverer will be here by then."

"Deliverer?" I pressed.

"The deliverer will be made aware of your activation. He will come to collect you and take you to a place that's location is confidential. There you will activate your remaining powers so that you can gain each Dragongod and Dragongoddess's blessings. Only with their blessings will you be able to fully wield their elements."

The adults looked at me. But if they expected me to respond, I would disappoint them. I furrowed my brows in concentration and let the words sink into every corner of my mind. Standing from my seat, I began to pace the room. The person I thought I was…was a lie. My entire life…was a lie. I felt the tears coming, but I balled my fists and dug my fingernails into my palms. I would not cry. I faced my parents.

"Will I ever see you again?"

The priest answered softly, "Once you leave this place, it is best that you remain on the path the prophecy has laid out for you. That means you should stay away from them."

I watched more tears cascade down my mother's flushed cheeks. My father stood in silence; his gaze downcast. I attempted to contain my fury, but my heart wouldn't allow it. "How long will it take for the prophecy to be fulfilled?" I demanded.

Priest Benigno took a moment to answer. "That I cannot say."

"So, it could be years before I can see them again?"

"Quite frankly, you may never see them again," he responded without hesitation.

His words punched me in the stomach. Mother rushed to my side and pulled me into her. From over her shoulder, I looked at my father.

He didn't protest. Because he agreed.

My mother pushed slightly away from me and grabbed me by the shoulders. Her silent tears had transformed into audible sobs.

"That's unfair," I snarled.

"Unfortunately, we do not get to decide what is fair and what isn't," Priest Benigno said. "The prophecy was written centuries ago." He glanced at me. "I know you have questions, and I admittedly do not have all the answers. But you will find them. You will become who you were born to be. You will save us all." He looked at my father and tipped his head, a silent acknowledgment that he was done. He backed up toward the door, sighed, and walked out the door, leaving me in shock, my mother crying, and my father silent.

After a moment, my father, with determined eyes, looked at me—his only daughter. He crossed the room and wrapped his arms around me. I inhaled his familiar scent of wood and spice. "None of this seems fair now, but we will be together again. The world will be right again. Until that day, we must be brave. We must keep moving forward, for our lives and the lives of others. We can make final preparations tomorrow. For tonight, let's just be us." He grabbed my hand and guided me to his favorite chair. Together, we sat in front of the fire and shared distant memories through our laughter and tears until the fire went out.

*   *   *

I willed my eyes open then blinked repeatedly. They burned with the glaring of the sun shining on my face, or maybe it was the lack of a peaceful night's sleep. My eyesight focused, and I took in the familiar surroundings of my own bedroom. I sat up, pushing the wool blanket off of me. Bits and pieces of the previous night's conversation drifted in my mind as I just sat and breathed. I sent Anahita a prayer that it had all been a dream.

A soft tap at the bedroom door brought me back to reality. My mother slowly opened the door and peeked her head through. "May I come in?" she asked.

"Of course," I answered. I shifted my body and swung my legs over the bed to make room for my mother.

"I wanted to see how you're doing…with…all of this," my mother said softly as she sat beside me.

So, it hadn't been a dream. Instead, I was living the nightmare. I paused, not sure what to say to her. I looked into her eyes, finding a mixture of love and worry.

"This all doesn't make sense. Until yesterday, the thought of being Dragonborn was impossible. I never entertained the idea because no one in our family had dormant blood. And now I'm a Dragonheir? Of a goddess?"

"It's a lot to take in. We had planned on easing you into it. We were going to explain it all little by little leading up to your Partition."

I uttered the words I'd been thinking but hadn't dared say out loud. "Am I even your daughter?"

At that moment, my father appeared in the doorway, leaning against the frame. His expression remained neutral while my mother's face fell. I processed their emotions and felt guilt immediately for even thinking about the question, but how could I not? I had to ask. Father exchanged a glance with my mother, and I silently noted the subtle differences between my parents and me. My mother's short golden hair fell to her shoulders, and her skin was tanned from multiple trips to the market. My father's short dark brown hair was cropped clean to his neck, streaked with gray. His eyes were like my mother's, a light blue green, the color of the sea under the shining sun. I looked down at my red hair that fell past my shoulders in thick, messy waves with streaks of gold and orange. My eyes were a dark brown like the rich chocolates my father would splurge on when merchants from the Kingdom of Earth visited. I'd always cherished my fire-like hair and brown eyes, but they now made me feel self-conscious, like I was an intruder in their home.

I continued to note the differences in appearance. My lips were fuller, and my nose sharper compared to my parents. Both of their lips were thinner, and their noses more rounded at the end, a clear indication of Waterion descent. In contrast, my skin was paler, and a light dusting of freckles appeared below the corners of my eyes. No matter how long I stayed in the sun, my skin would maintain its light color. It could have been worse though. At least I didn't get sunburns.

My father shook his head and broke the silence. "Until now, you've never had a reason to question your parentage. There might be a few differences between us that cannot be explained. Your hair, your eyes, your skin, for instance."

"I just thought I took after our ancestors," I mumbled.

"You take after *your* ancestors. But I don't want you to think for one second that we are not your parents. We will always be your father and mother regardless of our differences. Because it's not our appearances that make us family." He kneeled before me and placed one hand over his heart and his other hand on mine. "It's what's in here that connects us. Our hearts make us family."

I took a hold of his hand and squeezed it. "How long have you known?" I asked.

"Priest Benigno showed up on our doorstep many years ago," Mother said. You were just a baby. We tried for years to conceive a child with no luck. It seemed the Dragongods had other plans for us." A slow smile began at the corners of her mouth and was met by my father's smile that stretched across his face.

"He, Benigno, explained the situation several times. It was ludicrous," my father said laughing.

"We thought he was crazy," my mother added and chuckled. "A Dragonheir? A prophecy soon to be fulfilled? Utter nonsense!" I joined in their amusement with a smile of my own, but I couldn't quite bring myself to share in their laughter.

"It sounded crazy," Father admitted, his laughter subsiding. "But with each passing year, we discovered new differences between you and everyone else. From your appearance to your intelligence. From your compassion to your stubbornness." He stood and sat beside my mother.

"You were determined to succeed in anything you did," Mother added.

"Because of you," I pointed out. "Not because of some ancient heritage."

"Maybe," my father mused. "Regardless, you are who he said you were. We can't hide from it. Your journey begins now, my honeybee."

I could tell my father was trying to keep his feelings in check even though she could tell he was proud that his daughter was the savior to all six kingdoms. He'd never been an overly emotional man, so to see him struggling at maintaining his composure was new.

"May I go for a walk?" My question was met with uneasy glances between them. "I just need a moment to myself," I explained. I understood their apprehension at the thought of me going off somewhere by myself. I was a wanted woman after all.

"I think that would be all right," my father said. "But be quick about it. If you're not back shortly, I'm coming to look for you."

"And stay close to home," Mother added. She stood and headed for my small dresser. She opened the top drawer and pulled out a pair of long gloves. She then grabbed my hooded cloak that hung from one of my bedposts. "You'll need to conceal your scales."

I contemplated changing out of last night's clothes, but what did it matter, all things considered? I hopped off the bed, shoved my feet into my shoes, and bent down to tie the strings. I straightened and grabbed the items my mother offered to me. After fastening the hood close enough to my head that my scales were hidden, I tightly wrapped my arms around my mother and pressed my lips to her warm cheek. "Be back soon. I promise." I left my parents still sitting on the bed and descended the stairs leading into the shop portion of our home.

My senses all took in the comfort of my home from the view of the various herbs on the counter and the smell of the spices sitting on the shelves waiting to be purchased. A slight pain rose in my chest, as I put the moment to memory. Then I stepped into the sunlight of the day. My legs refused to move after the old oak door to the apothecary closed behind me. My back stayed flushed against it while I gathered my thoughts. The door was newer than most of the shop doors within Medora. A storm had claimed the town one distant summer, and the previous door was destroyed along with the windows and a portion of the roof. My father took me with him to locate a tree of solid oak, strong enough to withstand harsh storms. I remembered clearly the heat of the day and the laughter from silly stories. It was the perfect day. How many of these memories would I recall after I left my home?

The spring sun ricocheted off the ocean waves which would have blinded me had I not pulled my hood down to shade my eyes. When I'd finally reached the docks, I lifted my hand to block the glare when a sudden breeze floated through the air filling my lungs with the familiar scent of saltwater. I welcomed it since I was starting to sweat with all the layering I had on.

Tears welled up within my eyes, and I gulped to keep them at bay. I couldn't break. I wouldn't. I was strong and would get through this. My parents raised a strong-willed child, and no prophecy would change that.

Just like she said she would, I found Dwyn sitting at the edge of *our* dock. In the early mornings, we'd plan a rendezvous before our private lessons. The particular dock was currently out of commission, and by *currently*, it was pretty much permanent. The boards were faulty, so no one dared carry heavy crates of goods across them. We knew the flimsiest boards and where to step to safely make it to our spots.

Dwyn sat at the end of the dock. Her long hair was pulled into a knot at the base of her neck. She wore a modest pale blue dress with intricate stitching all over the skirt. Short sleeves enveloped her long arms just past her elbows. Her bare feet dangled over the docks, splashing in and out of the water. She was an absolute vision in the sun compared to me and my tangled hair and disheveled clothes. How did she look so perfect, like nothing happened last night? She acted nervously last night, but now? As cool as a spring rain shower.

"Good morning," she said when I sat down beside her. Her face twisted into confusion when she finally took in my appearance.

I hated this. How did one say goodbye to their dearest friend? A friend that needed protection from stupid boys like Nile Ford and a mean world.

"Good morning," I greeted, plastering a fake smile on my face. "I know. I know. I look like a fresh daisy ready to be picked." I twirled for her.

She pursed her lips. "Yes, that's exactly what I was thinking," she said. "Spill it. What happened after I left?"

"I had an interesting turn of events after Priest Benigno found us."

"And do those events have anything to do with your need to hide behind a hood? And why are you wearing gloves? It's not too warm, but it's definitely not cold." She eyed me suspiciously. So, she hadn't seen the scales last night.

My mind searched for an excuse but found nothing. "I need to tell you something else." I grabbed a strand of hair that had fallen into my face and nervously twisted it as I sat down beside her. I carefully took off my shoes and dragged my toes against the cool water. I drew in a deep breath and sighed.

"We're in trouble. I knew it," she said, taking mental notes of my actions now instead of my clothes. Her eyes began looking at me from top to bottom then left to right. "That's why you haven't changed."

"No. We're not in trouble." I exhaled. *Gods give me courage*. "I have to leave."

"Leave?" she asked, taken aback. "You said we weren't in trouble. Did you give back the basin and dagger? I mean, you apologized, didn't you?"

"Kind of. And we're not in trouble. All is forgiven."

"That makes no sense. You're not lying, are you?"

"No!" I said and laughed.

"You're worrying me now," she said slowly.

"You always worry about me," I pointed out. The pain that had formed in my chest began throbbing.

"Because you're not as well-behaved as everyone believes you are," she teased, and her lips curved into a graceful smile.

"If only I had your reserved nature, I'd be quite the lady."

"You are no lady."

"You're quite right," I agreed.

A tremble overcame her voice as she spoke. "What we did was wrong, but they cannot take you away from your home."

I placed my hand on her shoulder to steady her. "Trust me, Dwyn. It's going to be fine."

Her eyes darted back and forth, searching my face for more. "I cannot stop this, can I?" she asked.

"You cannot." I wished she could. I'd give anything not to be a Dragonborn, let alone a Dragonheir.

An unnatural, awkward pause followed, filling the air between us. I couldn't take the silence. "Remember the time Quinton Thornhill tried to kiss you outside of Old Pringham's tailoring shop?"

"You kicked him in the knees and pulled his hair," she finished the memory, and a light chuckle slipped between her thin lips. A faint smile touched her eyes briefly.

"If he, or any other boy for that matter, ever says anything inappropriate to you, you punch him square in the nose and kick him where it counts."

She brought her feet out of the water and hugged her knees. Tears started to well within her eyes. She struggled to keep them at bay.

I, too, brought my feet out of the water like she had. I twisted, crossed my legs beneath me, and looked my dear friend in her eyes. We stared at each other for a moment, and a knowingness settled between us. This was a goodbye.

"Will I ever see you again?" A single tear trickled down her rosy cheek.

There it was. The question I feared. Because I truly didn't know the answer. At least not unless the prophecy the priest mentioned was fulfilled. Would I fulfill my destiny? What if I didn't? I tilted my head toward the sun. My heart was breaking with each breath I took, but I managed to put strength into my bones. Dwyn wasn't just my friend; she was a sister. I released a deep, heavy breath. "I don't know."

She wiped her cheek. "All because of a basin and dagger."

I paused, thinking. I *needed* to tell Dwyn. Dwyn was rational whereas I would leap to conclusions. Dwyn always knew what to say when I fumbled my words. She knew how to steady my emotions. I confided in her. I laughed with her. I cried with her.

"Listen. What I'm about to tell you is going to sound absurd, but here it goes. My life is taking an abrupt turn into unknown territory." I glanced at her, and my stomach began to twist and turn from nervousness. I took off my gloves one at a time, exposing my scales. I heard a slight intake of breath, but that was it. I looked down at my scales that now glistened in the sunlight.

"I am supposedly a Dragonborn. But not just any Dragonborn. No, that would be too simple. I am *the* Dragonborn." I adjusted my voice, doing my best impression of Priest Benigno's gravelly voice. "I am the Dragonheir of Nimerah destined to rid the world of evil and bring in a new era of peace." I leveled my voice, "At least, that's what I'm guessing Priest Benigno meant by a prophecy." With our eyes still locked on one another's, I pushed back my hood.

Dwyn's eyes widened slightly, but she didn't react any more than that.

"So, how does it feel to be best friends with a Dragonheir?" I asked with an awkward laugh. "At least…that's what they say I am."

I closed my eyes for a moment, waiting for Dwyn to comment. The silent pause was deafening. Being Dragonborn was one thing…But to be the heir of Nimerah? I'm not sure how I'd handle it had our roles been reversed.

"I guess I'm honored," she finally said.

"Excuse me?" I asked, bewildered.

"I've always known you were different, Emera. Ever since I met you, you've just had this presence about you. Everything seems to work out for you. You're different. I just didn't know you were a Dragonborn. You always made it sound like that wasn't possible."

"It wasn't until last night."

The awkward pause returned. I understood the gravity of the situation and that news like this didn't just happen, but her silence left me on edge.

"So…Do you know where you're going?" she asked.

"Some secret location that no one knows about. The deliverer—as Priest Benigno called him—will come tonight and whisk me away. It's all ridiculous, really."

"Secret location. Sounds…*adventurous*. And you're to save the world," Dwyn said. I couldn't place her tone.

"I don't know. Maybe? Yes? I'm to fulfill some prophecy, and usually, prophecies mean saving the world, right? Although I don't know how I can," I replied.

"With powers, one would assume."

"Powers that I don't have," I insisted.

"Yet." She lowered her feet back into the cool, blue water and began kicking at the waves. She looked straight ahead, her eyes searching—for what, I couldn't say. She seemed deep in thought. I just stared at her, willing her to speak.

"This deliverer. He comes tonight?"

"That's what I was told."

"I guess this is goodbye then," she said softly.

"I guess it is."

And with that, Dwyn rested her head on my shoulder, and we silently watched the waves roll in.

*　　*　　*

After giving Dwyn my last goodbye—which had followed eight goodbyes before that—I stood by the fire back home. The spring air was warm enough that a fire wasn't necessary, but the crackles and twisting of the flames seemed to ease my heart. It didn't do much for my mind though. It was still a thunderous storm of electrifying thoughts.

A strong arm gently wrapped around my shoulder and pulled me closer. My father was there, holding me as the tears began falling. It was the first time since I'd heard the news that I let those emotions slip.

"I need you to be strong," he said gently.

"Always," I said, sniffling. I raised my arm and wiped away the tears. Father was right. I needed to show the strength he had instilled within me. I was my father's daughter, and I would make him proud regardless of what was to happen.

A crash behind us had both of our heads turning toward the door.

"Struan!" my mother cried out as she ran into the shop. Her heavy footsteps shook the staircase, and she stopped at the entryway to catch her breath. She bent over, placed both hands on her knees, and gasped for air. She reached one hand to her chest to steady her breathing and swiped her hair, now drenched with sweat, out of her eyes with the other. After a few seconds, she looked up to my father and me.

"Cult…ists…com…ing," she said between each ragged breath.

"But the deliverer isn't here," my father answered.

"And I don't have my things packed," I pointed out. My voice cracked. It was too soon. We still had hours before my departure. There was still so much more I wanted to say to them.

"There's no time," my mother responded. "I was visiting Yarela Blackwell when I saw horses outside the church and more in the distance. They had the marking the Dragonpriest showed us. It's them. They're here. Emera must go now."

CHAPTER

THREE

Father turned me toward him and cupped my hands in his face. "Remember that you are strong, brave, and smart. There are no bounds to what you are capable of. *You are our world, but the world is yours*," he repeated the words he'd said earlier to me. I held onto the words as we embraced. I lingered more than I should in his warmth, holding onto his earthy smell of wood and spice. He let go, and my mother quickly grabbed my hand, turning me to face her. She gave me a rushed hug and quickly kissed my cheek then pulled back and looked me over.

"You are more than we could have ever dreamed of for a daughter. I love you so much." She tried to keep her composure but failed. Her silent tears became sobs.

"I don't want to go," I mumbled, my mouth wet from my tears. As much as I tried to be strong, I couldn't hold back the tears. "I'm not ready," I stammered.

"I know," she breathed. She lifted her hand to my cheek and touched it tenderly. Our hearts were breaking together. She pressed her forehead to mine. It was her final act of affection.

My father grabbed my hand and led me down the stairs. I glanced around quickly one last time and put it all into memory: my family's shop, my home, my life. With a mental goodbye, and the sound of my mother crying in my ears, I rushed after my father who was already out the door. The door slammed behind me, and my anxiety rose. I could hear shrieks from the townspeople and the thundering of hooves getting closer. The stench of burning wood filled my nostrils. I squinted and looked as far into town as I could manage. People were fleeing as flames engulfed the church. The dark smoke ascended into the air and spread, blanketing the surrounding shops. The sound of the cultists continued to get louder as they closed the distance between them and our shop.

"To the docks!" my father shouted. He again took my hand and forced me to run. We weaved between houses and shops doing our best to stay off of the main road. We couldn't risk being seen by the cultists who were surely almost to the shop.

"What about mother?" I panicked. She was still there. Bile instantly rose into my throat, closing it off, and I began coughing. All of the destruction was because of me. And I was some powerless Dragonheir that couldn't do anything to help.

"She knows what to do. She can handle herself," Father assured me. "We're almost there."

We made it through the southern part of town and made it down the ramps to the docks. Small merchant ships sat silent, no sign of crews to be found. We kept running toward our family's dock. But as we neared it, I tripped over a coiled rope and fell to my knees. My left kneecap connected hard with the rough wood, and a piercing pain shot up my leg from my ankle. I took a deep breath and pushed down the pain. I couldn't let it slow me down. I pressed my palms on the damp wood and started to push myself up when a golden tan hand with red scales appeared in my line of vision offering assistance. I lifted my head and looked into red eyes speckled with orange. A cultist.

"Father!" I screamed. Unaware that I had fallen, he stopped abruptly, turned, and looked at the stranger.

Father stared at the mystery man and fear gave way to relief as he ran toward us.

"Where have you been?" he demanded. The stranger took a step back lifting his hands, palms facing outward in defense. My father wasn't the largest of men, but even so, he did have a commanding presence when he wanted to.

"I was held up," the stranger said with an edge to his voice. This was no cultist because somehow, my father knew the man. I took in his appearance more closely. He could only be a few years older than me. His messy black hair was cut short. It was longer on top with slight curls hovering over his brows that he swept to the side with his free hand. His sharp jawline was covered in a week's worth of facial hair, and his lips were pressed together in a fine, annoyed line.

"Held up?!" my father yelled. "This is my daughter's life we're trying to save!"

Father's relief had turned to rage. He bent down and pulled me to my feet, but I struggled to put weight on my injured ankle. The throbbing pain started to become a distraction. I wavered and sat on a nearby crate. My father, nor the stranger, seemed to notice my injury. They were too busy staring each other down while chaos continued to erupt all around us.

"You don't think I know that?" the stranger argued, his voice low and laced with irritation. "In case you weren't aware, cultists are infiltrating the town," he added sarcastically.

"Oh, we're well aware," my father seethed. "We need to get her out now. What's your name, boy?" With the wave of his hand, my father gestured for the man to reveal his name.

"Captain Calian Westbow," he said between his teeth, "not '*boy*'." Captain Westbow relaxed his jaw a little. Okay, like a smidge. Okay, it *barely* moved, but it did. "I have a horse just west of town, past the stables in the tree line. We need to get there quickly. We need to move."

"Um…hello?" I said waving my hands. Both men looked at me. "We have a new problem."

Captain Westbow's gaze fell to my ankle. It had already started to swell, making my shoe tight. There was no way I was walking to his horse.

"I'll carry you," my father insisted.

The captain snorted. "I'll carry her," he said. He gave no time for my father to argue. He hastily bent down and picked me up with little effort. I winced in pain from my ankle but held in any visible signs that I was hurting. I could feel the thick, hard muscles under his clean white shirt as he held me close. He gave off an earthy scent that was tinged with smoke. The smell reminded me of an autumn campfire. It was intoxicating.

He quickened his pace in response, exiting the docks and heading toward the stables on the western edge of town. I stole glances at him as he carried me. His eyes which were once alive like fire were now dimmed to simmering embers. He seemed annoyed at the predicament. Like I could help it.

Father ran behind us, turning every so often to ensure none of the cultists had followed us. I felt helpless. Not only was I not equipped with god-like powers, but I also had an ankle that didn't work and no idea what the cultists even looked like. I envisioned elongated teeth, gnarled hands, and leathery skin. In a world where humans descended from Dragons, anything could be possible.

The cries from the townspeople had died down, but the smoke above the church now covered more of the town. Was it my imagination, or did the smoke appear to be a mix of gray and blue? It was as if it had joined another cloud above...

"The shop!" A high-pitched scream escaped my lips. I thrashed in Captain Westbow's arms. I needed to get to my father. The newer smoke cloud looked close to the shop. But the captain strengthened his grip on me. He continued running, darting between buildings and down smaller, rougher paths. One would think my ankle would be bobbing up and down, but the ride—I guess I could call it that—was incredibly smooth given the circumstances. He was lightning fast.

"Keep quiet," he growled. "Do you want to give us away?"

"Don't you tell me what to do!" I snarled. I again tried to get out of his arms but to no avail. His grip held strong.

"I will absolutely tell you what to do."

"That is my *home*!" I yelled.

"Correction. That *was* your home."

I began to beat my fists against his chest. I didn't even know this man, and I already hated him. However, hitting him was like hitting a brick wall. Stupid muscles.

"You're going to hurt yourself doing that," he commented and grinned. Stupid grin.

"My mother is in that shop!" I spat.

"And what do you think you can do about it?" he demanded.

My cheeks flushed because he was right. There was nothing I could do. I was so useless, and it was embarrassing. Here I was in the arms of some guy being carried to a horse because I couldn't even walk. What kind of Dragonheir couldn't even walk?!

"We're almost there," he said. We rounded another corner onto a worn-out path that led to the West Edge Stables. My father was now several seconds behind us. We went through a clearing and then over a shallow winding stream. Slight energy burst within my core and flared to life. A quick buzzing moved throughout my body, then quickly calmed, soothing my muscles. I relaxed and again felt at peace like I had in the church.

With the anxiety and dread waning, I craned my neck to see over Captain Westbow's shoulder. My father gradually slowed his pace and looked behind him. Something had drawn his attention. My eyes surveyed the path beyond him and landed on an image. Coming into view was a man in a billowy black shirt tucked into black trousers. Across his waist was a red sash of what looked to be vibrant silk. His long legs wore black riding boots to his knees. His hood had a cowl neck and a thin veil over his eyes, so I couldn't make out any of his facial features. On his chest was an outline of a Dragon in white with a crown sitting atop its head. Three slashes across the Dragon's middle were the same red as the sash. Fastened at each hip were curved blades, and strapped to his back was a shortened scythe. To fight him would undoubtedly mean one's death.

So that's a cultist, I thought. I felt my fingertips tingling. The calming energy in my core spread and became fluid-like. Captain Westbow must have picked up on what was happening because he stopped and looked me straight in the eyes. He then tilted his head, angling his neck to hear the commotion behind him. He had incredible hearing. Without warning, he ran faster. He actually ran *faster*. And that meant he was leaving my father further behind.

"What are you doing?" I demanded.

"Getting you to safety."

"We cannot just leave my father back there."

"Why not?"

"Are you serious? He'll be killed. He has no weapons. Turn around!"

He didn't, and all I could do was watch my father because the stupid captain was not letting go. Behind me, my father glanced left, then right. He darted behind an abandoned wagon filled with empty fisherman's crates and crouched low to the ground as if preparing for an attack. His brown tunic and trousers helped camouflage him from sight. His hand flew over his mouth, no doubt to conceal his heavy breathing. He waited silently for the cultist to run by.

Finally, Captain Westbow and I cleared the edge of town going past the stables. Coming into view was a large stallion kicking at the ground just beyond the tree line. Its silky mane fluttered in the slight breeze, and its smokey gray coat glistened in the sunlight. It was the most beautiful horse I'd ever seen. The closer we got to it, the larger the horse became.

"Get on," Captain Westbow said, and he hoisted me up in front of the smooth leather saddle.

"Seriously?" I asked incredulously. "We need to go back! We must help him!"

"You are going nowhere except on the horse. Get on."

"But my…" I started.

He gave an exaggerated sigh. His eyes flared a vibrant red. "Leave that to me."

By this time, the cultist had gotten to the stables and stopped. He sniffed at the air and began looking around. He literally *sniffed* the air. My father was no more than five feet away from the deadly assassin, still crouched by the abandoned wagon. I watched my father while holding my breath as he shifted his weight, readying himself to pounce. The cultist walked past the wagon, and my father shot out, tackling the man in black to the dusty ground with a loud thud. Had it not been for the calming feeling swimming beneath the surface of my skin I might have passed out.

Wait. I looked at my hands.

Was this me connecting with my water element? I had no such serenity until we'd passed over the narrow running stream earlier.

"Do not make any movement, Emera. Do not make any sound. Just…Don't do anything," Captain Westbow said.

I opened my mouth, but he gave me no time to respond. He spun on his heels and took careful, calculated steps to a neighboring tall tree. He cautiously peeked around, positioning himself to where he was half behind the tree and half to the side. My father and the cultist were caught in a wrestling match on the ground. My father attempted to grab the scythe from his back but to no avail. The cultist was quick, rolling from out beneath my father. His hand steadied on the blade at his side. My father's body went still, but he showed no fear. I knew in my heart he was just trying to buy us time.

"Hurry! Get out of here!" he shouted. He couldn't see us, but he knew we were out there.

The cultist looked to the tree line, trying to figure out where I was. That's the moment Captain Westbow, his right hand lowered to his hip, had taken hold of his dagger, the metal a shining onyx. I watched in disbelief as the blade warmed to a fiery glow. The cultist's head had just twisted to the tree when the captain threw his dagger which buried itself between the cultist's eyes.

A perfect throw.

I sucked my breath, my eyes widening in shock. I had never seen such deadly accuracy.

I gathered my thoughts and broke my stare. "Father!" I yelled. I took hold of the reins, and the steed, as if knowing my intent, immediately trotted out of the trees and closer to the stream. My father ran toward me. His eyes paused on the dead cultist in shock at what had unfolded. He picked up his pace toward me and quickly made it to the stream just as I did. I dismounted, jumped over the stream, and embraced my father fiercely.

"You will save this word, honeybee," he murmured into my ear, and I felt my heart breaking again. It was different than with my mother. I loved my mother. Truly. But the bond I had with my father was different. He taught me everything. I didn't know how to navigate the world without him.

"Emera," my father whispered. "You must go."

"I can't," I replied. A large lump gathered in my throat, closing off my airway. The serenity from before had vanished. I mustered all of my energy to croak out the next words. "I can't do this without you." I dropped my chin to let the heavy tears that had filled my long lashes cascade over my cheeks. My father's hand lifted my chin.

"You can, and you will," Father said. His hand lowered and disappeared just below the collar of his shirt. From behind the fabric, he pulled out an amulet on a twisted chain and placed it in the palm of my hand. He enclosed both of his hands around mine, indicating the amulet was special.

"According to the priest, there are only three of these in existence. Keep it hidden. Keep it safe. When the time is right, you will know who to give it to." He walked me to the horse and helped me back up into the saddle. After what seemed like an eternity, I lifted my eyes, and my attention was drawn to the stream beside me. Curiously, its current was now faster. Small waves had formed, crashing into rocks.

Captain Westbow had reached the horse by this point. He gracefully mounted it and sat behind me. His legs split, and he pulled me into him and placed his hands on my shoulders, steadying me. My breathing began to even out as did the stream's current.

I looked at my father. He raised two fingers and pressed them to his lips. I repeated the action. The captain gave the horse a slight jerk and squeezed its sides. The horse began to gallop away, and we left my father in the clearing as the town behind him burned in flames.

CHAPTER

FOUR

I awoke from a fitful sleep, my back still pressed into Captain Westbow with drool encrusted on my chin. Wonderful. The picture of the perfect goddess.

The warmth of the captain's body was a brief reprieve from the cold wind piercing my face. The sun was down now, and the moon had found its way amongst the stars that were suspended vibrantly overhead. I peered above but immediately regretted the decision. My vision blurred, my head became dizzy, and my body swayed. I was going to be sick.

"I'm going to throw up," I said hoarsely.

"We need to cover more ground. Hold it in."

I pressed my lips together and held back what I truly wanted to say to him.

"I'm going to cover you and the horse with the contents of my stomach if we don't stop."

"Fine." He pulled the reins, and the horse came to a standstill. He effortlessly dismounted while I shakily swung my leg over the horse. I slid down, but my knees buckled, and I tumbled to the ground while he stood watching, his lips in a straight line. I pulled myself up just before I emptied my stomach onto the lush grass.

"This is the Dragonheir that's going to save the six kingdoms," he mused.

My fury began rising as I grabbed a handful of dirt and threw it on his perfect white shirt and into his perfect white teeth.

"So mature," he coughed.

"You're insufferable, Captain."

"I've been called worse."

"Challenge accepted."

Captain Westbow threw his head back and a deep, almost growl-like laugh rumbled from his throat. "Dragongods help us." He smirked and continued dusting the dirt from his shirt. He must have decided it wasn't worth the effort because he quickly lifted it above his head and discarded it on the horse. The horse gave a rumbling bray like a groan. I didn't speak horse, but I was pretty sure the animal didn't appreciate being used as a clothing rack.

"There's a small pond over there," he said, pointing east of where we stood. "I'm going to wash up." He crossed his arms. "And you should probably do the same. You look terrible," added. He dropped his arms to his sides, and I finally noticed his strong, muscular physique. Good Gods, he was a glorious sight. It made me want to throw up again, I was so annoyed by it. I gave him a disgusted look while lifting myself to stand.

One corner of his mouth curved upward into a lopsided grin, clearly satisfied by my reaction. He turned away from me, his toned back and broad shoulders now fully in my sight. Stupid perfect muscles! I bent down, took another fistful of dirt, and threw it again. "Gods, help us," he repeated and chuckled. He sauntered away to the nearby pond, leaving me stewing in my anger.

"Ugh!" I shouted and stomped my feet into the dirt. He was right, the kingdoms were in trouble if I was to be their savior. I took a deep breath, letting the cool air swirl within my lungs. As I exhaled, I lifted my eyes to the night sky and let the breeze caress my face.

"Why me?" I asked no one. And no one answered me.

The horse whinnied, but I didn't count it. What did the horse know? I stretched out my hand and stroked its thick neck. It whinnied again, delighted at the touch. "Does the big mean captain not pay enough attention to you?" I asked. The horse angled its neck and gave me a look that said *exactly*. I giggled, which was the first positive sound I could manage since yesterday. I attempted to locate a pleasant memory from that day; one that included my mother and father. Searching the outermost corners of my mind, nothing of substance came to me. It's funny how people remember negative experiences more easily than positive ones.

I gave the horse a last pat and headed to the pond. When I got there, I found the captain kneeling on the outer banks. The light of the water hit his face, illuminating his features. I couldn't believe this was whom I had to travel with. I'd made up my mind that he was a rotten scoundrel if there ever was one. A good-looking, rotten scoundrel.

I sent up a silent prayer. *Please help me with this one*, I begged Anahita.

Watching him rub the dirt from his skin, I decided that washing my face was a good idea. So, putting one step in front of the other, I meandered down to the pond to join him. I strolled around the edge of the pond and stood opposite of him. I felt the heat of his stare, so I kept looking straight ahead then dropped my eyes to the water when I knelt by the pond's edge. A stranger reflected back at me. Dirt was caked on her face. Evidence of sweat and tears showed in the form of streaks in-between dirt. This person was so foreign to me. She was nothing like the girl I knew just hours ago. No, that girl was gone.

I placed my hands delicately into the water, and the cool liquid coursed through my fingers. With the water cupped in my hands, I brought it to my face, doing my best to wash away the pain and anxiety I felt deep in my bones.

The atmosphere shifted and the air stilled. The trees stood motionless as the wind died down to nothing. Even the crickets ceased playing their songs. The fluid-like energy that I had felt twice before began to pulse within my fingertips and gradually flowed up the length of my arms into my shoulders. I lifted my hands out of the water and watched as the pond began to quiver. The air altered, creating a breeze that sang what could only be described as a soft, soothing lullaby. The low-hanging branches of the trees swayed, and everything felt right in the world. I reveled in the night's tranquility.

"Your activation is coming along," Captain Westbow interrupted, bringing me out of nature's enchantment.

"What?" I whispered. I brought my hands out of the water, sat back on my heels, and leveled my gaze at him. He was no longer next to the water but a few feet back. The calm feeling that I had was gone, leaving irritation in its place. Couldn't he just go away? Go talk to his horse, or something like that.

"You've connected to your water element. The Dragongoddess Anahita approves. There's a calm presence here. She's allowed the connection."

"Allowed?" I asked skeptically.

"The Dragongods are arrogant like that," he answered casually. "They must give you their blessing before you can wield their element at its fullest. Because of your chaos heritage, you don't have to have a blessing to exhibit the element, only to fully control it. It's usually easy to receive the blessing of your descended Dragongod or Dragongoddess—for some it's instantaneous. You lived in the Kingdom of Water, so the Dragongoddess Anahita allowing the connection makes sense." He pointed to my head and arms. "It also explains why your scales are blue and not purple," he finished.

I felt silly that it hadn't registered until now that Nimerah was a Chaos Dragon, so her scales would be purple. And I had blue scales, and blue was the color of Anahita.

"Getting Nimerah's blessing…That will be the challenge," the captain mused.

"How so?" I sat down fully and took off my shoes. I placed my feet into the cool water and let them soak.

"You must have all six blessings from the Elementals before you can receive hers."

"And how do you know all this? It's not like she could have told you because everyone knows she's dead. Killed at the end of the War of Three. She sacrificed herself for humanity."

"That's what we thought. New evidence has come to challenge that claim."

"The prophecy?" I asked.

"The prophecy…And you," he said.

"You seem to know a lot about all of this," I pointed out. I leaned back from the water and sat back on the lush grass. I wriggled my toes, letting the blades maneuver through them. They were soft and cool to the touch.

"I know a lot of things," he smirked. Satisfied with his appearance after one last look in the water, the captain stood.

I snorted in response to his arrogance. "You're here because my Dragonblood activated. But activation doesn't mean connection. All I did was touch the water."

"Look, when my activation occurred, I connected quickly to my fire element. I seemed at ease in its presence. In just a short time, I could manipulate it. Vukan was more than willing to give me his blessing, it seemed. Water is your dominant element due to you living within the Kingdom of Water. If your activation is anything like mine, within a day or two, Anahita will give you her full blessing, and you'll be able to wield it. I'm very confident that your Dragontrials will start with hers."

"Dragontrials?"

Captain Westbow sauntered toward me as he spoke.

"You must undergo a Trial which will be given to you by each of the Elemental Dragongods and Dragongoddesses. These Trials are their way of testing your ability to obtain their blessings. Normally, a Dragonborn is put through the Elemental Trial after they've arrived at the university within the kingdom of their element. Being that you're a Dragonheir of a Chaos

Dragon, you must go through a Trial that each Elemental Dragon develops. I say '*develops*' loosely. Even the Dragoncouncil doesn't know how they choose to test you or when it will occur. We just hope to put you in a situation that they deem is appropriate for your test."

His domineering presence hovered over me. I lifted my chin, angling my neck so that I could get a better view of him. The moonlight behind him darkened his face. He looked mysterious and handsome and...*Get it together, Em!*

I looked away from him. "How can they do that if they aren't alive?" I asked.

"Their spirits remain in the Dragonsoul Plane. They are not allowed to cross into Eternal Resting since they are the guides of the Dragonborn." He held out his hand. I took it, and he pulled me to my feet.

"Are you...a Dragonheir like me?" Dragonheirs were stronger and held more elemental magic than Dragonborn. My understanding—which seemed limited at this point, thus making me agitated—was that Dragonheirs were the equivalent to a niece or nephew and Dragonborn were the long-distance cousins. Something inside me hinted that Captain Westbow was more powerful than a Dragonborn.

"Yes. That is why I was tasked to retrieve you from Medora."

"Lucky you," I murmured.

"Lucky me," he replied evenly. We both realized that he was still holding my hand. He dropped it, turned his back to me, and walked away.

I bent down and grabbed my shoes before following him. "Did you undergo a Trial?"

"I guess you could say that. I used my fire to save a *friend* from drowning beneath a frozen lake," he said reflectively. I couldn't place his tone exactly, but I caught a hint of annoyance. His emphasis on the word 'friend' made me think it wasn't actually a friend that he saved. "Instead of melting a hole to get him out, I ended up melting the entire lake."

"I guess that'll do it," I said and shrugged. As interesting as his Trial was, it wasn't appropriate for me to ask about the details. We weren't friends. "You said my water element is probably my dominant, yet after I touched the pond, the air shifted, and I heard what I swear was a song. Will I have other experiences such as that when I touch water?"

"To be honest, I don't know. You're the descendant of a Chaos Dragon which means you'll be more powerful than an Elemental Dragon. Chaos magic isn't the same as elemental. It's more."

I stopped. I let his words sink in. *More powerful. It's more.*

He paused momentarily and twisted around. "You may be able to affect other elements slightly, but you won't have…How do I say this? You won't have direct access to them until each Elemental Dragongod blesses you with its power. You won't have full power over them until Nimerah blesses you." Then he continued his stroll back to the horse.

Priest Benigno didn't mention that, I thought. Either the priest didn't know everything, or he was unwilling to share everything.

I quickened my pace to catch up to him. I wanted—no, *needed*—to know more. "You're not descended from a Chaos Dragon, I take it?" I asked him, pushing Priest Benigno out of my head.

"No. Only you."

I thought about his answer, and for some reason, it annoyed me. How was he supposed to train me properly if he didn't know how to wield each element? "Great," I replied sarcastically. "So, one element down, five to go, huh?"

"Yes."

I began to massage my temples—which was a little difficult considering I still held my shoes in one hand. "This is just so much information for someone who didn't think she was even a Dragonborn."

"That's understandable. You've…"

"You don't get it," I cut him off, and I jumped in front of him, forcing him to stop moving. "I hated the way Priest Benigno spoke about the Dragonborns. Like they— *we*—are better than humans. Now I'm one of them?"

"Look, you've been through a lot in the last two days." He paused his words and looked down. "It's good to see your ankle has healed," he said to distract me. I took the bait and glanced down at my ankle. I hadn't noticed the pain was gone. In fact, I'd completely forgotten I'd injured it.

"Interesting," I whispered.

"It seems that you have some healing abilities as well. That would come from your light element."

I sighed. "I have many other questions," I told him.

"I'm sure you do." He stepped around me and continued forward toward his horse.

"Whatever I ask, you answer me truthfully, Captain," I said as I trailed him. "I'm tired of being kept in the dark."

"Of course," he replied. His answer came as a relief. I thought back to my parents and the priest. Their withholding information had placed us all in danger. Had I known who I was and my potential powers, I might have been able to conjure the elements to help. If Captain Westbow was correct, I could have conjured my water magic to put out the flames. I could have saved the church, the shop, the town. The *people*. Lives had been lost. There had been too many flames to think otherwise.

"Where are you taking me?" I asked, filling the silence between us.

"To the northern forests of the kingdom," he responded nonchalantly.

"For my training."

"Correct. Not all of your training will focus on the Trials, though. We will need to assess your non-magical abilities as well."

"I'm good with a bow, and I know how to hunt," I offered. "And just the other night I moonlighted as a thief. Stole a basin and a dagger. Would have gotten away with it if it hadn't been for, well, you know, the whole activation thing. I was very sneaky if I do say so myself."

His facial expression didn't change. He was a tough audience. "We will get you a bow," he finally said. "You'll also need combat training."

"Seriously?"

He whipped around, not knowing I was right behind him. I bumped into him, and our feet tangled, causing us both to lose balance. He fell backward, and I went down with him. He wrapped his arms around me so that I would fall on top of him. Our bodies were pressed together tightly when his back contacted the ground.

Captain Westbow spoke, clearly annoyed with the situation. "If your elemental magic is weakened, and you have no bow or blade, how will you defend yourself?"

Regardless of his irritable behavior, my limbs went weak. The hairs on my arms stood up, and my heart pounded louder and louder. *Good gods, Em! This was insanity! He is a stranger,* I thought. Yet, we hadn't moved. We were still lying there.

I cleared my throat and willed the electric energy away. I had to change the subject. "Please don't take this the wrong way, but how do you plan on training me if your only elemental magic is fire?" I held my breath and braced myself for a verbal attack. Instead, he pushed me off of him and stood.

"I have been trained by the Dragoncouncil on how to elicit a Trial and how to train each element. Plus, I have people there that can help."

"Sounds good, Captain," I said and pushed myself up from the ground.

He tilted his head slightly. "Please, call me Calian. We need to keep moving." He left me planted in my spot.

The constant moving and back-and-forth banter wore on me. Was it too much to ask to stay in one place for a while? If I asked, he would surely think I was weak.

"I think the horse is tired, Captain—uh Calian," I called to him. Maybe that would do it.

"His name is Dhruv," Calian yelled back over his shoulder. "And he's never tired."

CHAPTER

FIVE

Calian was right. Dhruv was never tired.

We rode the rest of the night into the early morning. The morning air was crisp, and the sky was clear of clouds. Gold outlined the northern mountaintops as the sun began to wake from its slumber. The sky was a mixture of deep purples and blues as night faded away. Sleep never called for Calian. He remained focused on the road ahead.

"How are you not tired?" I asked. I was exhausted from the laborious ride.

"Dragonborn do not need to sleep as much as humans. Dragonheirs, less than that."

"But I'm a Dragonheir, and I'm exhausted," I whined. I knew I sounded like a child, but I didn't care. My inner thighs hurt along with my neck and shoulders, and my eyelids continued to get heavier and heavier. I threw my head back and rested it on his shoulder. Calian radiated heat like a fire in the dead of winter, no doubt from him being the Dragonheir to Vukan: The Dragongod of Fire.

"We're close to the camp. It's just over this hill. Then you can sleep as long as you'd like." I took note of his shaky voice, but I didn't comment on it. Something was off. We'd just entered the Northern Forest of The Kingdom of Water with the hill leading to our destination just ahead. You'd think The Kingdom of Water would be all shoreline against the ocean, or prairie lands with lakes, rivers, and streams. No. The northern part of the kingdom was overrun with a dense forest inhabited by thick, voluminous trees as tall as small mountains. Most didn't dare to venture too far into the Northern Forest as it was difficult to navigate. Rumor had it that many adventurous folks attempted to travel through the forest to trade with the small, scattered villages said to be built within the trees. Some even attempted the trip to the Realm of the Dragondead just at the northeast edge of the forest. But all the rumors ended the same: the travelers ended up lost, never to return home. I shuddered thinking about the image of random skeletons littering the forest floor.

"I don't understand why I'm tired, and you're not," I continued, hoping to take the edge off of him. "Aren't I more powerful than you?" I asked jokingly.

"Not yet," he answered, clearly distracted. His eyes began to dart back and forth. "The activation process of each element is demanding on one's energy. You'll likely feel drained, emotionally and physically, for a day or two after each new element activates..." his voice became softer in the last few words. His arms tensed around the reigns. My heartbeat picked up its pace. I seemed to channel Calian's unease.

"You need to steady your heartbeat."

"I'm trying."

"Try harder." He slowed Dhruv to a halt.

"I can't try harder when your anxiousness is suffocating me," I said through gritted teeth. "It's like I can feel your anxiety flowing through my veins."

"Interesting" he murmured in reply, clearly ignoring my frustration. "Empathic abilities are from Endrit, the Dragongod of Air."

"Fantastic!" I whispered sarcastically. "How do I turn it off?"

"You can't. Try breathing deeply. Inhale through your nose and out your mouth." He closed his eyes and took in a deep breath, inhaling through his nose and out through his mouth. "Like that."

I did exactly as he'd shown.

"Again."

I repeated the breathing technique a second time when Calian suddenly straightened in his seat, his spine going rigid. His alert response overloaded my senses. I desperately attempted breathing deeply a third time, but it was no use. Calian was on high alert, his blood pumping faster and body temperature rising. I could feel my own body reacting the same. It was a weird sensation.

"I thought each Dragonheir only received one elemental power," I managed to say between heavy breaths.

"Each will receive two. Dragongods had two powers. The secondary power is not as dominant."

"What are the others?"

"Strength from Dhara, Healing from Endrit, Shapeshifting from Vukan, and…" He stopped talking abruptly, not bothering to finish the list. "We have company," he murmured. My body froze.

Calian looked toward the western edge of the forest, and my eyes followed to where he was looking. There, through the dense tree plumage, a shadow stood. Knowing we'd discovered it, the shadow quickly dashed out of sight. Calian quickly dismounted Dhruv, handing me the reins.

"Stay," he said.

"I don't think Dhruv is going anywhere."

"I wasn't talking to Dhruv," he said, and I could swear his eyes twinkled. Stupid twinkles.

"Very funny," I mumbled. I scrunched my nose and threw him a gesture I'd seen my father use a few times throughout my life. Mostly when he'd encountered unfair trades and unruly customers and occasionally after he'd had a little too much to drink at the tavern. Dwyn's voice filled my head. *You are no lady*, she'd said.

"Gods, help us," he said.

"Quit saying that," I hissed.

He smirked and pivoted to face the area the shadow was last seen. He carefully surveyed the surrounding area, looking and listening intently for the shadow's new position. If he found it, he didn't let on. I, too, scanned the area for any trace of it. I didn't see anything.

Suddenly, a long, thunderous howl interrupted the calm of the forest. The tops of the trees rustled, and numerous flocks of birds took flight.

"Lightenion Wolves," Calian said. "They've been keeping watch on the camp since we arrived."

"Beasts as large as cattle and as fast as horses?" I remembered those details from hunters that visited the shops. I never believed them because the stories sounded so far-fetched to be true. Yet, as an aspiring adventurer, I'd hung onto their every word.

"Precisely."

"Then we need to get out of here."

"We can't."

"And why not?" I demanded. He lifted a single finger in the air and closed his eyes.

"Because we're being hunted," he said. And with that, I froze. My once-boiling blood instantly became still.

"What's the plan?" I asked quietly.

"Slow, steady movements. Dhruv is fast, but I'm not willing to test his speed against a Lightenion Wolf."

"You would think The Kingdom of Earth would have the fiercest wolves," I said.

"And why is that?" he asked with a single eyebrow lifted.

I straightened my back. "Because they breed large animals for fighting in underground pits."

Calian brought his hand to his mouth in an attempt to stifle his laughter. "How much do you know about the six kingdoms?" he asked.

My face must have turned red. "From the traders coming into Medora."

"Remind me to tell you more…*accurate*… information."

A snap of a twig brought us back to the wolf.

"I think it's time for your first lesson, Almighty Dragonheir."

I looked him square in the eyes. "Now?" I asked with disbelief.

"No better time than the present, I suppose."

"Shouldn't we—oh, I don't know—be focusing on getting out of here…*alive*? Emphasis on *alive*!"

"That's exactly what I'm trying to do. But I'll need your help to do it," he said bluntly.

"And how am I supposed to do that? I've only connected to my water element. I can't possibly use any elemental magic right now. Can't you just use yours?" I asked exasperated.

The quick snap of twigs interrupted our verbal squabble and drew our attention behind us. The shadow had returned, and at its center were two vibrant large glowing yellow eyes. It stopped and lingered just within the darkness of the bushes and towering trees.

Calian quickly turned to face me. "I can use mine, but yours will be much more effective if what I'm thinking is correct."

He had me there. "What power do I have that can help us?" I continued to stare into the eyes of the unknown creature.

"You might have the power of telepathy. It's the secondary power from Anahita."

"That makes zero sense to me," I said flatly.

Calian shot me an exasperated look. "How do you think Water Dragons communicate underwater?"

"You want me to read its mind?"

"I want you to talk to it," he said. I finally looked down at him.

"With my thoughts." It meant to come out as a question, but the tremble in my voice made it sound like a squeak.

"Yes."

"And if I fail? It seems my powers are coming in randomly. There's no way to tell if I can do this."

"Only one way to find out."

I nodded. Mustering whatever small amount of courage I could find—truthfully, I wasn't as brave as I thought I was—I started to slide off of Dhruv.

"No," Calian said. "Stay on the horse. As much as I'd like to not test the theory of which animal is faster, I'll do it if it means any chance at your survival."

I shifted back into the saddle and patted Dhruv on his neck. "Let's hope it doesn't come to that," I said. "All right. Here goes nothing."

The yellow eyes were still suspended above the ground, watching, and waiting to see how its prey would react. They were now smaller and more menacing with dark pupils positioned near the top of the eye. I imagined that the wolf's enormous snout was tilted downward, and its body was ready to attack. The tilt of its eyes suggested it was locked onto our every move. It never blinked.

I closed my eyes and steadied my breathing. I inhaled slowly and deeply while focusing my mind. I felt a wisp of energy within my mind and willed that energy into the form of a ribbon and pushed it outside of my being. The energy continued forward, weaving through the air, searching for its destination. I could feel the wolf's life force and extended the ribbon to wrap around it. The life force guided my ribbon toward the wolf's mind. Once within the wolf's mind, the ribbon became a seed that I planted, forming a telepathic tree with roots growing and spreading. I created a single thought for the wolf.

We are not your enemy, I spoke.

The Deceiver is not welcome here, it replied. My eyes immediately opened wide in shock. I did it. I actually made contact with the wolf. A small feeling of pride rose within my chest.

"Emera?" Calian said. His voice seemed so distant.

The Deceiver? What do you mean? I asked the wolf.

The Deceiver, it repeated. The wolf's eyes lifted and out of the shadows a nose appeared followed by very pointy fangs. The rest of the wolf's head emerged as it slowly walked toward us. Its eyes were wide and vibrant, and its ears were back, almost flush with its fur. It was the largest wolf I'd ever seen. It was just smaller than Dhruv. Its black fur was so dark it almost appeared blue in the sunlight. Its razor-sharp fangs were moist, and they parted to emit a low growl. Protruding from its monstrous paws were claws as long as eagle talons. Its long, bushy tail hung still behind it. I did everything in my power to hold my mind in place, to keep the telepathic tree planted, as I sat in awe and fear.

I don't understand, I replied. *We truly mean you no harm.*

The Deceiver is not welcome, the wolf answered.

Let us pass, and we'll leave this area.

Yes, leave. The wolf shifted on its legs, indicating it was ready to attack if needed.

I severed the mental connection and attempted to steady myself on Dhruv. The telepathy had used so much mental strength that I was dizzy. My body began to sway, so I closed my eyes and braced my arms on Dhruv's neck. Dhruv didn't seem to notice. He remained unmoving beneath me. I continued to gather my thoughts when I felt a touch of warmth on my knee. I opened my eyes to see Calian staring at me, his hand steadying me from falling. "We must leave now," I breathed. "He called me the Deceiver."

"That doesn't make sense," Calian said.

I shook my head to dislodge the gruesome thought. We needed to get away from the Lightenion Wolf who had silently crept closer to us. I needed to focus.

"If we do not get over that hill, he will likely kill us. He *really* doesn't want me here."

"His wish is our command," Calian replied. He hoisted himself up onto Dhruv and quickly urged the horse forward. I turned to watch the wolf. Although its eyes had softened, it still stood watching and waiting. I heard a distant voice in my head.

Do not return, Deceiver, the wolf threatened.

CHAPTER

SIX

Calian and I raced over the hill to put as much distance between ourselves and the large predator. After a final turn around a grove of Watergreen Trees, into view came a small military camp. A wall constructed with logs formed a perimeter around a couple of dozen tents. In front of the wall were several portable frames with projecting stakes. I'd seen these contraptions in the books traders brought into my family's shop.

"The barrier seems on the short side," I mused.

"It's mostly for keeping out wild animals," Calian replied. Considering our location was nestled away from civilization, it made sense.

We rode to the eastern side of the camp where a gate stood, marking the camp's entrance. The gate was no wider than two horses and just as tall as the barrier. Standing just above the gate on what I assumed to be a platform was a man with a bow and an arrow ready to be released.

"Password?" the man called down to us.

"You've got to be joking," I said softly. I watched as the stranger's lips widened into a smile, exposing his well-kept teeth.

"There is no password, Fin!" Calian yelled back. He shifted his weight behind me.

"That's not it," Fin replied.

"Fin, so help me, Gods, you better open this gate," Calian growled. I giggled. Calian leaned forward and looked at me from the corner of his eye. "You find this amusing?"

"Very much so," I laughed.

"Still waiting," Fin cried.

In a split second, Calian's hands began to burn. A faint red glow pulsed from his palms. His eyes turned a vibrant red, and the left corner of his mouth curled upward.

"Now, now," Fin said. "Don't do anything irrational, Cal. It's not our fault you weren't here to vote on a password."

Calian brought back his arm, but before he made any other movement, Fin shot the arrow at Calian. With the reflexes of an Earthean Tiger, Calian grabbed it right before the arrow pierced his chest. Calian looked down at the arrow in his hands, just inches from his heart. He tossed the arrow to the ground and ever so slowly raised his gaze.

"Fin, Fin, Fin," Calian chuckled. "Is that the best you got?" He dismounted Dhruv and flames erupted from his hands. He twisted and turned his wrists, letting the flames dance around his palms and through his fingers. It was the first I'd seen him manipulate fire, and he did it effortlessly. Would I be able to do that?

"Not even close," I heard Fin reply. But Fin was nowhere to be seen. Calian scanned the area. He studied the spot where Fin had been. I began to say that I thought Fin had retreated when another arrow flew past Calian's left ear. I heard him snicker and paid close attention to the trickle of blood that slowly dripped down his neck. The arrow had just grazed him.

"Well, at least he missed," I pointed out.

"No, he didn't," Calian said. "You're going to pay for that, Fin!"

"Gentlemen," came a female voice from behind the gate. "You are both acting like children and, quite frankly, are not providing Emera with a great first impression." The gate opened fully, and the woman stepped into my view. I gasped as I gazed into the shockingly vibrant blue eyes of the most beautiful woman I'd ever seen. Her rich, dark ebony skin reminded me of a winter night. Her dark, silky smooth hair was half down, caressing her shoulders while the other half was pulled back into a simple braid. It was the perfect style to show off her exquisite facial features which included captivating eyes, full lips, and strong cheekbones. As she walked, her long, deep blue dress hugged her slender frame until it reached her hips and fell to the ground sashaying around her. It reminded me of the most exotic waterfalls in the Kingdom of Water. Her neckline was high, embellished with silver thread, but there were no sleeves, leaving her shoulders exposed which showed off her dazzling blue scales. She was an absolute vision of beauty, and I couldn't help but feel inferior in her presence as I looked down at my tattered, dirty dress.

"Emera knows all about rough first impressions. She's fine," Calian remarked. I ignored him.

"Captain Calian Westbow, you help that woman down from that horse this very minute," the woman ordered. I loved her already.

"She's not *that* helpless," Calian said in defense. The woman shot him a warning glare. Calian sighed and offered me his hand. I pushed it aside and slid off Dhruv on my own. I gave Calian a wink as I brushed past him. "No thanks," I said sweetly.

Calian turned to the woman. "See what I mean?"

The woman smiled. "We're going to be great friends. Come, Emera." She extended her hand which I gladly took. "My name is Morwen."

Fin came strolling through the gate. My eyes widened at the sight of his hair which was red like mine. I hadn't met many people with red hair. However, there were differences. Whereas mine was a deeper red with hints of gold, his was lighter with an orange tint. His eyes, a light hazel, lit up with admiration and respect as he and Calian embraced like dear friends. His smile widened beneath his red facial stubble, drawing more attention to his square jaw. What truly caught me by surprise was that he had no scales. Fin wasn't a Dragonborn.

I did my best to hide my surprise. It wasn't uncommon for humans to live amongst the Dragonborn, but to see them joking, laughing, and hugging a Dragonborn? That was new to me.

"Let's get you settled," Morwen chimed, interrupting my thoughts.

She led me through the gate and into the camp. Calian grabbed Dhruv's reins and followed behind us with Fin at his side. The two quickly engaged in conversation while Morwen led me forward. The path continued at an incline with field tents on either side. Most of the tents were small, big enough for only one or two men, but as we walked further up the path, the ground leveled out, and a few larger tents came into view. We passed soldiers, male and female Dragonborn, from different kingdoms. They all had different scales, but they wore the same crest. A deep purple shield with a silver and black Dragon at its center. Most were just exiting their tents, ready to take on the day. Others were already sitting next to small fires, eating their morning meals. They talked and laughed with one another. In comparison to the last couple of days, it was a welcoming view.

When I passed by, many paused their conversations to see who the newcomer was. The people took note of

Calian's presence, lifted a fist, and placed it over their hearts in solidarity. Calian's welcome was much warmer than mine. Hushed voices trailed after me as I walked through the camp.

"Ignore them," Morwen said.

"It's difficult not to, considering my appearance. I am filthy."

"Oh, it's not your appearance they're gawking at."

"No?"

"They've been waiting for your arrival. They just don't know how to handle themselves." She patted my arm for comfort.

"I'm not a queen," I said.

"No," she mused. "You're more than that."

I had no response to give, so I changed the subject. "Who are they? They don't look like any type of royal guard from any of the kingdoms."

"They're not. Some are mercenaries; many are from the Nimerian Legion that Calian is captain of."

"I've never heard of that," I replied.

"Pretty sure they made it up," Fin joked. He and Calian had closed in on us.

"She's got a lot of catching up to do," Calian declared from behind, ignoring Fin's remark. Morwen turned to give him a quizzical look. He explained, "Neither her parents nor the Dragonpriest assigned to her dared to divulge any useful information."

"He's right," I admitted.

"No matter," Morwen assured me. "Calian will teach you what you need to know. If anyone can train you promptly, it's him. He was my teacher."

"He's smarter than he looks," Fin added, which was followed by, "Ouch!"

"You're a Dragonheir?" I asked while the men behind us behaved like boys.

"Morwen Elderbrook, Dragonheir of Anahita, at your service," she said with a smile.

"Elderbrook? As in King Calder Elderbrook of The Kingdom of Water?" I was thrown off balance by the realization that hit me. An inkling had told me she looked familiar, but I'd ignored it. I quickly dropped to one knee and lowered my eyes to the ground, placing a fist over my heart.

"Here we go again," Fin said with a long exhale.

"Princess Morwen. I apologize. Please excuse my ignorance," I breathed.

"Emera, please. There is no need to apologize. In fact, if anyone should be bowing, it should be these two," she said and laughed as she gestured to the men walking behind us. "Especially that one," she pointed at Calian who rolled his eyes.

"It's likely that Cal won't bow to anyone," Fin pointed out.

"Well, that's unfortunate," I remarked.

"Funny," Calian replied.

Morwen chuckled, helped lift me to my feet, and put her arm in mine. "When it comes to matters of the prophecy, I am not a princess," she said. "I hold no power or reign over you. How about we fill you in on some of those details? Shall we?"

"Yes, please. That would be wonderful."

"Good. There is someone you need to meet."

She guided me to the last of the tents—the largest ones in the camp that were arranged in a semi-circle. The tent in the center was the largest, made for an entire gathering hoisted up by three large poles. Hanging from a post just beside its entrance was a flag of purple outlined with a white border. At its center was a black outline of Nimerah's head on a silver-gray circle. This tent was dedicated to Nimerah. I could assume I was about to enter an area of worship. I followed Morwen into the tent while Calian tied Dhruv to a post.

Once inside, the smell of Twilight Orchids greeted me. The orchids were only known to grow in the City of Nimerah but had apparently been brought to the camp. Tapestries of purple, silver, white, gray, and black fabric hung from the inner walls of the tent. Another banner devoted to Nimerah hung behind a long altar. On the altar was a large bust of Nimerah with smaller statues of each Elemental Dragon on either side of the goddess's bust. Makeshift pews from logs were positioned in six rows with a small aisle separating them. We were standing in the camp's sanctuary.

At the end of the aisle, standing over the altar with outstretched arms was a hooded priest in deep purple robes the color of eggplants.

"Welcome, Emera," came a comforting, feminine voice from beneath the purple hood. So, I was wrong. She was a priestess. The priestess met me halfway down the aisle and without warning, embraced me like we were old friends. "We have been waiting for you. Please, sit." She gestured to a pair of wooden chairs at the back of the sanctuary with a small table between them. "I hope you had an uneventful journey. Would you like some water?"

"Absolutely. Thank you." The Priestess poured water from a metal pitcher sitting on the table. She handed me the water, and I gulped down the smooth liquid that cured my thirst. I looked up into her thoughtful, piercing gray eyes. Her tawny-colored skin glistened in the light, showcasing her white scales marking her as originally from the Kingdom of Light. She lowered the hood of her robes revealing dark brown hair woven into intricate braids which was another trait of Lightenion citizens.

I quickly glanced between her and Morwen then looked away, catching my reflection in the pitcher at the table. My hair was still matted to my forehead from dried sweat while my face was adorned with dust and dirt. My lips were chapped from the wind when riding. I was a mess.

"I wouldn't say that it was uneventful, but we survived," Calian responded from the entrance, pulling me from my self-consciousness and back into the tent. He ran his hand through his dark hair, and my heart skipped when his dark eyes met mine. I looked away in an attempt to conceal my embarrassment.

"Well, at least there's that," the priestess answered, glancing at Calian. She looked me over from head to toe. "My name is Rehema. I'm the camp's Dragonpriestess which I'm sure you've already guessed. Your being here means you've started the activation process. What elements have you connected to?"

"Well, Priestess Rehema…" I began.

The priestess held up her hand. "Just Rehema, please. I don't abide by those frivolous formalities like many others who are called to serve the gods and goddesses."

I smiled. "Got it. *Rehema*, I have shown signs of water magic. Water seems to be my strongest element. We believe I've already started manipulating its life force. It seems to calm me whenever I call it if that makes sense. It's helped me shift the atmosphere and talk to wolves."

"Those godsdamn wolves," Fin muttered.

Rehema paid Fin no attention. "Wonderful!" she beamed. "However, you need to complete each Elemental Trial so that we can then figure out how to get Nimerah's blessing. That's what I'm here to do," she said proudly. "Considering you've done so well with your water element in just three days, I think it's safe to say the other elements will come readily to you once you've completed the Trials."

My mind paused on the fact that she said three days. Had it really been only three days since I was in Medora unaffected by the heavy weight of a prophecy and duty.

"I understand this is all new to you, Emera. I am here to help you in any way that I can," she said warmly.

Calian straightened from the post he was leaning on and walked toward us. "We'll start right away," he said. "We need Nimerah's blessing if you're to be as powerful as the prophecy claims.

"Once we get that blessing, then we can train you to be the powerful Dragongoddess you were born to be," Rehema added.

"Pfft." I covered my mouth quickly, but the damage was done. At the mention of the word *Dragongoddess*, I spit the sip I'd taken onto Calian's face right when he leaned in to grab the pitcher of water. Fin and Morwen laughed loudly, and Rehema stifled a giggle, doing her best to appear composed.

"I'm so sorry!" I said, but my laughter spilled out.

"Apparently," he said and dragged his hand down his face to wipe the water away.

The laughter faded, leaving a bout of dizziness in its place. I held my breath and closed my eyes to keep the room from spinning. "Dragongoddess?" I asked Rehema, my eyes still closed. I felt more and more lightheaded. Exhaustion had finally caught up with me, rolling through my limbs like an ocean wave. I swayed slightly.

Ignoring the fact that I'd just sprayed water all over his handsome face, Calian leaned down and placed his arm around my shoulders, steadying me. I leaned into him since it was the only thing I could do to stay upright.

"Who do you think you are, exactly?" Morwen asked.

"Nimerah's Dragonheir," I answered heavily.

"You're not just a Dragonheir," Rehema explained. "You're her *daughter*."

My eyes flew open, and I whirled my head to face Calian. "Daughter? You lied to me." I accused him.

He raised an eyebrow. "No, I didn't," he answered.

Heat rose to my face, and I could swear steam was coming out of my ears from the anger and irritation I felt. "I see no difference," I told him. "Anything you fail to share with me is essentially lying. And now I don't feel bad at all for spitting water in your face." He didn't have to know I never felt bad about it to begin with.

He rolled his eyes. "It's not my fault your so-called loving parents didn't tell you anything regarding your true heritage," he said. "So don't blame me for their incompetence."

"Their *incompetence*?" I seethed. I shoved him away from me, and he fell downward, landing on his back. I could feel the temperature rising around us all. How dare he disrespect my parents? They were loving and devoted to raising a mysterious child as their own.

Rehema stepped between us. "Excuse the lack of transparency with the captain," she said, trying to smooth over the situation. I didn't say a word. Calian didn't say a word. We just glared at each other breathing heavily, our hearts beating loudly. I wondered if everyone else could hear them.

"Maybe you should rest," Morwen suggested gently. "We can fill you in later."

I clenched my teeth and curled then uncurled my hands. I took a deep breath and exhaled loudly. "That may be for the best," I said. I looked at everyone in the room and then at Calian, my *Deliverer,* still on the ground in front of me. He finally looked at me, and I held his gaze. His nostrils flared, indicating that he was still trying to calm down.

"I've had enough of talking," I said calmly. "I am tired, I am angry, and I miss my home. I'd like to rest."

"Yes," replied Morwen, already having moved to my side. "Let's get you to bed." She stopped in her spot and scrunched her nose. "Would you like to wash up first?" she offered. So not only was I tired, but I also stunk. Great.

"I'm not sure I have the energy, to be honest." I sighed deeply, and my knees buckled. I fell into the chair. Sleep pulled at every corner of my consciousness. Morwen held her arm out as I struggled to stand.

"No," said Calian, having gotten up to his feet. "I've got her." He scooped me into his arms before I could protest. What was his deal with carrying me everywhere?

"We'll discuss this more once you've had adequate rest," Rehema called after us while Calian exited the tent.

Just outside, a breeze chilled my face and filled my lungs with Calian's scent of wood, fire, and spice all mixed into one. The anger within me was now a pile of dying embers. I opened one eye and peered up at him. The dark circles under his eyes exposed his need for sleep.

"Where to now?" I asked.

"Our tent."

Well, that woke me up a bit. "*Our* tent?" I managed to spit out.

"Yes. Tents are limited in case you didn't notice. There are a few, however, with only one occupant. Would you prefer to sleep with them? A stranger?"

"You're a stranger." My eyelids fluttered, but I forced them to stay open.

He smirked, "Not as much as everyone else, I'd suppose."

"Fair point, but it's still weird. Plus, I'm still mad at you." I wasn't. That was just another thing he didn't need to know. His eyes flashed with amusement. I shivered from the brisk, spring air and burrowed myself deeper into his chest. If he didn't like it, he never let on.

"What about Morwen?" I asked. Surely, she wouldn't mind if I stayed with her.

"She shares the tent over there." He gestured to the tent on the opposite side of the path from us. "With Fin."

"Oh," I said. Then it hit me. "Oh! They're together?"

"They're Dragonmates." I mulled his words over in my mind. A human and a Dragonheir? Dragonmates?

He carried me into one of the larger tents beside Rehema's sanctuary. Two cots sat on the opposite sides of a fire pit placed between two of the larger poles holding up the tent. One cot contained blankets that were strewn about making it obvious that Calian slept there. The other cot had a small pillow atop a folded blanket. Next to each cot was a chest for clothing and supplies.

"I thought Dragonmates were just love stories to make desperate Dragonborn feel better about being alone," I said groggily.

Calian laughed and sat me down on the barren cot, and I promptly laid down. He moved the pillow beneath my head, and I relaxed into its softness. Granted, it wasn't as soft as the pillows back home, but in comparison to sleeping on Calian's shoulder, it was a cloud.

Calian grabbed the edges of the blanket and gave it a light toss to unfold it. He then lifted it above me and let it fall, letting it spread over my body like a cocoon. "You sure have some wild stories about us Dragonborn. A little prejudiced if you ask me," he said.

"I'm not prejudiced. I just don't like their pompous attitude and how they look down on humans," I replied. I closed my eyes; a long yawn finally broke from its cage. "Which is why I'm quite surprised that a Dragonheir and a human can even be Dragonmates since Fin isn't a Dragonborn," I said.

"Astute observation," he replied. I stuck my tongue out at him. "Classy," he chuckled. He turned his back and walked toward his cot where a small table with a lantern sat. I heard him snap his finger and thumb together then he turned to face me, the candle now lit within the lantern. Show off.

"Fin is not the only person here that is not a Dragonborn. This camp is a mixture of humans and

Dragonborn." He sat the lantern on the chest next to my cot. I felt its warmth instantly.

"That sounds nice," I said and smiled. It was a nice thought: humans and Dragonborn working together peacefully.

"It is. That's the goal, right? Human and Dragonborn living together equally."

"It's a nice thought. I'm not sure how achievable it is," I said skeptically.

"Very achievable if you or I have anything to say about it." He sat in a chair next to the fire pit. He looked down into the ashes.

"What about Rehema? Can I room with her?" My words began to slip away as sleep clawed at my consciousness. I wanted to protest more about the living arrangement and opened my mouth to do so, but I stopped. What did it matter? I had been at Calian's mercy from the moment he offered his hand at the docks. He was probably the most powerful Dragonborn here, anyway, so staying close to him could ultimately mean my survival.

"She lives in a small tent next to the sanctuary. Part of the lives of Dragonpriest and Dragonpriestesses is to sleep and worship in solitary. Whether you like it or not, you're stuck with me for the moment."

I yawned. My eyes were growing heavier. "What about guests?"

"Guests?" He looked up at me, his brows wrinkled in confusion.

I felt my face flush. "Of a romantic nature?"

Calian threw his head back and let out a deep laugh. The corners of his eyes were crinkled from how tight his eyelids were closed. "That is the furthest thing from my mind at the moment, so don't worry about that. Look. You'll have your side, and I'll have mine. I'm sure I can get a blanket or something and hang it between us for privacy."

"I appreciate that."

"I'll see that it's done." He stood up and began to walk back outside, but he stopped and faced me once more. Our eyes met, and his pupils seemed to focus. Every bit of his facial expression turned serious. "Besides, if anything were to go wrong while you're sleeping, I'm close to you," he said softly.

His sincerity caught me off guard. "What could go wrong?"

"Someone could infiltrate the camp to kidnap…or kill you."

"That would be very wrong," I admitted.

His voice lifted as he started out again. "Or your magic could go awry, and you could end up killing others," he said in jest over his shoulder.

"That doesn't make me feel better," I said evenly.

"Probably not, but we must be prepared for all scenarios. Now, go to sleep, Emera." He left the tent, and I was comforted by the silence.

He didn't have to tell me twice. I closed my eyes and drifted into nothingness.

CHAPTER

SEVEN

When I finally awoke, my senses registered the sound of chatter, the smell of fresh rain, and the taste of my dirty teeth. I lifted my eyelids and found two blankets strung up as a makeshift wall between Calian's cot and mine. He was—dare I say, gentlemanly—enough to keep the fire pit on my side.

My heart twisted briefly with the realization that everything had been real. I hadn't been dreaming. I was no longer in Medora at the apothecary. My mother's humming and my father's laughter would soon become a distant memory. A tight pain in my chest manifested itself; my body's way of saying it mourned the absence of my parents.

I lifted myself up slowly until I perched upon my elbows. I surveyed the tent and saw that Calian was not there. I didn't know the time, but the bright sun shining through the gaps of the tent's fabric told me it was at least daytime. I really hope I wasn't out long.

I sat up fully and pushed the blankets aside. Sweeping my legs to one side of the cot, I tensed. My back was stiff, and the rest of my muscles ached. The soreness was just more evidence that the past few days had, in fact, occurred. I wished they hadn't, and that I was back home at the apothecary.

An elongated groan parted my lips, slicing through the quietness of the tent. I stretched my arms high and straightened my back to alleviate whatever soreness I could. I rolled my head from side to side and hunched then shrugged my shoulders. Having dulled some of my body's pain, I stood and walked toward the opening of Calian's tent.

Correction: *our* tent.

I could make out some laughter from the soldiers, their voices full of vivacity. Up until this point, I hadn't questioned their presence at the camp, but listening to them made me wonder what exactly they were here for.

Battle? Were we about to enter a war I didn't even know had started?

I pushed open the entrance flap and stepped into the midday sun. The brightness stung my eyes, so I lifted my palm to shield what part of the light I could. It took a couple of blinks before my eyes adjusted and the stinging subdued. I took in the scenery including the soldiers engaging in conversations as they walked through the camp, the horses tied to small posts outside the numerous white tents, and the looming trees of the forest beyond. I listened to the birds singing, the cling clang of swords, and the crackling of fire from the small forge. The camp was alive. It was vibrant and animated. A stimulating energy hovered above it all.

"You're finally awake," said a gruff voice from behind. I turned to see Calian walking up the path. His short, wavy black hair glistened in the sun like raven's feathers. He was ready for the day with his brown boots, tan trousers, and a white linen shirt that was untied at the top, exposing the upper part of his chest.

He grinned as he got closer. Well, it looked like he grinned. The sun was in his eyes, so he could have been wincing. I wasn't sure due to my gawking at the peek-aboo his chest was playing. Then I realized he'd said that I was finally awake.

"Wait. What do you mean *finally*?"

"You've been asleep for two days."

"Two days!"

"I'm not surprised. Actually, I thought it might take you longer to recuperate. A lot has happened the past week, so it's natural for your body to need the rest."

"Two days," I repeated quietly.

He waved me to follow him, and we entered Rehema's tent of worship side-by-side. Upon our arrival, Rehema stood from her seat at the back. Her deep purple robe's silver stitching mimicked scales with sparkling black threads lining her neck and the cuffs of her sleeves. It swayed at the bottom with her every move, making her look more like a regal Queen than a Priestess.

Morwen, who was also present, rose from praying at the altar and greeted me with a friendly embrace. She wore a soft long-sleeved shirt the color of sea foam. The color was quite the contrast compared to her light beige pants and knee-length brown boots. Her hair was pulled back completely, exposing her beautiful face and flawless skin. I bit down on my lip to hide my jealousy.

Rehema and Morwen both sat on the wooden pews. I chose to stand. I'd had enough time to rest, and my legs were begging to be used.

Calian leaned against the tent's largest pole at the center of the sanctuary. "Were you able to get any leads on her mother's whereabouts?"

"Mother…right," I muttered to Morwen. "I'm still trying to wrap my head around an ancient goddess being my mother."

"You'll get used to it," she insisted.

"Unfortunately, only Nimerah herself can answer that. I have not been able to make any headway on the matter," Rehema told Calian, hanging her head slightly in defeat. She spread her hands out on her upper thighs, smoothing out her deep purple robe.

Morwen grabbed my hand. "We were hoping," she said gently, "that once we brought you here, you would be able to help us find her."

"I told them it sounded ridiculous," Fin remarked. "I mean, how would you know where she is?" When had he shown up? He was sneaky, I'd give him that. He had to be an assassin. His all-black, fitted leather attire with hood and cowl further proved it. It also could have been the variety of daggers attached to his hips.

"Fin has a point," I admitted. "I'm not sure what I can do."

Fin elbowed Calian in the side. "See? I have a point," he quipped.

"Don't let it get to your head," Calian replied, rolling his eyes. I suppressed a laugh.

"We have much to do," Rehema said, clapping to get our attention. "I need to notify the Dragoncouncil within the city that you've made it here safely. If you don't mind, I will see you out so that I can begin meditating. I will need complete isolation if I am to contact Dragonmaster Anwir. Maybe he has new information about your mother's location." With her arms spread wide, she hastily ushered us toward the opening of the tent like a mother hen even though she couldn't have been that much older than any of us. "Please leave me in peace."

Once we were outside, I turned to Calian, causing Fin to almost run into him. "Dragonmaster?" I asked.

"Dragonmaster Anwir is the Dragonpriest that read the prophecy once the ancient script was found. He is head of the Dragoncouncil. He is the one that assigned me to you."

"Remind me to thank him later," I joked. Wait. Was I...? Was I flirting? I shouldn't be surprised. The last time

I was with him, I was nestled in his arms. The memory made my face flush.

Behind me, Fin chuckled, and Calian looked at me suspiciously. Great. I was arguing with myself, and they were watching the entire time. They definitely thought I was insane.

I cleared my throat. "Can someone please explain to me this prophecy now that I'm here? What am I supposed to do? Save the six kingdoms?" We started down the path into the camp. My stomach grumbled. How long had it been since I'd eaten? I couldn't remember.

"It would seem that way, sweetheart," Fin replied behind me.

I spun on my heels and waved my finger at him. "No. Immediately no. Do not ever call me that," I said. Morwen threw Fin what looked to be an annoyed glance. I'd have to help her master that skill.

Fin ignored her and swooped down in a low bow before me. "I apologize, Your Highness."

"And add that to the list of what not to say or do in my presence. I'm not a Queen," I said.

He stood up straight, "Would you like me to call you Dragongoddess instead?"

"Gods, no!" I laughed. This was all ridiculous.

"Oh, great Dragonheiress of Nimerah?" He winked.

"You can stop now, Fintan," Morwen said and punched him in the shoulder.

By this time, Fin and I both convulsed with laughter. "My sincerest apologies, my love," he told Morwen. He took her hand and kissed it. It was the first bit of affection I'd seen from them, and it just looked right. Morwen just shrugged.

"It's a Dragonmate thing," Morwen said with an eye roll and a hint of a smile. Fin grabbed Morwen's waist and dipped her over his arm. He planted a long, passionate kiss on her lips.

"More like a Dragonass thing," Calian added.

"Language, Calian," Morwen said after she was upright again.

Deep within my soul, a light of joy flickered in the darkness of my despair.

*   *   *

"I cannot give you all the specifics of the prophecy, Emera. But I can tell you what I know," Rehema offered.

Morwen and I had spent the day roaming throughout the camp so that I would be accustomed to my new surroundings. Calian and Fin had parted ways with us to check in with the soldiers on patrol after Cook—the camp's cook—claimed someone had broken into his food chests. Rehema found us once she'd heard from the Dragoncouncil. She'd insisted on privacy and thought a stroll out of camp would do some good. Morwen had bid us farewell and sauntered off toward her tent.

Rehema and I stayed close to the camp. She guided me to what she claimed was her favorite spot—a large crystal-clear pond surrounded by lush foliage and beautiful flowers of varying colors. It was the perfect spot to sit and daydream.

"Whatever you can tell me is better than nothing," I told her.

"It has been prophesied that when the people of the six kingdoms grow divided, the Second Chaos Dragon—who we have determined is Ragnar since he was the second Chaos Dragon in existence—will rise again by the blood of the Daughter of the Chaos Dragon and the ring of Six. The Second Chaos Dragon will bring power to the Dragonborn. You are the daughter of Nimerah. Along with the Ring of Six, you will resurrect the second Chaos Dragon and restore peace and balance to the six kingdoms."

"Resurrecting Ragnar seems like a lot for someone who just found out their true heritage," I pointed out. "What is the Ring of Six?"

"The Ring of Six is the other Dragonheirs. Calian, Morwen, and Erjon—he's on his way back from The City of Endrit—make up three of its members. We have yet to locate the other three, but once we do, you'll have great power on your side."

I'd at least have help. That was somewhat reassuring. But I still had one gnawing question. "What I don't understand is why Calian, or my parents, or Priest Benigno couldn't tell me any of this."

Rehema sat on the grass next to a large Water Crest tree. Its white bark shimmered in the midday sun, and its dark green leaves hung low, creating a peaceful ambiance with ample shade and a cool breeze.

"That was an order from the Dragonmaster. Only the Dragoncouncil is allowed to speak of the prophecy aloud. We Priests and Priestesses do not question the council."

"That sounds ridiculous." She smiled knowingly. I could tell she wanted to agree but couldn't.

I sat beside her and crossed my legs into a more comfortable position. "There's something else that you're not telling me."

Her eyes darted back and forth nervously. "This is all so new to you. And you've been through so much. I think that—"

"I can handle it," I assured her.

She pursed her lips and huffed through her nose. "Quite right. The prophecy ends when you defeat the one whose deception hurts most. In that final act, the bonded will die."

My mouth gaped open in response. I sealed my lips and straightened my back, sitting taller. I uncrossed my legs and stood. "Someone I am bonded to—or will be bonded to—will die. Because of me. That's just wonderful," I said sarcastically. I paced back and forth. Rehema didn't move.

"Peace will be restored, and the six kingdoms will unite."

"At the cost of someone I love or will love? Because that's what that means, right? Someone I'm bonded to?" I could hear my voice getting louder and louder. "I've lost so much, including my family and my home, and now this prophecy is demanding I lose more? How is that fair?" I yelled. Rehema didn't flinch, but I still felt awful for my outburst. It wasn't her fault. She didn't deserve my anger.

"I'm sorry, Rehema," I said quietly.

A quiet moment passed before she opened her mouth to speak. "You will survive this. You're your mother's daughter, after all."

"That's reassuring," I said sarcastically. "I don't even know her."

"It is imperative that you receive your blessings. You will need all the Dragonmagic at your disposal. You must have each blessing—along with Nimerah's—to perform and live through the ritual." She finally stood and sauntered toward the tent's entrance. I gulped loudly. Did she really just say *and live through it*?

Rehema leaned back and hollered over her shoulder, "I can hear you brooding, Calian Westbow. I'm finished." She crossed back to me and gently took my hands in hers.

"I have every bit of faith in you, Emera," she insisted. "Your power grows within you. Once it is unleashed on the world, no one can stop you from saving it." She let go. "And no matter what happens, your strength will see you through." I felt the tears coming. Her confidence in me reminded me of my father. Gods, I missed him so much.

"Now, do me a favor and clean up," she scrunched her nose as Morwen had done. "You stink." She smiled sheepishly. "No offense."

I laughed even though tears fell down my cheeks. "None taken." She was right. A foul odor seemed to hover around me like a thick fog.

"I'll make sure Calian gets you some hot water, and I'll have Morwen find you more suitable clothes. Fintan will get you something to eat." We both nodded at each other and then she left me standing there, my cheeks soaked and my nose a bubbling mess. I wiped my face with the back of my hand. I was going to bathe anyway, so what did it matter?

A large, tanned hand with red scales dropped in front of me. Calian stood, waiting for me to take his hand. I did so, and he lifted me to my feet.

"So, what will we focus on today?" I asked. He hesitated, taking in my appearance.

"Today you'll start with assessing your skills," he said slowly. "If you're up to it."

"I am."

He nodded, and we walked silently back to our tent. I was surprised to find Fin lounging on Calian's cot. Calian, however, was not surprised.

"Have you heard of boundaries?" Calian asked.

Fin feigned ignorance. "What are those?" He sat up and rested on his elbows. He whistled lowly once he saw how disheveled I was. "I'll go find you food," Fin said more seriously. He stood and darted out.

I threw my hands up in the air. To hell with it all. "What do these Trials entail?" I asked Calian. My stomach grumbled. I needed food. How long had it been since I'd last eaten? I couldn't remember.

"Each will test your elemental magic, and the gods will determine if you are worthy of it." He proceeded toward the center of the tent and leaned on the pole. I wondered if the weight of his stupid muscles would cause it to fall over. He crossed his arms in front of his chest. The pole didn't budge.

"Let's say I pass with flying colors?" I chortled at my own joke, but Calian didn't seem to appreciate my humor which was seriously rude. I was the one destined to save the world while losing everything. Shouldn't I be able to laugh every once-in-a-while?

"What happens after that?" I asked.

"We travel to the City of Nimerah once your training is complete. But you have to have Nimerah's blessing before we can move out. We'll stay as long as we need to. This camp is full of soldiers to protect you at all costs for as long as it takes."

I'm not sure how I felt about others blindly willing to lay down their lives for me, a stranger. "What will I do in the city?"

"Meet with the Dragoncouncil."

"To ensure that I'm fully capable of defending the six kingdoms?"

"I suppose so." He took a brief sniff, and his nose scrunched up and his eyebrows wrinkled. "Rehema's right. You do need to wash up. I'll bring in some warm water and cloths." He nodded and left.

I began to feel suffocated sitting alone in the tent. I needed to step back outside into the sun and fresh air, but when I stood to do so, Morwen walked in with what appeared to be my new training attire and a small tray of fresh fruit, sausage, and a cup of water—she must have run into Fin. I hastily grabbed the plate and inhaled the food like a rabid wolf. I ate quickly, barely stopping for air as I scarfed down the sweet grapes and plump strawberries. Once I'd finished my meal, I gulped down the water. I sat down the cup and made eye contact with Morwen. As embarrassed as I should have been for my lack of manners, I wasn't. And her eyes held no judgment.

Without a word, she handed me a pair of black pants that could have been mistaken for tights, a long-sleeved black hooded tunic with a cowl neck, and a sleeveless linen shirt.

"Thank you. For everything. The food. These…" I looked more closely at the clothes, turning them over several times in my hands. They were heavier than I'd anticipated, but they were clean. At this point, anything was better than my dirty, tattered dress and worn-out shoes.

Pinned under Morwen's arm was a pair of black boots. They didn't look as worn as those boots the soldiers were wearing. In fact, they didn't look like a soldier's boots at all. These were slender and appeared to be knee-length.

Morwen spoke as she handed them to me. "Your feet look to be about the same size as mine, so I brought you a pair of my boots. I hope these are more comfortable than any of those that the soldiers wear. Even the women's boots are stiff. Oh! And there are some undergarments folded within the pants. I thought I'd hide them just in case Calian was in here."

"Thank you. I truly appreciate your kindness."

"Anything for the Dragonheir of Nimerah," she smiled.

"Just Emera is fine."

"Of course. No need for lengthy titles between friends." *Friends.* It was probably premature to believe we were friends, but I wanted to be. As much as I missed Dwyn, Morwen's immediate warmth and welcoming started to make up for the loss I was feeling. My upper lip began to quiver. The familiar tug of sadness began to pull at me, attempting to drown me in more tears of sorry. I ignored it and raised my chin. This was my life now. I had to accept it.

Sensing my struggle, Morwen filled the silence with conversation. "This has no doubt been a difficult process for you. I grew up learning each Dragongod and Dragongoddess. I studied our history. I know of Dragonmagic—elemental and chaos. When I was told at my Partition about the prophecy, I wasn't all that surprised. But you had no such upbringing, and I'm sorry for that."

"Don't be sorry. You didn't even know I existed."

"True. But the sentiment is still there." She gave a friendly smile.

Calian suddenly appeared with a bucket of water and rags. "Gregory had some boiling water left over from breakfast. It's not boiling, but still warm enough, I think."

"It will be fine. Thank you," I assured him.

"I'm going to check on Rehema. I'll meet up with you in a moment." She put her hand on my shoulder and gave a light, reassuring squeeze. Then she left, leaving me with Calian. He sat the bucket near my cot and tossed the rags next to my pillow. He stood straight, looking directly into my eyes. They moved slightly back and forth as if he were searching. I cocked my head slightly, confused.

"Is there something wrong?" I asked.

"I'm just trying to figure you out."

"Not much to figure out."

He cleared his throat. "Right. Well…Um…I'll leave you to it."

"I shouldn't be long," I said and grabbed a rag from the pile. "I'll meet you…Where?"

"Head toward the front gate and take a left at the horse troughs. Walk until you see the training ring." Before I could confirm, he left.

"You'll find it, Em," I reassured myself. I undressed, dipped the rag in the water, and pressed it to my skin. As much as I wanted to relish the lukewarm water, I made haste to finish scrubbing my skin. Once I looked somewhat presentable, I soaked my hair for a few minutes before drying it with a dry cloth. Time was wasting. If I didn't figure out how to use my magic and receive each blessing, the six kingdoms were doomed…*apparently*.

The clothes Morwen gave me resembled nothing of my previous wardrobe. The pants were thick, but somewhat stretchy, easily sliding over my curves. I tucked a thin white top into them before grabbing the black long-sleeved tunic. Over that was an additional layer: a black leather corset. I laced it up, cinching my waist. I found it somewhat odd, but it was still better than my dirty, tattered dress. Lastly, I stepped into the boots and laced them. They hugged my feet a little too tightly, but they would no doubt stretch a little after wearing them a day or two. The tunic had a hood, so I lifted the hood over my head; the top of it hovered just above my eyes.

"I'm definitely not the person I was," I said to no one.

*   *   *

Morwen and I departed for the training ring once I'd disposed of the dirty bath water. We rounded the horse troughs and headed down the path Calian said was to the training ring. This area of the camp was cooler than where the tents stood, probably from the height of the trees blocking out direct sunlight. Not that I was complaining.

The temperature within the Kingdom of Water always stayed pretty neutral. It was never too hot, nor too cold in the kingdom. I wondered how the weather would fare within the City of Nimerah which was at the center of the six kingdoms.

The sounds of grunts, groans, and the occasional yell became louder the closer we got to the ring. It was a large area with a small pathway leading to its center. A wall of rocks and stones were piled up to my waist, serving as a boundary for whatever training went on inside the ring. A few chairs lined the rocky perimeter as well as a large tree stump. Besides the narrow dirty path, the rest of the ring was grassy with patches of dirt.

Fin was crouched low on the southern end of the ring, wiping his nose with his thumb. I focused in on the blood that now stained his shirt. A quiver of arrows hung from his back. A large, slender bow lay close to his feet. Across from Fin stood Calian with a smug look of victory planted on his face. And he was shirtless. I stopped dead in my tracks. Sweat glistened on his chest from the sun. "Holy Gods," I breathed.

"Dragonmagic is an unfair advantage, Westbow," Fin coughed.

"Your enemy will use their gifts to their advantage. If that's Dragonmagic, then you need to be prepared for it," Calian retorted. Fin looked just as serious as he gathered his composure and stood, giving one final wipe of his nose and wiping the blood on his shirt. I glanced back at Calian. His eyes were once again a fiery red. I could feel the energy permeating from his body and saw it gather at his hands. His muscles tensed and all focus was on Fin. I hoped Fin could take it. An additional blow from Calian, and he could be out cold. Or worse.

I inhaled sharply and slowly sat on a nearby tree stump. I stared in awe as Calian created fire within his palms. It continued to grow until the flames, rolling and flickering like waves, were poised and ready to be unleashed. He was powerful, and I couldn't take my eyes off of him. He shifted his weight and pulled his arm back, gathering energy, and shot balls of fire toward Fin. Fin dove, barely missing the flames, and somersaulted beside his bow. In the blink of an eye, Fin knocked an arrow and shot at Calian. Calian bent back, the arrow narrowly missing his left shoulder. A low growl of frustration parted his lips. Fin smiled.

"Aren't you supposed to be one of the strongest Dragonheirs?" Fin taunted.

"Aren't you supposed to be the fastest archer?" Calian replied.

"I am."

"Then why did you miss?"

"Who says I missed?" Fin threw Calian a mischievous grin. Understanding registered on Calian's face, and he looked down to see an arrow protruding from his left rib cage, just under his heart. I released the breath I'd been holding. Fin had shot two arrows simultaneously.

"Touché," Calian chuckled.

Fin dropped his shoulders and relaxed. He walked toward Calian who sat on a nearby chair. For someone who had been shot with an arrow that narrowly missed his heart, Calian seemed unusually calm. He closed his eyes, steadied his breathing, and squeezed his fists. Fin leaned over, placed one hand behind Calian's right shoulder, and gripped the arrow with his right hand. Fin pulled the arrow quickly while Calian let out a groan. Blood rushed from the wound and trickled down Calian's bronzed skin. He placed his hand over it and pressed tightly.

"No need to worry, Emera," Calian said.

"I'm not worried. I'm sure a big strong man like you can handle a flesh wound," I replied nonchalantly.

"Just making sure you aren't going to cry on me now," he joked.

"Never."

"Ouch," Fin said and laughed.

"As much as I'd love to chat, I believe we need to see what Emera can do," Morwen reminded them.

"Let me grab my shirt," Calian said, and he walked to the edge of the ring and grabbed a shirt hanging from the rocks.

"Wouldn't bandages work better?" I asked.

"He won't need them," Fin answered.

"Why?"

"Because he will just use his fire to cauterize the wound."

"Well, that sounds awful."

"He's a strong guy. He's the strongest Dragonheir to date I'm told," Fin replied and shifted his gaze away from Calian to look at me directly, "Until you."

"I'm not strong."

"Yet," Fin added.

"We'll see."

"See about what?" Calian asked, holding his hand to where the arrow punctured him.

"How quickly she can beat you," Fin answered. He meandered to the rock wall and hoisted himself up. He sat next to a small brown bag and pulled out an apple. He took a loud crunch before adding, "I doubt it takes long."

"I'm not sure I deserve that confidence, especially without my *mother's* blessing," I said. It sounded weird to call her mother. Maybe I should say Dragonmother.

"Let's see about that," Calian said. "Each Trial will require that you create the element you are calling on. Before we attempt to initiate one, I want to assess where you are with any other skills."

Fin waved his hand furiously. "Oh! Me first! Me first!" I hopped off the wall, grabbed his bow, and threw it at me. "Take this."

I didn't expect the bow to feel as light as it did. A touch of the smooth yew wood and the tight string sent my mind back home, hunting with my father. I could have stayed there, savoring the memory of a fresh kill.

But a sudden jab brought me back. "Ouch!"

Fin laughed and held an arrow in my face. "Shoot it," he said.

I snatched the arrow from his hand and smirked. Fin winked and walked to where Calian—who was now eating an apple—stood. I looked down at the bow that I gripped in my hand. Forget magic. This, I could do. With a deep breath, serene focus washed over me as I readied the arrow and drew the taut bowstring to my chin. Pulling it back, time seemed to momentarily pause. My gaze narrowed, honing in on the apple Calian was eating. I waited for the precise moment.

Noticing my pause, Calian held the apple out and gestured with his hands. "Well? Are you going to show us what you can do?" With sudden release, I let go, and the arrow propelled forward, slicing into the air and hitting its target. Calian dropped the apple, and a faint thud could be heard when it hit the ground.

Fin beamed, a wide smile spread on his face, and Morwen whistled lowly. Calian stared at the apple for a little while before he slowly raised his eyes to mine.

"I told you I was good with a bow," I said.

"That you did."

The world around us faded into a blur as our eyes remained locked on one another's.

Morwen coughed, pulling us out of whatever trance we'd been under. "Can we move on?" she asked.

"Yes, of course," Calian answered.

"Good," Morwen said. "Emera, do you mind if I see what abilities you have with water?"

"Sure. Is this my Trial?" I asked.

"No. Once I see how well you do with water, I can plan out the Trials," he answered.

I couldn't help it. I grinned and said, "And what makes you qualified to plan out these Trials?"

He instantly focused his expression and didn't hesitate to say, "The Dragoncouncil. Now, listen to Morwen. She's going to guide you to connect you to your water element." I dropped my smile and nodded.

Morwen stood close behind me and spoke gently, "Close your eyes. Clear your mind. Take a deep breath, inhaling through the nose and exhaling through the mouth. Your water element is one of tranquility and peace. To harness that magic, you need to be calm and grounded." I let my mind go blank and felt the cool, fluid-like energy I had before.

"Good," Calian praised, his voice more distant. He must have been on the other side of the ring now. "Now, a couple of more times. But on the last inhale, I want you to focus your mind on one single element: water."

"I can already feel it," I whispered with a smile tugging at my lips.

I could still feel Morwen close. "That's wonderful, Emera," she said. "Hold onto that feeling. Let it flow within you. Welcome it into every fiber of your being. With that flow of tranquility, I want you to manifest an image of water—a river, a rainstorm, anything—and draw that power from your core to that image."

Calian added, "Create that image."

"Easy for you to say," I mumbled.

On the last inhale, I attempted to conjure an image of running water, like a small stream in a forest. But before the image could take hold in my mind, my peace morphed into the familiar anxiety I knew all too well. The uneasiness grabbed hold of my chest, whispering negative words of discouragement.

What if I couldn't do this? What if Rehema was wrong to invest so much faith in me? What if I failed, and the six kingdoms burned?

My breathing became rapid as a wave of energy dwelling in the pit of my stomach released itself and filled my body.

"Calm down, Emera. Stay calm. Steady your breathing," Morwen instructed. But I couldn't.

I heard the breeze pick up into a howling wind, whipping my hair around me. Behind my eyelids, I could see the sunlight fading. The temperature chilled, and tiny prickling sensations stung my face. Fresh water dropped from above, and rain ensued.

I heard Fin let out a whistle. "My gods," he exclaimed.

"Open your eyes, Emera. See what you've created with your water element," Morwen said in awe. She didn't know of the thunderous storm currently taking over my mind, body, and soul.

I opened my eyes and witnessed my internal struggle coming to life. Dark clouds swept across the sky at a rapid pace, harboring a rainstorm. My intuition told me that it wasn't just a rainstorm coming. Within the dark clouds, I saw flashes of light. I heard a slight rumble as the storm came closer.

I turned to Morwen. "I didn't imagine a rainstorm!" I yelled over the deafening wind. I suddenly felt a shock in my palms, so I looked down in fear to see my fingertips emitted sparks and were making crackling and popping noises. "Back up, Morwen!" I demanded.

A panic-filled scream tore from my lips, and I hunched over, pulling my hands into my stomach to examine them. The energy from my fingertips pulsed stronger and stronger. The electric power begged to be released.

"Emera!" Calian yelled.

I lifted my chin, and faced Calian who stood several paces ahead of me, a confused look on his face. "Something isn't right!" I shouted.

The build-up was unbearable, and without warning, my magic unleashed from within me. Lightning shot from my palms and crashed into a nearby tree, cutting it in half. Fin leapt from where he was sitting just before the top of the tree came crashing down. Had he not moved, he would have been crushed. Rain continued to fall faster, and the droplets were now the size of gold coins.

Fin hopped off the wall, grabbed Morwen's hand, and shouted, "We better warn the others!" Worry seized my heart. I closed my palms and pulled in my arms, hugging my core. I closed my eyes and tried to get the storm to stop. But I couldn't. Tears fell from my eyes, painting a salty line from my eyelashes to my chin.

"Emera, you must control yourself!" Calian yelled, though I had difficulty hearing him. The thunder and wind made it impossible for sound to travel. "Emera!" he yelled again. I opened my eyes and watched while he pushed against the wind, reaching his arms out to grab me. The slight curls of his hair were wet and plastered against his forehead. I stood when he reached me, and the moment he wrapped his arms around me, thunder roared, and lightning crashed.

"I can't make it stop!" I cried.

"Yes, you can! Remember that night in the forest, and how you were able to calm yourself and the atmosphere around you? You can do that now!"

The wind continued to blow with fury. Tents started lifting from the ground and flying into one another. I watched as horses galloped into the forest with a group of soldiers running after them, looking at me as they passed. The fear in their eyes punched me in the gut.

I pushed away from Calian, closed my eyes, and concentrated. With everything I had left, I pulled at the energy raging within me and called upon the element of water once again. This time I envisioned a small stream of calming energy and took hold of it. I forced my chaotic emotions back down while letting the calming energy flow freely. The wind calmed, and the rain stopped.

I opened my eyes and began to inhale deeply. In through the nose, out through the mouth. In through the nose, out through the mouth.

Sunlight seeped through the disintegrating storm clouds. Surprisingly, I wasn't wet. At all. Calian, on the other hand, was drenched. He stood in front of me and grabbed my upper arms. He looked me up and down then our eyes connected. "Are you okay?" he asked. Was it my imagination, or did his voice shake with…*fear*? Was he *afraid* of me?

I nodded slowly. "What did I create?"

"Chaos," he answered, and a smile spread across his face.

CHAPTER

EIGHT

"Dragonmagic can be unpredictable if not wielded properly. Especially chaos magic." Calian rubbed the back of his neck and spoke as if the past moments were a normal part of his day. "We just witnessed the raw power you have when calling upon only one element. Imagine what you could do if you wielded *all*?" We walked out of the training ring and back into the main part of camp.

"I'm confused. Didn't I just use the element of air? That wind was very strong."

"You did."

"I shouldn't have access to any other elements without the blessings, right?"

"Nimerah might be testing you. Maybe she's given you a little bit of chaos magic to see how you wield it throughout your Trials? Because chaos magic works with elemental magic and blends it. It would explain a thunderstorm with high winds and lightning instead of just a rainstorm. You used the chaos magic to make your water magic, and what appeared to be air magic, stronger and more potent. Your emotions then took over, and...well..." he gestured towards the destruction left from the storm. "It's okay, Emera. This is all new to you. There are bound to be mishaps," he said. If I didn't know any better, I swore Calian was trying to make me feel better.

"This looks to be a little more than just a mishap," I mumbled. I could still see the soldiers' fear in my mind.

"If you let your emotions dominate your magic, you become chaos itself. Powerful, yet undisciplined. Who knows what you could do?"

"You mean destroy," I said in defeat.

His hand brushed against mine. "I didn't say that."

My heart did a flip-flop from his touch, but I managed to keep my face neutral. "You didn't have to. If that was just a kernel of what I could do without control, I'd hate to see me at full strength when I do have all my elemental powers as well as my Dragonmother's blessing."

Calian stopped. His lips parted into an open smile exposing a hint of his perfectly straight teeth. "Dragonmother?" he asked.

"Just feels better than calling her mother," I replied. We started walking again, and I noticed that most of the tents within the camps were still standing although they sagged from the weight of the rain on their tops. Still, the vacant areas meant some tents were torn down or blown away leaving soldiers without shelter. Buckets were strewn about the camp along with various clothing articles, plates, papers, and more. I felt guilty.

"I'm sorry," I murmured.

"Don't be," said Calian gruffly. "Had the soldiers secured their tents properly, all would be standing. That's one way to tell the difference between a seasoned soldier and a new one."

"It's still my fault."

"Do not apologize for this. They knew what they were getting into when they volunteered."

I figured arguing was a moot point, so I stopped talking altogether. We closed in on the tents atop the small hill.

Rehema came running out to meet us. She looked hysterical. "Was that…you?" she asked me.

"Afraid so," I mumbled.

"That's wonderful!" she cried. She clasped her hands together and looked to the sky. "Blessed Nimerah. The world will be saved." We all continued inside the tent and sat down in the back. Well, Rehema and I sat down.

"I don't have her blessing yet," I told her. "I think I'd know if I did."

Rehema still beamed, her face lit with joy, "But we're getting there! You'll have her blessing in no time."

Morwen entered the tent. Her clothes were wet with dirt and mud. Her wet hair was pulled back into a braid. Even soaked, she was beautiful.

"I believe it's safe to say you're very close to obtaining Anahita's blessing. Once you do, I reason that the other gods and goddesses won't be too far behind. I'd wager that Dragongoddess Ilmari will follow. That was some powerful magic, Emera. Well done," she said and clapped her hands.

Well done? Aside from her being oblivious to the destruction I'd caused; she hadn't seen the fear in the soldiers' eyes.

"Where's Fin?" I asked her. *Did I hurt him?* That's what I really wanted to know.

"I helped a few soldiers locate their supplies, and Fintan went to go find a couple of stray horses. He definitely has the advantage when it comes to not spooking them." She smiled. I saw the admiration in her eyes. They shined like the brightest stars on the darkest of nights when she spoke of Fin.

"I should go help the soldiers secure the fallen tents," said Calian. He looked at me, "I can have someone bring you…" His voice trailed when he discovered that despite the heavy winds and rain, my clothes were perfectly dry as were my hair and skin. I just shrugged. I had no answers. And quite honestly, I was tired of trying to figure out how or why things happened to me.

Fin entered the tent just then. "All horses have been accounted for. There is still some debris and damaged tents, but nothing we can't fix."

"Good," Calian said and addressed all of us. "We need a solid plan for Emera. I think she should begin her Water Trial. She's already connected with Anahita, so it's the best one to start." He looked between all of us, waiting for us to agree with him.

"She didn't get Anahita's blessing after that? Or Ilmari's?" Fin asked. "That was some powerful wind and rain," he reasoned.

"No," Calian answered. "She created them, but she couldn't control them." I looked down in shame.

"Don't worry, Emera," Morwen said. "I think you're more than capable." She grabbed my hands and pulled me closer to her. "But let's take a break." She smiled and squeezed my hands in hers. "I think emotions are running high right now. It might be best if we resume the course tomorrow with your official Water Trial." She turned her head and looked at Calian. "Don't you think," she said with a warning tone to her voice.

Calian squinted his eyes just a little, thinking carefully about how to respond. "Agreed," he said. I let out a breath I didn't realize I had been holding. I didn't need to rest physically—although my strength was depleted. I needed more mental rest.

Rehema looked at Calian. "I've made contact with the Dragoncouncil. You are to head north to the City of Dhara to retrieve its Dragonheir. Emera must be through all of her Trials by the time you leave which will be in five days."

I snorted. "What?" I cried.

"It seems unwise to rush her Trials," he said, every word drenched with disdain. "Are you sure you intercepted the message clearly?"

Well, that was the wrong thing to say to Rehema.

"Do you doubt my abilities, Calian Westbow?" Rehema challenged.

Calian ignored her question. "I was specifically assigned to her so that I could train her. I was not assigned to anyone else. Fin can retrieve the Dragonheir so that I can stay and prepare her for what comes next," I caught a spark in his eyes. They were ready to ignite into flame.

"It would be wise to watch your tone. I am only the messenger." Rehema didn't seem like the sort that was annoyed often because she always seemed to be in a joyous mood, but I could tell she wasn't interested in arguing with Calian.

"Emera cannot be pushed into Trial after Trial. She's emotional and undisciplined. In case you didn't notice, she brought in a thunderstorm *without* Anahita's or Ilmari's blessings. Can you imagine what would happen when she receives Nimerah's blessing while I'm gone?"

"Excuse me," I interjected.

"I trust that the Dragongods—especially Nimerah herself —will ensure that nothing too extreme will come to pass," Rehema responded evenly with just a hint of irritation.

Calian scoffed, "You priests are all the same. Blinded by your faith. With her instability and raw power, she could kill everyone in this camp."

Wait a minute. Was he serious?

"I wouldn't do that," I insisted. They both continued to talk over me.

"Who would be left to fulfill your precious prophecy should she be pushed into the Trials too quickly, and she fails to be blessed by your precious Dragongods?" he demanded. Flames twisted in Calian's eyes; his anger palpable.

Rehema rose from her chair. "Do not dare question the Dragoncouncil, Calian Westbow. Your life was nothing without their guidance!" It was the first time I'd seen her visibly upset. Her voice boomed throughout the tent. I could swear the entire camp was silenced by her words. I gave Calian a look that said, *I agree but cool it*. He stopped arguing but continued to glare at her. I looked back and forth between them, but all I could do was put my hands in my lap and bear through the awkward silence. Maybe once they calmed down, we could discuss how unsurprisingly Calian was right. Undergoing all of the Trials in one short week seemed hasty.

He sighed heavily, his eyes returning to their normal gray. "Fine," he growled through clenched teeth.

I stood abruptly. Did he just give up?

"Wait. That's it?" Calian and Rehema finally acknowledged my existence. I turned to Rehema and kept my breathing even to keep my frustration under control. I failed. "You are," I accused her, "just ordering him to go? Because he's right." I turned and pointed at him. "Which I hate admitting, thank you very much." I focused back on Rehema. "I just had my first assessment, and I almost destroyed the camp!" I flailed my arms like a madwoman.

"The Dragoncouncil has spoken. Calian must leave for the City of Dhara in five days," Rehema replied. Whatever patience she had with me had expired in the argument with Calian. That was fine with me. I had no patience to offer her in return.

"Would it really be an issue if I go instead?" Fin asked Rehema.

Rehema leveled her voice as if she were talking to children, "Calian is whom the Dragoncouncil appointed, therefore, it is his responsibility," she said flatly.

"Oh, sure," I agreed. She detected my sarcasm because she gave me a scathing look.

"Emera," Calian warned. A spark of fire came back to life in his eyes.

"What?" I snapped.

"I agree with you. Okay? But in the end, Rehema is right. If they say I have to go, I go." I knew he was speaking to me to calm me down because I could feel the temperature rising within the tent. Somewhere in my brain, my voice of reason was telling me that I needed to subdue my anger.

I didn't listen to the voice.

"Is the council supposed to mean something to me? Because I don't care what they say," I spat. Calian opened his mouth to speak, but I claimed the opportunity to express my frustrations before a sound came from him. "So far, you've made it clear you think me being the *savior,* or whatever you want to call it, is ridiculous. You've insisted we must train me properly to conquer the Trials so that I can receive all these blessings so that I'm powerful enough for a prophecy I just learned about," I paused and took a breath. "And now you're standing down to this council instead of ensuring I'm ready to complete each Trial successfully?" My blood boiled under my skin.

He didn't answer for a moment. When he did, his voice was low and still. He held his hands up in surrender. "Are you finished?"

My heart began racing, and all I felt was intense warmth creep from my chest to my neck and face. In a fluid motion, heat shot from my head to my fingertips, and my hands spread out. Balls of flame began forming in my hands.

"Absolutely not!" I yelled. And just like I'd seen him do many times, the fireballs exploded from my hands toward Nimerah's banner at the opposite end of the sanctuary. The fire crashed into it, and the banner instantly burst into flames.

Rehema gasped, Morwen smiled, and Fin said, "Whoa."

Calian continued to look at me. He slowly closed the distance between us. I raised my hands to my face and inspected them. There was no trace of a fire. They looked and felt completely normal.

"I never liked that banner," Fin joked. He looked at me, and after seeing how visibly upset I was, his grin vanished. "Sorry. It's how I deal with terror. Because you're terrifying, and it's amazing. Any minute you could probably blink us out of existence."

"Let's hope not," Calian said to Fin, but his eyes remained locked onto mine. "Breathe, Emera. You're letting your emotions control you." I breathed. In and out. Inhale and exhale. "It seems like Vukan appreciates your…tenacity. We will follow up with your Fire Trial after Air."

I took some deep breaths and slowed my heart. "Which will come after Water?" I asked. My question came out more like a statement.

"Fantastic!" Rehema cried. She clapped her hands in merriment and threw her arms around me in a deep embrace. She lowered her voice and whispered in my ear. "I understand your *reluctance* to perform each Trial so quickly, but I assure you that the chaos power of Nimerah will guide you."

"Rehema's right," Calian closed the distance between us. Any other soul would have crept cautiously like Rehema did as she passed me to salvage what was left of the banner. Calian didn't hesitate though. He walked right up to me and placed both of his hands on my shoulder to steady me. "We'll get you through this."

The snap of a twig indicated a stranger had entered the tent. All of us turned our attention toward the entrance. The man assessed the situation quickly, looking around the tent and back to me. His light gray eyes were the color of summer rain clouds rolling in over the sea which harmonized with his cool taupe complexion. He wore a contemplative expression as his eyes surveyed the room.

Fin gestured toward the stranger. "We can get Emera through the Trials, and once you leave, I can take over her physical training, I'll work with her regarding her Dragonmagic, and I'll urge Er-jon here to assist us both," he said. A playful twinkle shone in his eyes.

"Er-jon?" I asked the stranger.

Erjon tilted his head. "It's pronounced Air-yon," he said, clearly bored with Fin already. So, this was the other Dragonheir Rehema mentioned. Another member of the Ring of Six.

"But that's not how it's spelled," Fin insisted.

Erjon's expression remained unchanged. Something told me that Fin had mispronounced Erjon's name before, yet Erjon remained unbothered. He stood there silently, observing me. He was just a little shorter and more slender than Calian, rivaling Fin's frame. He wore plain light gray clothes of the same style Calian wore. There was an obvious difference between this Dragonborn—how I knew that I wasn't sure—and the other two men in the tent. Whereas Calian was the picture of physicality and power, and Fin, the picture of speed and agility, Erjon's gift was his intellect. I wasn't sure how I knew that exactly, but I did. Erjon was smart.

"Has she produced any other elements of her Dragonmagic?" Erjon asked.

"She has," Calian responded.

I waved my hand to get Erjon's attention. "I'm right here, thank you," I remarked.

"Well, have you?" he asked.

"Water, Air, and now Fire…" I rattled off.

"We should have hoped for her to be further along than just three elements." He brought his hand to his face and cradled his chin, tapping his lips in thought. "I'll see if I can locate Nimerah herself or determine if there is another path to obtaining your chaos magic should you not pass each Trial prior to Calian leaving." His arrogance filled the space abruptly like a thick fog, and I felt like I would suffocate. He seemed very sure of himself.

"Good. Sounds like we've got a solid plan," Calian said and nodded.

So that was that. I had one week to pass the Trials and receive the blessings from the gods.

No one said a word for a few minutes. Finally, Calian broke the tension. "Morwen insists you get a break. What are your thoughts?" I felt like this was a test, but I was tired. I needed to regenerate. Did Dragonheirs do that? Regenerate their magic?

"A break should help. But tomorrow, we are beginning first thing in the morning," I insisted.

Calian nodded in affirmation and said as he was leaving, "I think I'll go change my clothes and then see if Cook has had any other issues with theft." And with that, he left the tent and Erjon followed on his heels.

"I think I'll go rest," I told Morwen. "Can we speak later?"

Her eyes brightened. "Of course," she said.

I smiled at Rehema and waved at Fin before leaving. I exited and walked into the sun's friendly rays, squinting to adjust my eyes to their brightness. The ground began to dry out from their caressing touch. Inhaling deeply, the smell of nature swirled within my lungs. I exhaled and looked down the path. Despite the gnawing feeling that I'd never be worthy of any blessing, the vitality of the day gave me a sense of peace with my new life. I could see soldiers continuing to get their supplies back in order, and a few even nodded as they looked in my direction. Their nods brought back the guilt of what I'd done.

And the good feeling's gone, I thought.

I dropped my chin and took a step, almost knocking over a woman who walked up to the worship tent.

"I'm so sorry! Please forgive me. I wasn't paying attention."

Her startling eyes held no anger. She nodded and smiled. I formed a faint smile of my own and gave a quick, shy nod. She paused and fully nodded with what seemed like a small curtsy. The unspoken conversation between us eased my guilt, and I felt a sense of serenity wash over me.

Although going back to the tent and resting was the smart decision and the right decision, I needed to clear my head. I was angry, frustrated, and now anxious that I wouldn't be able to successfully complete each Trial before Calian left. I desperately wanted a bow. I hadn't hunted in weeks, and I yearned for the chase. But I didn't have a bow to go hunting with, so I took off for the stables. If anyone would listen to my troubles without trying to give me unsolicited advice, it was Dhruv. Yes, I wanted to talk to a horse.

But when I reached the stables, Dhruv wasn't the only familiar face there.

"I thought you were going to change," I said.

Calian stood brushing Dhruv's mane. The horse's eyes were glazed with satisfaction. "It seems I changed my mind instead of my clothes," Calian quipped.

The serenity I had felt coming from the woman with striking eyes had vanished. I stopped dead in my tracks when I realized that Calian made me feel betrayed. Or maybe it was that he hadn't put up much of a fight to stay.

"How could you do that," I asked softly.

"Do what? Brush the horse? Dhruv may look like a fierce beast, but he's a bit of a softie when it comes to having his coat brushed." Dhruv sighed in agreement. Yes, the horse sighed.

"You know that isn't what I'm talking about."

Calian continued to brush Dhruv as I ran my hand along Dhruv's mane. "You'll be fine, Emera. You'll get through the Trials successfully," he turned and flashed his perfect teeth. Stupid teeth. "You worry too much, especially about yourself."

"It's not me I'm worried about, Calian. It's everyone else!" Dhruv snorted in agreement. Even the horse knew I was dangerous.

"Everyone else has been trained to handle themselves in all types of situations."

I stomped over and planted myself right in front of him. "You didn't agree at first. What changed your mind?"

"Besides remembering that I made an oath to lead Nimerah's heir as her general, so I should probably complete the missions I was assigned to do?"

I didn't have to see my face to know the shock I felt was plainly visible. I felt the breeze come through my mouth as it gaped open. A gnat must have flown in as well because I choked on one…or my spit.

"Excuse me? General?" I choked out.

"Your general," he confirmed. He retrieved an apple from his pocket and fed it to Dhruv who neighed in merriment.

I pushed my thoughts to the side. "Well, besides that."

Calian changed the subject abruptly. "It's not ridiculous."

"Come again?"

"I don't think you being Nimerah's heir is ridiculous. I admit that I thought that at first…" He quickly mounted Dhruv in one fluid motion and looked down at me.

"You don't have to admit anything. It was clear to me," I retorted. "I know that I'm not as powerful as I should be. I know that I have a lot to learn. But you came in with your powers, strong muscles, and know-it-all attitude and *laughed* at me."

"Strong muscles, huh?"

I threw him a foul gesture. Like Dwyn had said, I was no lady.

"You pretty much said the whole world was doomed because I'm the one responsible for its survival. And you know what the worst part was? It was that I didn't argue because I agreed with you. It was so obvious that I didn't know anything when I met you! I felt foolish around you. I could just feel you mocking my every word and my every move. And yet...I hung onto your every word. I listened to everything you said because deep down, I felt that you were the one who could help me accept this role I've been forced to play. And..."

"I'm sorry."

"Being a *goddess* is a whole other level. But...Wait. What did you say?"

I looked at him. Really looked at him. The quick-witted playfulness in his eyes was gone, replaced with a look of remorse. He took an audible gulp.

"I said that I'm sorry. I didn't know you felt this way."

"Well, you did. And before you go find the next heir, I thought you should know. I would hate for them to feel as I did." I leaned into Dhruv and rested my head on his neck for a short moment. Then I turned and left Calian Westbow.

*　　*　　*

"There's a large fire by the kitchen tent. A soldier named Jensen has some honey ale the men are playing cards for. There's music and dancing. The men are celebrating." I was currently sitting in Morwen's tent. I had risen from my cot after the sun had fallen below the tree line.

"Celebrating what?" I asked curiously.

"Not what…but *who*," she grinned.

"Me?" I was horrified, to say the least.

"Think of it as a belated activation celebration, if you'd prefer that, over the coming of Nimerah's heir."

"I just destroyed their tents and supplies."

"They don't care. It's what they signed up for." Her words brought back my conversation with Calian right after the storm. I wasn't sure a celebration was in order, though.

"I appreciate the invitation, Morwen, but I'm not sure I'd be good company."

"That's where you're wrong. You'd be the best company compared to everyone else," she smiled. She then threw her elbows out and jumped around like she was dancing. How very regal of her. I snorted and then laughed at her ridiculousness.

What could it hurt to have an evening free of all things Dragonheir and prophecy? I thought. "All right. I give in! Just stop doing that, please," I said and laughed louder.

Morwen stood and joined in my laughter. She pulled me beside her, and we both strolled out of the tent into the night air. The smell of burning wood and cooked meat and the sounds of laughter and music greeted us when we arrived at Cook's tent which was the only other tent the size of Rehema's sanctuary. Half the tent was open for soldiers to line up and get their food. A line had already formed, and the man I finally learned was Cook stood behind a cauldron suspended over a fire, serving the night's stew. To the left side of him was a grill over a wooden box with meat sizzling on a cast iron pan. A few men played a lively song using a variety of instruments while others were laughing and telling stories. It looked like a gathering for a family celebration.

"I'll grab us some stew. Why don't you find us a place to sit?" Morwen asked. She headed toward Cook while I surveyed the seating arrangements. Small tables were scarce. There were mostly benches arranged in an arc around a large fire. Fortunately, I passed by a table right when a drunken soldier got up to relieve himself, or so he said. I'd seen men like him pass through the docks of Medora. He wouldn't remember where he was sitting if he even made it back. I gladly took the small table and inhaled deeply. The cool night breeze was refreshing regardless of if it was tainted with smoke. We sat just outside the fire's reach, so I could still breathe in the forest air, a mix of pine and wood. The fragrance was so different from the sea salt and lilies of Medora, but I embraced it just the same. I looked all around me. Despite the laughter and loud conversations, the night promised relaxation.

But the night quickly broke its promise when I caught a glimpse of Calian talking to Fin and a handful of soldiers on the other side of the fire. He was seated on a tree log with Fin at his left side. He spoke animatedly, gesturing with his hands when he talked and throwing his head back when he laughed. He paused every so often to take a drink from his tankard. The men soldiers hung on his every word, waiting for their chance to impress their captain with what I imagined would be jokes and tales of heroics.

I figured the women soldiers would be fawning over him, but I was surprised to find that most treated him like the other soldiers. Only a couple batted their lashes at him. Not that those women would get his attention. They didn't seem like the type Calian would want.

Wait. Was I *jealous*? No. Impossible.

Calian turned his head and saw me, so I quickly looked away just in time to see Morwen with our stew and two tankards of water.

"Cook says it's the finest venison in the forest. I think he's telling tales again," she chuckled.

"I'm famished. I'll eat anything." My stomach grumbled in agreement. I started shoveling spoonfuls of stew into my mouth.

"You weren't kidding," Morwen said.

I stopped and saw her gaping at me. I smiled, shrugged, and took a drink. The liquid hit my mouth, but it was bitter tasting, so I choked a little down. Surely Morwen didn't get us some of the honey ale. "You got us water, correct?" I asked.

"That is correct," she answered between her bites of stew.

"Hmm. Just tastes funny, that's all."

"I wouldn't be surprised if Cook added a *special ingredient* so that it's the best water of all the six kingdoms," she joked.

"Yeah, right." I continued to eat and drink. I got used to the taste after a while. It was more manageable once I started taking a bite of stew in between each sip of water. The more I ate and drank, the more wonderful the stew became.

"This is the best stew I've ever eaten," I exclaimed. No wonder everyone loved Cook. It was melting in my mouth like the finest chocolates from the Kingdom of Fire. I had some once when a trader came through Medora.

"It's okay. I've had better," said Morwen. She looked up and eyed me suspiciously.

I sat my spoon down. "What? Am I not allowed to like the stew?"

"Liking it is different than saying it's the best," she replied, her brows suddenly furrowed with skepticism.

"So, you say," I said and hiccupped. I tore my gaze from her and looked around the campfire. The once dull colors of the night became vibrant and lively. The music came alive. I saw the waves of the notes coming from the instruments. I watched in wonder as soldiers twirled and clapped around the campfire, the colors of their clothing transforming into vivid blurs of emerald greens and ruby reds against the twisting of the flames.

"Those flames are beautiful," I gushed. Orange, gold, red, and yellow created an autumn tapestry before my eyes even though it was still spring. The smoke curled itself around the tips of the fire.

"They…are…" Morwen said slowly.

"They make me feel all warm and relaxed just looking at them." I closed my eyes and let the heat spread over me, blanketing me in its warmth. I rose from the table and wrapped my arms around myself. I ran my fingers up and down the sides of my clothing.

"Emera, are you okay?"

I opened my eyes. "I am more than okay, Morwen. The music, the atmosphere, it's all exhilarating."

"Something is definitely off," she said, her tone serious. Too serious.

"Nothing is off! Come, let's dance!" I yelled. I moved my body like the dancers from the Kingdom of Fire. My hips led the way, swaying with the music. What was it about that kingdom that was so sensational? Chocolate? Dancers? It wasn't fair.

"Emera, maybe I should get Calian," Morwen's voice was shaky, but I couldn't figure out why. She had no reason to be concerned. I was in full control of my emotions. In fact, I bet I could use my magic without issues.

"Oh, he would just ruin the fun! I feel alive and free!" I raised my arms above my head and began to twist and turn them while I continued to sway back and forth somewhat seductively. From the corner of my eye, I watched Morwen grab my stew and sniff it. She shook her head and then lifted my tankard of water. She sniffed deeply, but immediately pulled away, her face contorted in an awful grimace.

"That's not water," she claimed.

"No! It's Cook's *finest* water," I sang. As I did, beams of light emitted from my palms into the starry night sky. Everything around me suddenly stopped: the music, the laughter, the dancing. Everyone looked up in wonder. Or terror. I couldn't tell. I ceased swaying and twirled instead. The breeze picked up, and the beams of light stopped. I circled my hands high and called to the stars. I called to the element of light, and a shower of fallen stars cascaded over the camp. It brought the soldiers back to their jubilant selves. They clapped and cheered, and the music played once more. Everyone danced as stars fell around them. It was truly magical. I reveled in my glory. I'd done something right for once.

"Morwen," came a growl from behind me.

"Here we go," I groaned. "Sir Grumpy is back." I ignored him and continued dancing in my spot. I was not going to let Sir Grumpy Westbow ruin my good mood.

"I don't know how it happened, Calian," I heard Morwen say. "One minute we were enjoying our food—well, as much as one can enjoy Cook's stew—and the next, she was saying it's the best stew she's ever had."

"Something is definitely wrong if she thinks that's the best stew," Fin added.

I whirled around and faced Fin, pointing a finger in his face. "You sneaky assassin. I need to know the ways of your sneakiness, Fin. Is that a word? *Sneakiness*?"

"She's drunk," Fin declared. He grabbed my finger and lowered it. I responded with a giggle.

"I'm not sure that's entirely accurate," Calian replied. I could feel the heat radiating from him. His Dragonfire was more distinct than the campfire in ways that I couldn't explain.

"She said the water tasted funny, but I didn't think much of it," Morwen admitted.

"You didn't think much of it?" he snarled, a spark of anger in his voice.

No, no, no. That would not do. He would not speak to my friend that way. Maybe if I could get him to see reason, he'd see that this was not Morwen's fault. That I was just having a great time for once.

"Look out, everyone!" I shouted. "Calian's about to lose his temper!"

I sashayed up to him and leaned in, my lips lightly brushing against his ear, "Your eyes are turning red. Someone's hostile."

"You have no idea," he breathed. The temperature between us rose.

And it wasn't from the campfire.

I knew his eyes were ablaze, and I just had to see them. So, I pushed back and grabbed his face with both hands, pulling him eye-to-eye, our noses almost touching. I laughed at how surprised he looked as I stared deep into his fiery red eyes.

He didn't let me admire his ruby-red eyes long because he took a hold of my shoulders and guided me to where I had been sitting earlier. I giggled and plopped down.

"Give me the tankard," he demanded. Fin handed it to him, and he grabbed it forcefully. He lowered his nose to the rim and inhaled. "Where did you get this?" he asked Morwen.

"From Cook's assistant. I requested two tankards of water before getting some stew. The woman had both tankards ready once I returned."

"You!" Calian pointed to a soldier on his way into the kitchen tent and waved the soldier over with this finger. The music stopped and everyone stared as the soldier diverted his route and walked over to us.

"Yes, Captain?" the soldier responded, pulling nervously at the collar of his shirt.

"Cook's assistant, get her for me," Calian ordered.

I scoffed. "Don't be rude. Say please, Calian." He ignored my reprimand.

Seeing that Calian had no intention of saying please, the soldier responded, "I'm the assistant, Captain."

I cackled. "You don't look like a woman," I pointed out.

"Acute observation," Fin commented and angled his head to the side. He lifted the back of his hand and pretended to wipe something from his mouth, but it was evident he did it to hide his smile. I winked in response.

"That's not true, soldier," Morwen stated with a scowl. "The assistant is a woman. I spoke with her earlier." The soldier's face flushed. He was obviously flustered at the accusation.

"You look like a ghost," I giggled. "Calian, you're scaring him. See? He's so pale!"

Calian glared at me, and Fin bit back a laugh.

"I'm s-s-s-sorry, milady," the soldier stammered, clearly nervous. "I'm the assistant. I t-t-t-took a break to…um…um…" he looked back to Calian.

"To *what*, soldier?" Calian barked.

The soldier lowered his chin. "Relieve myself, sir," he whispered.

"We ladies are not children. You don't have to whisper around us," Morwen responded. She pinched the bridge of her nose. I nodded in agreement.

"Of course, sorry, my lady," the soldier apologized.

"Here," Calian shoved the tankard into the soldier's chest. "Take this to Dragonheir Erjon. He's meditating in his tent. Ask him what's in it. It smells like Stormshade was mixed into the water. See what he can make of it," Calian ordered.

"Yes, Captain," the soldier responded. He turned on his heels and left.

"I'll go with him." Morwen declared. She looked at me, "I'm so sorry, Emera." She didn't wait for my response before she hurried after Cook's assistant.

I waved my hands around. "It's fine! I'm fine! We're all fine!" I scanned the crowd of soldiers. They definitely thought I was a lunatic. After a lengthy pause, the crowd went back to ignoring me and the music began again.

Calian leaned down close. "You're not fine," he asserted.

I raised my finger and poked the tip of his nose. He wasn't impressed. He grabbed my arm and pulled me from where I was sitting so quickly that I braced myself for impact, my hands hitting his chest. I looked up into his fiery eyes which were slowly becoming the color of dimming embers. I began to breathe heavily, so I closed my eyes to steady myself. The light, airy feeling I had previously experienced immediately dissipated, leaving me with pressure in my chest that traveled to my stomach.

"I think I'll go talk to Cook and let you deal with her," Fin said slowly and took off for the kitchen tent. "Good luck," he called over his shoulder to Calian and then he finally let out the roar of laughter he'd been holding inside.

"Yeah. Good luck, Calian," I teased. I frowned as his eyes traveled across my face, searching. He opened his mouth to speak, but before he could make any sound, a sharp pain hit my stomach. I was no longer in a joyous mood but instead was now panicked. I looked down, convinced I'd see a knife, but there was nothing. The pain intensified quickly, and my legs gave out. I grabbed Calian's arms and held him tightly as I slumped forward. My vision caught a red substance on my shoes. I brought my hand to my nose and pulled it back.

Blood.

The sharp pain in my stomach intensified, and my mouth forced out a piercing shriek.

"Calian," I pleaded. What was happening to me?

Calian, still holding onto me, yelled with such force I could have sworn that the ground shook beneath our feet. "Fin!"

In any other state, I would have argued that in no way could the Dragonheir of Vukan do that. Shaking the ground seemed more like the element of earth to me. But I said nothing because I was probably dying. I should worry about that.

I rolled my head back and my eyes grew heavier as I looked for Fin. I finally found him conversing with Cook.

"Fin!" Calian yelled again. The music and noise from the crowd of soldiers stopped at once. They were probably annoyed at all the disruptions—not that they'd say it since Calian was their commanding officer.

Fin whipped his head in response to Calian's yell and the ground's rumble, and his eyes went wide. But he wasn't looking at me. He was looking at Calian. My head was pounding, and my eyes hurt. But I still turned my face and fought to see Calian through the slits of my eyelids. In his eyes, I found fear mixed with anger. They were glowing the brightest red I'd ever seen.

CHAPTER

NINE

"It's definitely Stormshade," said a calm male voice.

"What do we do?" asked a worried female voice.

"I'm so sorry," replied a remorseful female voice.

"This isn't good," answered a tense male voice.

I didn't know who was speaking. I couldn't remember their names. But I knew what they were feeling.

"Stop talking, all of you," said a commanding voice. Now that voice I knew. Calian was there. He would fix this. "I can't think with the incessant chatter. It's distracting."

I felt him close to me. Maybe I was lying on a cot with Calian kneeling beside me? Even if that wasn't the case, it comforted me to imagine it being true. It was the only thing that eased my mind. Because my body was not at ease whatsoever. The pain felt like I was being stabbed over and over. I arched my back and screamed again to alleviate the pain. A rough hand brushed the hair from my forehead. Was it Calian? Normally he radiated heat, but this touch was unusually cold. If it was him, it meant my head was unusually hot.

"I'll notify the council," the first female voice replied. "They may resolve to send someone else to the City of Dhara." Council? That voice. It belonged to…to…Rehema! I fought to hold onto my consciousness. Quiet weeping filled the silence when I wasn't screaming. All the voices in the room began speaking simultaneously.

"Is there a remedy?"

"How could an assassin get into the camp?"

"Only one that I know of."

"What is it?"

"A woman, you said?"

Sniffle. "Yes." Sniffle.

"Dragonmagic is the only remedy. Chaos Dragonmagic."

"With brown hair?"

Sniffle. "I think so." Sniffle.

"She's too far gone to heal herself. Her Dragonmagic isn't that strong. She needs chaos."

"I'm afraid that I do not know how it's possible to get it."

The conversations quieted, and Calian whispered, "Fin, please escort Morwen to her tent."

"Of course," Fin replied.

"No, I need to be here for Emera," Morwen insisted.

"You've done enough for Emera already." The words hung in the air for an awkward moment, his tone unreadable. Was he blaming her? I was the one who drank Cook's water.

"Calian, that's not necessary. Morwen didn't know." I tried repeating what Fin just said. Morwen didn't know.

"He's right. I should have paid more attention. I let my guard down. And for that, she could…"

"Don't say it," Calian snarled. Calian would never let anyone tell him he'd failed. If I died, which seemed inevitable at this point. What would Calian tell the council?

"I'll escort Miss Morwen to her tent," the first male voice said. I couldn't remember his name. Why couldn't I remember his name? Air? Air-jon? Airy-yon? No. Get it together, Emera. Think, think, think. Erjon? Yes, Erjon. The Dragonheir that seemed to know everything.

"I'll go see if Rehema has conversed with the council," Morwen said sadly. With Erjon and Morwen leaving that left Fin, Calian, and me. Surely, Calian could help me. He was the strongest Dragonheir here.

"Make it stop," I whimpered. My body convulsed. I couldn't stop shaking.

"Emera. As much as it hurts, you must try to use your Dragonmagic. Tap into the chaos and heal yourself," Calian pleaded.

"I don't have her blessing," I groaned. The convulsing stopped. Temporary relief flooded my body.

"Cal, we have to prepare for the possibility…" Fin said softly. I could sense both men close to me. It was good that Fin was there to console Calian. I was sure he was distraught that he'd failed his duty.

"No, she won't," Calian whispered. Despite the mind-numbing pain, I focused all of my remaining energy on their exchange.

"Then you know what you have to do."

"I'm just a Dragonheir," he insisted.

"You and I both know you're more than that," Fin argued. Wait. Calian? More than a Dragonheir?

"That's not possible," he growled. Was it possible?

"You and I both know you can," Fin retorted. Can what? Enough with the cryptic statements!

"I've only ever healed myself that way. And it was only a couple of times. I've never healed another person." Oh, how I wished I could see them. But my eyes refused to open.

"Would you rather she dies than try?"

"Gods, no!" Calian cried.

I suddenly turned on my side and started to cough profusely. "Please, Cal. Please," I begged between coughs.

"Cal," he murmured. He seemed surprised. Had I ever called him Cal? I didn't remember, but it felt right. I wanted to say it again, but I didn't say anything else because I was losing consciousness. I opened my eyes for a brief moment and looked at Calian, who seemed to be placing his hands on my chest. What was he doing?

"Help me. Use your chaos, Emera, and help me save you," he whispered before I took a ragged breath and plunged into darkness.

*   *   *

"Calian?" I managed to say his name. It sounded more like a croak than a word, but at least I spoke. Wait. Why wasn't I dead?

"He's not here," Morwen said.

I sat up but immediately regretted the decision. The interior of the tent was spinning uncontrollably, and I quickly became nauseated. I threw myself over my cot and emptied the contents of my stomach which wasn't much. "Sorry," I muttered.

"You have nothing to be sorry for. It is me who should apologize."

"You have nothing to apologize for. *It is me* who should have been more careful." I assured her.

I wiped my mouth with the back of my hand and rolled onto my back. I took a few breaths before opening my eyes again. It took a moment for my vision to adjust, but once it did, the spinning slowly stopped. I saw the early morning sunlight creeping in through the flaps of the tent that blew from th e chilling breeze. Did it mean I was only asleep throughout the night? Or had I been lying unconscious for days? I panicked. The Trials! Had Calian left!

Please, please let it be that I wasn't out that long.

"Calian will be glad that you are awake. He's been worried."

"He's still here?" I maintained eye contact with the roof of the tent.

"He is. You've only been out two nights. It's a miracle you're even…" her voice drifted, but I knew what she meant.

I shifted my weight and carefully lifted myself. I swung my legs over the side of the cot and firmly placed my feet on the ground. I wriggled my toes in the cool grass, letting the thin blades slide between my toes. I needed to get up. Even if he was still in the camp, Calian would leave soon. I needed to begin my first Trial quickly.

"You don't have to pretend that I wasn't knocking on Death's door." I took a satisfying breath and stood up. I wobbled a little bit, but I found my balance. Surprisingly, I wasn't sore or in any pain.

Morwen stood. "Don't you think you should rest?"

"All I've done is rest from the moment I arrived." I scooped up my boots by a trunk at the foot of my cot and looked back at her. "I'll be fine, really. I actually feel well-rested all things considered, so please don't worry."

"I'll try not to. Rehema has requested my presence. I just wanted to check on you first. I'm so glad you're okay." I saw the sparkle of a newly formed teardrop. I hugged my friend.

"I'm okay," I assured her. I gave her a quick smile and headed out for the training ring. I picked up my pace, almost running through the camp. Most of the tents were still closed, but others were open, showcasing their emptiness. I continued by Cook's tent on my way and saw soldiers lined up waiting for their meals. I paused when I saw the extinguished fire. Where flames had been now sat ash. Wisps of smoke rose into the air. I tried to recall the events from that night with the Stormshade, but they were hazy at best. I couldn't remember what had transpired except that I had been poisoned and lost consciousness from the pain. A lot of agonizing pain. Any conversation, and any other act, was forgotten. It was probably for the best.

I rounded the troughs toward the training ring when a hand grabbed me and turned me around.

I looked up to see Calian's face. He breathed a sigh of relief as he scanned my face with his soft eyes. "You're okay," he stated.

"I'm okay," I repeated and smiled. "I came looking for you. I want to begin the Water Trial."

"I'm not sure that's the best idea," he said.

"Aside from a slight bit of dizziness when I first awoke, I feel fine. It's like nothing happened. To be honest, I'm surprised I could even heal myself. I guess I've connected with more of my magic than we thought, and that means I need to finish each Trial quickly." I began walking toward the ring again, but he didn't follow. I paused and looked behind me. "You coming?" I asked.

He smiled so wide his lips almost reached his eyes. It was refreshing to see him smile instead of the scowl he often wore. "Okay then. However, your Trials will not be held within the camp. Today, we'll travel toward the river just west of here. We'll need Morwen to come with us to…"

"Make sure nothing goes wrong," I finished.

"To keep you safe if needed," he said.

Calian grabbed the arm of a passing soldier. "Please go get Princess Morwen and tell her she's needed at the stables and that she'll be going to the river," he said with command, yet respect. Despite Calian's rough exterior, he took pride in his soldiers, and anyone could see that the soldiers felt the same way. The soldier nodded and headed up the path toward Morwen's tent. "Now. I want you to meet someone." One corner of his lips curled slightly. He turned and walked toward the horse stables, not even telling me to follow.

"I have Dhruv saddled and ready to go. We head out now. We'll ride until the sun is directly overhead and stop to eat…That is…unless you're hungry now." He stopped and looked back at me.

"I'm not, oddly enough." Not only were my limbs healed with no trace of the poison, but I wasn't hungry at all.

"Let's go, then."

Dhruv was saddled, ready for travel with Calian's weapons and bags strapped to him. Because the camp was small, the term *stables* was used loosely. There was a small tent that contained horse feed, riding saddles, and other supplies. Most of the horses were tied at a post near feed and water troughs. They lounged on hay and grazed. I laughed because Dhruv looked completely out of place next to the other horses. He towered over them, his massive size sticking out like a sore thumb.

My breath caught in my throat when my eyes saw what stood next to Dhruv. It was the most exquisite mare I'd ever seen. Her coat was golden yellow and her mane a couple of shades lighter. She was a Lightenion Sun Mare which was a rare breed—I knew this because I'd met an equestrian once.

"She's beautiful," I breathed.

Calian cleared his throat and introduced us. "Emera, meet Zari. Zari, this is Emera."

"So pleased to meet you," I said. I glided my hand along her neck and ran my fingers through her soft hair.

Likewise, a strong feminine voice said. I pulled my hand away quickly as if I'd been stung and stared into her eyes.

Was that you? I asked.

Yes, my Kahina, she answered.

What does that mean?

It means queen, she said.

"You're talking to her, aren't you?" My ears heard that question.

"I am," I told Calian. "Just like the wolf."

I looked at Dhruv and attempted to say hello with my mind which felt completely silly. The horse glared at me in return.

"Either it doesn't work on all animals or Dhruv is ignoring me," I said thoughtfully.

"That wouldn't surprise me," Calian remarked. He mounted Dhruv effortlessly.

I, on the other hand, mounted Zari not-so-effortlessly. I almost fell backward but threw my hands back and steadied myself. I sat my hands on an object strapped to her rump. I positioned myself so that I could see what I'd touched. My heart leaped when I discovered a beautiful white bow, a white leather quiver, and white arrows. I lifted my eyes to Calian.

He just shrugged. "You should have a bow that matches your skill."

I beamed at him. I probably looked like a fool, but I didn't care. I grinned from ear to ear.

It's beautiful, Zari said.

Dhruv's eyes flickered toward the bow, but he looked bored. Apparently, this wasn't entertaining enough for him.

"Will I ever be able to talk to Dhruv?" I asked.

"Maybe. You'll need to be fully blessed by Anahita before then. The first horses were gifts from Nimerah to Anahita so that Anahita would have a trusted friend whenever she was in her human form. She made it so that Dragonborns of her blessing could communicate with their horse just as she could. She hoped that a bond would be formed as she had bonded with hers."

"I was able to communicate with a wolf, though. Why not all horses?"

"Anahita viewed horses as superior to all other animals. You must gain her blessing before you can speak to horses, and even then, it is up to the horse. I can communicate with all other animals, but not all horses."

Just then, the same soldier that Calian had sent to find Morwen came running toward us.

"Captain Westbow," he said slightly out of breath. "Dragonpriestess Rehema received correspondence from King Calder. Princess Morwen is unable to ride with you today."

Calian frowned. "That's unusual for the king to send anything through Rehema."

"Let's go then," I said. "She'll catch up if she can."

Calian's brows were still scrunched together with skepticism. "I guess," he said, and Dhruv took off.

I didn't have to tug the reins or nudge Zari. She just started trotting after Dhruv. When we were down the hill from the camp, we guided the horses west toward the river. Zari's gait was smooth and effortless. My father would be entranced by her. My heart twisted in my chest with pain at the thought of him. I wished I could see his smile and how it lit up his entire face. I'd relish in his sparkling eyes as he laughed at one of his jokes. I'd cling to the sound of his voice praising me for a straight kill. A thick lump rose within my throat, and I swallowed it back down.

Get it together, I thought. I seemed to think of those words a lot. I rolled my eyes and looked at Zari. If she'd heard me, she didn't let on.

Up ahead, Calian lifted his palm indicating that we needed to stop. Before I could say anything, he brought his finger to his lips. Something wasn't right. I could sense it.

I slowed Zari and came to a standing halt beside Calian.

The Deceiver is not allowed in our territory. The wolf's voice was back, and it was not happy we were there.

CHAPTER

TEN

"He's back," I whispered.

"Who?" Calian whispered back.

"The wolf. And he's not happy. What is with these wolves?"

"The Dragongod Endrit fought against Nimerah in the War of Three. Lightenion Wolves were his faithful companions. Seems like they've held a grudge."

"Well, we need to move. They're getting closer. I can feel them."

"Say nothing more," Calian said. With his voice low, he commanded the horse. "Dhruv, fly." Dhruv understood and took off.

"You heard him, Zari. Run like the wind."

Yes, my Kahina. Zari sprinted after Dhruv. I wasn't surprised to discover she could, in fact, run like the wind. Zari was quite a bit faster than Dhruv. She was a flash of lightning sweeping across the sky.

A deafening howl erupted from behind us and then several more howls joined in. I glanced behind me to see five Lightenion Wolves racing behind us. They were big. They were fast. And they hated me, the Deceiver.

"We'll keep going until we get to the river!" Calian yelled. "We'll need to look for a place to cross!"

Zari and I passed Calian and Dhruv. We flew out of the woods into the open grassland. The wolves were getting closer and closer to Dhruv. Any moment, the wolves would catch up, so I had to figure out a way to get us across…and fast.

I heard Calian shouting. He threw flames at the wolves while they nipped at Dhruv's tail.

"No!" I shouted, and Zari stopped. My demand caught the wolves off guard. The two in the lead looked at me, losing their concentration on Dhruv. They tripped and rolled over each other, tumbling through the grass. The three following leapt over the first two and continued their chase. I looked forward to the river and scanned the area. It was wide, and the waves crashed violently against each other. As much as I strained my vision, I couldn't find a place to cross, and we were running out of time. The three wolves continued to close the distance between them and Calian. I had to think fast. I was sure the other two would regain their composure and be after us again.

I looked toward the river, focusing on the rhythm of the rolling waves. My heartbeat matched the water's cadence, and the all-too-familiar tranquility flowed through my veins.

Then it came to me. The wolves. The water ahead. This was my Trial. Zari understood and took off running.

A man's yell, a wolf's howl, and a horse's bray cut through my thoughts simultaneously. I looked back to see that Dhruv and Calian were surrounded. Frenzied, disjointed thoughts clawed from my chest, fighting the serene magic that cocooned me. A quick idea formed in my head on how to get us out of this mess. Calian was doing his best to protect Dhruv and himself. He conjured the largest whirlwind of fire I'd ever seen. But there was no time to gape in awe at the sheer power he held. I needed to act.

I looked back toward the river. "Stop, Zari," I commanded.

Zari halted immediately. I dismounted and stood before the river. I closed my eyes, took a breath, and held out my arms. I prayed to Anahita, asking for her help. Then I looked back upon the river.

Come to me, I thought. I let myself be vulnerable to the river's life force. Would Anahita trust me with this request?

I opened my eyes and watched as water began to rise higher and higher, creating a wall of solid liquid. I'd seen waves that high back when storms tormented Medora during the fishing seasons. Its imposing size folded over Zari and me, but I held it together. With my arms now high above my head, I twisted myself, guiding the wave toward Calian, Dhruv, and the wolves.

"Calian!" I screamed as the wave loomed high above their heads. Calian looked up, and with quick reflexes, created a blazing shield of fire just as the wave crashed down upon them. The water, regardless of its weight, became nothing but steam when it hit Calian's shield. I released a sigh of relief that he and Dhruv were okay. However, the wolves that had been circling them were no longer standing. They were crumpled on the ground *dead.*

Calian let down his shield. A smile crept along his lips. He opened his mouth to speak, but I cut him off.

"Behind you!" I called out.

Calian turned Dhruv back toward the woods. Behind them, stood the first two wolves. They snarled in unison, flashing their sharp fangs. Dhruv took off toward Zari and me, and the wolves followed.

With what little grace I had, I leaped onto Zari. I wobbled but still managed not to fall off of her. We turned back to the river, its waves more restless than before.

"It's like it knows something's wrong," I whispered.

Zari didn't respond, but I swore she nodded.

I gave one tense final glance back at Calian. He nodded and his eyes sparked, a sign that he wanted me to go without him. To save me.

Absolutely not.

I urged Zari toward the raging river. *One more time, goddess*, I thought.

I raised both arms with my palms upward, and I closed my eyes and focused on a single image while drawing in my magic. I held the image in my mind and opened my eyes. I took a deep breath and separated my arms, stretching them out wide. At that exact moment, the waves calmed, and the river parted. I could see the floor of the river, and luckily, it wasn't that soft. There were rocks which were perfect for the horses to run on.

"Go, Zari!" I screamed. Zari ran even faster, kicking up sand and dirt as she charged through the parted waters on the rocky river floor. I held my arms outright as Zari and I made it to the other side. When we were standing atop the riverbank, she stopped, and I turned her to see where Calian was. He made it to the river, but the wolves were closing in. Calian turned and shot a large ball of flame. The ball hit its target, taking down one of the wolves. But there was still one more left. Dhruv and Calian were almost across the river, but the last wolf was so close, it could take Dhruv down in one leap. It was now or never.

I closed my eyes and took a deep breath. I held my magic within me, and as Dhruv closed in on the riverbank by Zari, I lowered my arms to my sides, letting the magic go. The water crashed down from the other side of the river to where Zari and I stood. Dhruv jumped onto the riverbank just in time for the water to swallow the wolves with such a violent force that no animal could survive.

I was quiet for a moment, taking in what I'd done. I jumped off of Zari and screamed.

"I did it! Oh, my gods, I did it!" I looked at Calian still sitting atop Dhruv, and I waved at the river like a lunatic. "Did you see that? Did you see it?" I squealed. "I parted the water and held it! Then it came crashing down once I let go. I had control, Cal! I was in control of my water element!"

Calian had already dismounted Dhruv and was running toward me. He outstretched his arms, grabbed ahold of me, and lifted me off the ground. We laughed as he swung me around. The atmosphere around us turned electric. Everything felt…*right*.

"I did! I saw it. You were magnificent! You..." Calian stopped twirling and lowered me back to the ground. "You called me Cal."

"I guess I did," I replied. His name lingered on my lips. I let it dance in my mind. *Cal.*

Calian brushed his hand through his hair and held it on the back of his neck. It was evident he didn't know what to say next. After a few minutes, he broke our silence. "Great use of control, Emera. I think you're getting the hang of it." He lowered his voice, "But don't do anything so foolish again. You could have killed yourself." Regret flashed on his face but vanished quickly.

I mumbled, "I just did what you told me to do. I calmed myself and pictured what I wanted to happen. It worked."

"It did, thank the gods."

The awkward silence that followed was agonizing. I didn't know how to process what he'd said. Weren't we just ecstatic about what I'd done.

Which was saving his life!

"So, what now?" I asked hopelessly.

His eyes softened. "I think you just passed your first Trial," he said with approval. "You're radiating light. And look at your scales." He pointed to my scales. They were blue before, but whereas they were dull and lifeless, they now shimmered vibrant shades of turquoise and sapphire blue in the sunlight.

Without thinking, I threw my arms around him again. "I have her blessing!" I screamed. This time, he didn't pull away. I felt his arms slowly rise and wrap around my lower back, and I breathed in his familiar scent of smoke and spice. I quietly inhaled, putting the scent to memory, letting it ground me in the moment. Creeping up inside of me was an electric energy. It took hold of me slowly and expanded, wrapping us in its embrace. Calian trailed his hand up my back and into my hair. I lifted my chin and peered into his eyes. I marveled at their golden red glow.

"Anahita's blessing has fully transformed you. Your eyes are like sapphires," he said in barely a whisper. A strand of my hair fell into my face, and he gently brushed it aside. His touch was electrifying, and a hunger that I'd never known erupted deep from within my core.

Calian shifted his weight, and he started to lean in. I could hear his breathing pick up for a brief moment. Gods! Was he going to kiss me? He was going to kiss me. I closed my eyes and prepared for our lips to meet.

Calian closed the distance between us but then abruptly pulled away. "Let's take a break while we wait for Morwen." My heart sank, and the energy between us vanished. "I think it's best for you to eat and replenish the energy you just used."

I didn't respond. What had I been thinking? Kissing Calian? I watched silently as he walked away to grab whatever he'd brought in the pouch strapped to Dhruv. He handed me some fruit, and we ate in silence underneath a large sun tree. We didn't make eye contact. Dhruv and Zari stood grazing from the tall grass while the sun lifted higher into the sky. The tree provided coverage from the sun's high rays. It was warmer out in the open than it was back in the camp thanks to the forest's dense trees. It wasn't terrible, but I took off my boots and stockings for some relief, and Calian had done the same. I watched Calian lay on his back with his arms crisscrossed behind his head.

"So. You said you'd tell me about the six kingdoms since I apparently don't know much about them."

He lifted onto his elbows. "What would you like to know?" he asked.

"Have you been to all of them?"

"Yes. It was part of my training. To put you in situations a Dragongod or Dragongoddess would approve for a Trial, I needed to speak to those with better knowledge than me. I traveled to each kingdom."

"Which one was your favorite?"

"That's tough. Each kingdom had something special. For instance, the Kingdom of Water was a very welcoming place. Everyone was friendly. And the Kaimana Sea? I sailed it for two days, and it was so relaxing."

I would be lying if I said I wasn't surprised. With Calian's quick temper and fire magic, I figured the Kingdom of Fire would be his favorite.

The corners of Calian's mouth raised slightly as he recalled his visits to each kingdom. "The Kingdom of Earth has the grandest forests you'll ever see with lush grass and the tallest trees. Their lands are home to numerous animals, but most are gentle creatures. The Kingdom of Air is adorned with the most majestic snow-capped mountains. It is said that one truly finds their Dragonsoul at the top of the highest peak. The Kingdom of Fire is the most entertaining. They have a celebration for everything with elaborate parties that include dancing, singing, and music. And they make you feel like you are one of them." He stopped and lowered himself back down to the ground.

"The Kingdom of Darkness would have to be my favorite. It was quiet and serene. Their night skies were full of the brightest stars. I believe I found myself there." I could just imagine a starry night sky with Calian sitting beneath it, contemplating the wonders of the world. It was a nice thought.

"And the Kingdom of Light?" I asked.

"The Kingdom of Light is the one kingdom I will be glad never to step foot in again," he said without hesitation. "They're pompous Dragonasses who believe they're better than all the other kingdoms."

I barked out a laugh. I made a mental note to steer clear of the Kingdom of Light if I could. I was still coming to terms with being a Dragonborn, the very same people I hated because of their holier than thou attitude. It sounded like I would not get along with anyone in their kingdom.

"You know, I feel like there's so much more to you. I'd love to know…"

A loud snore interrupted my thought. Calian was asleep. Much to my surprise, I wasn't that tired, so I stood and crossed to Zari, trying to clap off the stray blades of grass that stuck to my palms.

Morwen is later than we expected, I told Zari. *I'm going for a walk to pass some time. I just need to clear my head for a moment, but I'll be back soon.*

I'll be listening for you, Zari said.

I walked off down a path desperate for solitude. The grassy fields were open save for a small tree line with bushes. The lush leaves of the foliage were a deep green and provided coverage for smaller animals and travelers. I ventured further, wading through the bushes and basked in the cool shade of the overbearing trees. The rustling of leaves and the songs of the birds inhabiting the trees was a symphony to my ears. I leaned against a tree and closed my eyes, listening to their song. My thoughts drifted back to the moments with Calian following what had happened at the river and the wolves. He'd seemed so happy and relieved. He was quick to touch me, yet pulled away once he'd realized what we were doing. His mood swings were starting to take their toll on my heart. As much as I didn't want to admit it, I felt something between us. Didn't I? If only Dwyn was with us so that I could confide in her.

The slight crunch of a twig brought my attention back to my surroundings.

I froze where I stood, and my mind went blank. I felt a presence within the wooded area, and I prayed it wasn't a stray wolf. I cautiously opened my eyes and seeing that no one was beside me, I hastily searched the area. Whatever or whoever was there was watching me…I felt it. I pretended to look relaxed as I pushed away from the tree and carefully walked backward. I looked at the trees, the sky, the ground, the bushes, trying to appear like I was interested in my surroundings and nothing more. Maybe if I could reach Zari telepathically, she could wake Calian.

Zari!

Yes, my Kahina.

Oh, thank goodness I can reach you! I'm a little way west of the tree by the river. Please tell me Calian has gone looking for me, and he is making the noises I'm hearing.

He has not. He is still under the tree. Shall I wake him?

Yes. Okay, I'm—

Whatever I was going to say stuck to my tongue because a woman with brown hair and brown eyes slowly stood from behind a bush. She looked familiar, and I couldn't decide if it was because of her face which harbored full cheeks angling into a pointed chin, or if it was her clothing. I started filtering through the memories within my head. The effects of the Stormshade must have lingered on because I couldn't find her image within my mind. I let my arms go slack beside me, not making any other sudden moves.

"Hello," I said cheerfully. "I wasn't aware of other travelers in this area."

She said nothing. Her eyes looked at mine and then they surveyed the surrounding area and beyond me.

I kept the stranger in front of me as I walked backward. If I could just get past the bushes, I would be closer to Zari. I'm sure she was already on her way. Except—and the frightening thought left my bones shaking—she might not have been where I'd last seen her. She was a horse. She and Dhruv could have taken off for all I knew. I was alone with this woman.

I took a good look at the woman, and it hit me. Of course, I recognized her. She was wearing the same clothing as the man had that day. The same billowy black shirt tucked into black trousers; the red sash around the waist; the black riding boots that came to the knees. She also had the hood with a cowl neck—except it was missing the veil—and across her chest was the Dragon in white with three red slashes. She was a cultist.

And she had come to kill me.

I didn't even think. I just threw one of my hands at her and conjured a blast of water to knock her over. I turned and began running out of the tree line and back toward the riverbank, stumbling through the bushes. The cultist recovered quickly because the next thing I knew, I was on the ground face down, lying flat on my stomach. I pushed up onto my forearms and looked beneath me to discover my feet were tied together.

What in the name of Nimerah did she just throw at me?

I heard her quick footsteps getting closer, so I rolled onto my back and sat up. We locked eyes as she emerged from the bushes, and I threw my hands out, water exploding from my palms. She dodged behind a neighboring bush to avoid the blast. I took what time I had while the cultist readjusted herself and tried to free myself from the ropes at my feet. They were twisted almost into a knot, and I yelled out in frustration because I couldn't loosen them fast enough. I tried to crawl away, but I was out of time. The cultist was now between me and the river with a dagger pointed in my face, yet she made no attempt to throw it. "First the Stormshade. Now this. You're in my way."

Before she could finish, her eyes widened, and her back stiffened. The life behind her eyes faded as she slumped to the ground, exposing a knife protruding out of her upper back between the shoulder blades. My mouth gaped open in shock, and I slowly tore my eyes away from the cultist and up to the looming figure before me.

Calian's eyes blazed. He was terrifying yet mesmerizing all at the same time with flames dancing across his hands. "What were you thinking?" he said angrily.

"I was just clearing my head."

"Clear your head closer to me next time. As Nimerah's heir, you can't go traipsing off wherever you feel like it. Especially if you don't have full control of your Dragonmagic yet. This is what I'm talking about when I tell you not to do something foolish!" he growled.

"I didn't ask to be the Dragonheir!" I cried out.

He threw his arms up in response. "It doesn't matter that you didn't, Emera!" There it was. The electric feeling between us was back. Only this time, it wasn't desire. It was anger, and it pulsed between us.

I pounded my fists into the ground. "It matters to me! This is not the life I wanted!" I screamed, and my eyes pooled with tears despite my best. The fury I felt caused the ground to quake beneath me. Just a bit ago, we were elated at the progress of my magic, regardless that he thought I'd been too careless, and now we were back to him being indignant.

Calian dipped his head back and looked to the sky. He muttered what was probably a curse of some kind while running a hand through his hair. He lowered his voice, and the air became still again.

"What we want does not matter in this life," he said, defeated.

As a single tear fell down my cheek, I looked into his eyes. "What we want always matters. In this life and what comes after."

My anger fizzled because no matter how infuriating Calian was, he had my best interests at heart. The hostility drained from my body, and the atmosphere calmed.

"You believe there is more after death?" Calian asked mildly. I just nodded.

"I hope you're right, Emera. I truly do." He bent down and began detangling the ropes at my feet. After a few twists and tugs, my feet were free. I massaged my ankles where the ropes had cut into my skin. I should have put my boots on before I went *traipsing off*, as Calian put it.

"What do we do now?"

"We need to get back to camp and check on Morwen. We need to update everyone on her." He thrust his chin toward the dead cultist on the ground.

"She's the one responsible for the Stormshade. She's the one Morwen spoke to."

"I heard. And if she was able to infiltrate the camp without Fin knowing, it means we need to make adjustments to rotations and protection of the wall. It's even more imperative that we get you through the Trials." He stood completely and walked over to the woman. He filtered through her clothes and pulled out small knives and containers. Once he seemed satisfied with his plunder, he straightened.

"Let's go home," he said.

CHAPTER

ELEVEN

Dragonheir Erjon was an over-bearing, egotistical jerk. How he was an Airian and not a Lightenion was beyond me. He acted exactly like the people of the Kingdom of Light that Calian had described. Erjon sneered at me as I recalled how I'd lifted and parted the river. I tilted my head, inspecting the Dragonheir before me while I willed my irritation to simmer. He reminded me a little of Priest Benigno, however, Benigno was at least kind. I wondered if Erjon had an ounce of kindness in him. If he did, he didn't show it. His foggy gray eyes looked distant during and after I spoke. He either wasn't paying attention, or he didn't care. It was probably both.

He had woken me early in the morning after the sun first peeked over the horizon and informed me that we'd be attempting my Air Trial. As tired as I had been from staying up late into the night retelling the events of my Water Trial to Rehema, Morwen, and Fin, I couldn't wait to be back in the training ring to stretch my fingers and test my abilities with air magic. But whereas my friends had celebrated my newfound blessing the night before, Erjon didn't. I'd quickly found out that Erjon's charming personality wasn't easy to get along with.

I took a deep breath and exhaled. I needed to get Ilmari's blessing, and he was my way to get it.

He stood before me now, the sun barely above the tree line, wearing fresh gray silk trousers and tunic with long black boots that hit just below the knee. Unlike Calian and Fin who both dressed for a hard day's work, Erjon looked like he'd prefer to sit at a desk reading historical texts than be outside.

"The element of water is the easiest to manipulate. Even a new half-witted Dragonborn could do what you did," he said arrogantly.

"I'll be sure to tell Morwen that," I quipped.

Erjon ignored me. "Air requires concentration, intellect, and great skill." He brought his fingertips together, mimicking a church steeple. He brought the tip of his nose down in concentration, connecting it to the highest point of his fingers. "Hmm," he mumbled. "First, I need to see what abilities—if any—that you have in regard to your air magic."

I truly didn't like his tone and glanced quickly behind me to see if Calian…or Morwen…or even Fin was going to show up and rescue me. It was highly unlikely, considering all three were meeting with Rehema and the soldier that had stopped Morwen from accompanying Calian and me to the river. It turned out that Morwen's father hadn't sent a message at all. It appeared the female assassin I'd encountered after my Water Trial wanted me separated from Morwen, the Dragonheir of Water. In hindsight, it made sense. While I was stuck with Sir Better Than Everyone, the others were planning more safety precautions.

"Your mind is wandering. Pay attention," Erjon snapped.

I narrowed my eyes and felt heat flash behind them. I'd give anything to the gods to throw fire at him. I exhaled a hefty sigh and neutralized my expression. I'd play Erjon's game. I'd show him how powerful I was.

"I did create quite a powerful wave," I offered. I opened my palm and produced a small geyser of water.

He snorted. "Child's play," he remarked.

I didn't hesitate. "Then challenge me," I dared.

He paused, letting his hands fall to his side. "Well, we can certainly do something a little more challenging."

"I'm not scared," I said, and a thrill curved up my spine.

"You should be. Get your horse and meet me at the gate."

*   *   *

Erjon headed out of the camp, and I followed him in silence, not wanting to cause him to say something that would break my confidence. Besides, Erjon struck me as a solitary individual. There was no need for me to disrupt his peace and quiet. In fact, I appreciated it to a certain extent. Being the destined savior of the six kingdoms was emotionally draining, and I was tired of discussing my ineptness in regard to my magic.

We finally cleared the northern part of the forest, and that's when I saw that the northern part of the kingdom was covered with rolling hills that kept getting higher and higher leading to a rough terrain of marshes, fog, and cold temperatures. The towering trees I'd grown familiar with back at the camp had enshrouded the contrasting image before me. Through the misty atmosphere, I strained my eyesight to see that ahead of us stood a haunting mountain range with sharp, jagged mountains that spanned from left to right as far as the eye could see. A dense fog covered the highest peaks of the mountains making the range even more ominous.

"I didn't realize the camp was placed so close to this," I said, my voice barely above a whisper. It was the Obsidian Mountains that bordered the Eternal Resting of the Dragondead. The closer we got to the bottom of the range, the more eerie the scenery was. A whistling wind greeted us, blowing threatening whispers in our ears. The cowardly sun hid behind thick gray clouds, and the gnarled trees cast shadows on the dark, cold ground. Every instinct within me said to turn around. Yet Erjon kept moving forward.

Zari, stop, I said, and Zari immediately halted.

"What are we doing?" I called out to Erjon, breaking the silence between us.

"You wanted a challenge. I'm giving you a challenge," he replied nonchalantly. His horse slowed to a walk, but it didn't stop.

"I want a challenge that won't kill me," I snapped.

His horse stopped, and Erjon turned its reins so he could face me. "Then it's not much of a challenge, is it?" There was no trace of anger in his eyes or voice, only complacency.

I glared at him. "What is it you want me to do?" I demanded.

"We're going up there," he pointed to the mountain closest to us. "And then you're going to jump off."

"I'm going to *what*?" I blurted. Zari tensed slightly beneath me. "No, I'm not," I said flatly.

"Are you backing down, Daughter of Nimerah?" Erjon asked?

I lifted my chin and straightened my spin, sitting as tall as I could. "Never," I said, but I couldn't tell if my voice shook or not.

Erjon raised an eyebrow, and one side of his mouth curved up slightly. "Then let's not wait." He turned his horse back toward the looming mountain and began to trot toward it. The sun was just starting to lower itself, indicating it was just after mid-meal, so we needed to hurry if we wanted to complete the task prior to nightfall.

We reached the base of the mountain, and we—okay, more so me—were relieved to find a narrow path up which meant we didn't have to climb. Zari and I were both on high alert as we made our way up. When the horses could no longer safely continue, Erjon and I dismounted, covering the remaining part of the path on foot. Finally, just when I thought we'd never make a stop, we'd reached a cliff Erjon thought was suitable enough for the task.

I pushed the negative thoughts out of my mind and clenched my fists. *Don't think like that, Emera. You can do this. You created wind before, and you'll do it again. Create a wind to catch you and guide you down.*

I slowly tiptoed to the edge of the cliff and looked over. The drop would kill anyone or anything. An audible gulp released from my throat. I felt droplets of sweat form at my brow. My hands were cold and clammy. My confidence wavered at the thought of my imminent death. I closed my eyes and reached for my water element to calm me. I set my feet right at the edge of the cliff and held my hands out wide. But before I could step off, I felt pressure on my back, and suddenly I was falling.

Then it registered: *He pushed me!*

My mind went blank, and the ground didn't look so far away now as my hair whipped behind me and my limbs flailed. I screamed in panic because what else was I supposed to do? Pass the Trial. Right. I tried to quell my thoughts, but they bombarded my mind. I frantically searched for what Erjon had told me. *Air requires concentration*, he'd said. As terrified as I was of becoming a flattened pile of crushed bones, I had to concentrate. The ground was coming closer and closer, so I had to do something.

Against the harsh wind from the fall, I forced my hands out beneath me, palms facing the ground. I sent a silent prayer to the Dragongoddess Ilmari, requesting help to guide me through this. A sense of clarity washed through me, and I focused on what would help me the most. Could just wind carry me? What if I created it from my hands to push myself up? All I could do was try. I projected an image of air protruding from my hands into my thoughts and threw all the magic I had at it. I closed my eyes and braced for impact, sending final thoughts to my loved ones into the evening air.

But the impact never came.

I cautiously opened one eye at a time and beheld the sight before me. With my arms still thrust out below me,

I had created wind so powerful that it kept me suspended in the air, hovering just above the ground. Relief rushed through me, and I called back my magic, causing me to fall onto the hard ground face first. The impact stunned me and knocked the air out of my lungs—I never described myself as graceful. I laughed and cried simultaneously. My tears mixed with the dirt, staining my cheeks, but I didn't care. I did it! I had created wind powerful enough to keep me alive!

"Emera!" A distant voice shouted to me, but it wasn't from above. I lifted my head and strained my vision to see ahead of me. A figure loomed in the distance, moving closer and closer toward my position. I pushed myself up on my hands and knees then sat back on my heels and lifted my face to the sky. I drank in the light breeze that washed over my face. I looked ahead once more when I heard thundering hooves. Dhruv came speeding up to me, Calian riding atop wearing a look of pure fury on his face, his eyes a fiery red. He hopped off Dhruv quickly and kneeled beside me. His hands were all over me, searching for broken bones, bruises, and blood.

"I'm okay, Calian," I reassured him. He held my face gently and turned it left then right, inspecting my jaw and cheeks. "I promise, I'm fine. I'm perfect actually. I did it!

I passed my Air Trial. I passed Erjon's challenge!" He then grabbed my hands and held them up.

"You did. Look," he instructed. I looked at my scales. Mixed into my blue scales were now beautiful silver ones. He let go, and I turned my hands over and over, examining how brilliant they were.

"They changed," I exclaimed.

"So did your eyes," Calian remarked. "They're silver now. It appears that each time you receive a blessing, they change. At least you're not glittering now," he laughed.

I took my time getting to my feet. Calian held onto me. He said it was to make sure I wouldn't' fall over, but I wasn't so sure. I felt fine. I actually felt energized. How I would sleep through the night, I didn't know. Still, I let him help me. With his thumb, he lightly brushed the dirt from my cheek and then tucked a strand of hair behind my ear.

"Despite the outcome, he will answer for this," he murmured.

"Calian. It's okay," I breathed.

Footsteps indicated Erjon had made it down the side of the mountain. He approached slowly, somewhat cautiously. I guessed Calian was the only person who intimidated him.

"Reprimanding me seems uncalled for considering she has now been blessed by Ilmari," Erjon reasoned calmly. "I know that you have this attachment for her, but in order to truly test her and complete the Trials, we must do what is necessary."

"By killing her?" Calian snarled.

"Do you not have faith in her?"

In any other situation, Calian's stunned expression would have made me laugh. But what followed his reaction was hesitation. He *hesitated*.

"Why are you hesitating?" I demanded and pulled away from him.

His eyes widened. "I didn't hesitate. I am just thinking through my answer."

"Which is the same as hesitating," I retorted. "You don't trust me."

Calian's eyes dimmed, and he grabbed my shoulders, hunching over so that his eyes were directly in front of mine. "How can I trust someone I've just met?"

I staggered back from the force of his words.

"Seriously?" I asked roughly. "We've bonded since we met. Don't tell me you don't feel the same way!"

Ignoring what he knew was about to be an argument, Calian turned to Erjon—who remained silent with a passive expression—and spoke through gritted teeth. "You are to ride back to camp and notify the others of Emera's success. Then you are to ride to the City of Nimerah. You've been summoned by the Dragoncouncil for some reason."

Erjon paused. Just when I thought he'd say something, Calian took a step toward him. "Leave," he barked. Erjon nodded and retreated slowly to his horse. He mounted, gave a slight nudge, and the horse trotted toward me.

"Well done, Emera," Erjon said, tipping his chin down in a silent acknowledgement. And with that, he rode off toward camp, the blackening sky blanketing him in the distance.

I turned back to Calian. "What are we doing now?" I huffed.

"I've spoken to Rehema," he said irritably.

"Really? About what?" I asked sharply.

"We're going to retrieve a Dragonheir," he said.

CHAPTER

TWELVE

The City of Dhara was the most beautiful city I'd ever seen. Well…the only other city I'd ever seen was the City of Anahita when I was just ten, so I didn't have much of a comparison. Regardless, it was larger than the City of Anahita as I remembered, and the City of Dhara didn't smell like fish. The City of Dhara was nestled within the Arden Forest, the largest forest in all of the six kingdoms.

A river ran through the heart of the city with one bridge of pure white stone connecting the two sides. Trees with the most exquisite leaves of green, white, pink, and purple were everywhere. Houses were built into the largest of the trees from the bottom of the trunks to the top with winding staircases built into the sides of the massive tree trunks.

The likeness of the Dragongoddess Dhara was carved into the trees as well. A large statue of her sat perched on a white bridge.

We arrived just before sundown, having stopped for three nights to practice, rest, eat, and practice some more. My ability to control my water and air magic increased with each skill Calian taught me. I learned how to form icicles, hail, water shields, wind shields, blasts of water, and gusts of wind from my hands. I'd brought geysers up from the earth and created wind so strong, it knocked Calian on his butt. There might have been uncontrollable laughter when it happened.

His confidence in me had grown, which eased the tension between us. And it all momentarily vanished once my eyes fell on the lights glowing from within the residents' homes, I gasped. The lights gave an ethereal glow to the city.

I was mesmerized, and I couldn't help but wish Zari was there to witness it. However, we'd left Dhruv and Zari at the city stables located just outside the city walls with a stable boy named Holt. Holt, who had insisted he would take great care of her, told us the horses weren't allowed inside the city per the king's orders. The boy had looked innocent enough with his dark blonde hair, light blue eyes, and freckles resting on his upper cheeks and across the bridge of his nose. He'd reminded me of the young boys back in Medora. His calm, sweet demeanor with Zari had made me feel better, and I'd figured she was in good hands.

Now, walking through the city, I admired the flow of the beautiful river, all of the buildings and houses, and of course, the palace. It was a grand fixture of gray stone overrun by vines that bloomed with beautiful flowers. It stood further back into the city, but it was tall enough that a person could see it from wherever they were. It towered above everything save for a few trees that stood within its courtyard as well as the one it was built around—or into by the looks of it. The palace was divided by a colossal tree that grew up through its middle and extended into the sky. Four large towers connected by walls formed an additional perimeter of the city. Smaller bridges connecting the tree to the towers indicated the palace had additional levels within the tree itself. Elaborate stained-glass windows were carved into the tree with large balconies containing lavish furniture. It was an intricate design one had to see to believe. Leading up to the palace was a wide staircase that divided and wrapped around a large statue of Dhara before connecting once more and continuing to the palace door. The closer we got to the palace, the easier it was to make out the numerous people hustling about.

"Keep your hood low and pull down your sleeves," Calian said.

I tugged my sleeves over my scales and pulled down the hood of my cloak. "Sorry," I mumbled. "I was just taking in everything. The palace—this whole place —is breathtaking. I've never seen anything like it."

"I don't disagree, but we can't have people getting a clear look at your face and especially your scales. As of now, the prophesied Dragonheirs are still a rumor. Your eyes and scales say different."

"Understood," I said. I closed my eyes and scolded myself silently. In the darkness of my mind, I saw Erjon's smug expression. Of course, I should have known to cover all of my identifying markers.

Calian must have sensed my internal struggle because he cleared his throat to get my attention. "Tomorrow is the Partition. They're making last-minute preparations." He waved at two men wheeling in a small wooden staircase. Beside them, women were carrying large floral arrangements. Both men nodded, the women smiled, and we continued our way through the city.

"They'll have the Partition at the palace?"

"Kind of. I anticipate it happening in the market. It's a wide-open space where merchants set up…"

"I know what a market is, Calian," I retorted.

"Well, the market has a direct view of the palace. It will be there." He paused. "Why? Where did you think they'd have it," he asked curiously.

I shrugged. "A church? That's where it was supposed to be held in Medora."

"Medora is a fishing port. This is the City of Dhara, so it's bound to be different," he said matter-of-factly.

I glared at him. "Will we be staying at the palace since we're heading in that direction?" I asked, my temperature rising. My ears tingled from annoyance.

"No. We will be staying at the Arden Inn within the Market Quarter, which houses the market."

"Really?" I feigned shock. "The market is in the Market Quarter? Who would have known?"

Calian looked at me from the corner of his eyes, his head still facing forward. "All right, all right. Keep the sarcasm to yourself, thanks."

We passed more people readying the city for the Partition including priests and priestesses, citizens of Dhara, and the occasional city guard.

"Because the Market Quarter contains most of the businesses for food and trade, there's a large inn there called The Arden Inn. Hopefully, there will be room. Since the Partition is tomorrow, we might be looking for lodging elsewhere."

"Well, let's hope there's at least a couple of rooms left," I agreed. Calian chuckled under his breath.

By the time we crossed the white stone bridge into the Market Quarter, there were no carts of goods, and the businesses were vacant. The inn was perched on a small hill overlooking the Market Quarter. A statue of Dhara stood next to a sign that said *The Arden Inn*. The wooden exterior of the inn was adorned with vines, small trees with white, pink, and purple leaves as well as Dragon carvings. The windows were lit with fat candles in the windowsills. The large front door was painted a beautiful, vibrant green.

Calian opened the door for me, and I stood momentarily in the doorway. The interior room contained small tables and a small fire with benches and chairs of deep green velvet surrounding it. Despite the fire, the room smelled of spring: fresh flowers, grass, and the calm before a storm. Humans and Dragonborn were engaged in conversation with one another around the fire or while eating at the tables. It was a wondrous sight to see everyone getting along. The soldiers back in the camp had been Dragonborn, and the citizens of Medora had been mostly human. This was the most diverse crowd I'd ever encountered, and my intuition told me that there was no hostility between any human or Dragonborn here. My heart was light with relief, and I felt quite in tune with the atmosphere.

"We have one room left," the innkeeper told Calian, who was already paying for the room when I sauntered up to him. "We usually book up days out of the Partition, but we had a last-minute cancellation."

"Lucky us," Calian said and smiled kindly.

The innkeeper didn't miss a beat. "Lily will be here momentarily to take you to your room. You're in the main hall; my family's living quarters are downstairs, and the kitchen is to the left of the stairs. As I'm sure you noticed, all stables are outside of the city. King's orders. I thought it'd surely be a terrible idea…y'know? People come an' steal the horses, but he keeps part of the Royal Guard on watch there. So far, no issues. How 'bout that?"

"How about that, indeed," Calian replied coolly.

The innkeeper turned abruptly toward the stairs. "Drat," he said. "Where is she? She was just…" He stopped when a woman and a young girl trailing her came down the stairs. The woman's dark hair was pulled back into an intricate braid that sat like a crown atop her head, and she wore a sensible dress with an apron. She walked up to us and nodded. Calian and I both responded in kind. The young girl hid behind Lily's dress, occasionally peeking out to steal glances at us. She was different than the children of Medora who had long locks of wavy dark hair. This girl had short light brown hair that sat just above her shoulders and was cut bluntly across the forehead emphasizing her hazel eyes. She had rosy cheeks, and the twinkle in her eyes highlighted her innocence. I gave the girl a quick wink which seemed to ease her, and she smiled.

"Lily, please take these two upstairs to the empty chambers. They'll be staying one night."

Lily gave a smile and a short greeting before motioning us to follow. The little girl bounded up the stairs before us. "Please don't mind Willow. She's very spirited, to say the least." Lily lowered her voice, "We think she might be Dragonborn, but there are none within my family or Oren's." I glanced at Lily's arms and, sure enough, found no trace of scales. Come to think of it, I didn't see any on her husband's arms either.

"Who knows? She may be the first," I pointed out.

"Only time will tell. She is not due to enter the Partition for quite a while. Ah," Lily said and stopped in front of a green-painted door. "Here you are." She unlocked it, and Calian walked in first. "I'll leave you to it," Lily said. She turned and walked back toward the staircase, Willow following closely behind.

I closed the door and watched Calian inspect the room. He looked under the bed, out the window—which had a small balcony of all things—and the closet. "All clear," he said.

The room wasn't spacious, but it was of good size. It had one bed large enough for two people, a small fireplace, and a chair lined with green velvet. A wardrobe sat empty on the western wall while a matching chest of drawers sat next to the bed. Calian discarded the bags on the bed and began his attempt to light the fireplace. I sat my bow and quiver of arrows that I'd brought with me against the wall.

"Question," I said, interrupting the silence between us. "With each of us having fire magic, couldn't we just raise our body temperatures and keep ourselves warm? I know I don't have Vukan's blessing yet, but I did shoot that fireball. Surely, I can warm myself."

"We could. But that would take energy, and I'm tired."

"I thought Dragonheirs don't get tired," I said playfully.

"I didn't say Dragonheirs never get tired," he pointed out. "They just don't tire like humans. Dragonheirs can go for several days without sleep if needed. Doesn't mean we can't take the occasional snooze." He formed a ball of fire in his hand and tossed it at the fireplace. The ball hit the firewood, and the logs burst into flames.

"You seem grouchy."

"I'm not grouchy," he replied. "As I said, I'm just tired."

"Got it. Well, I'm not. I'll just go down to the common room and let you rest." I began to back up toward the door, waiting for him to stop me and tell me I was being reckless.

Calian opened his mouth to speak but stopped. Instead, he let out an elongated sigh and brushed his fingers through his hair. "Please don't go wandering out into the city. It's not safe for you out there."

"I won't, Father."

"Funny." He stalked over to the bed and threw himself on it. That was my cue to exit before he changed his mind.

Not that I'd listen to him anyway. Regardless of my joke, he wasn't my father.

After closing the door to the room, I strolled down the hallway and descended the stairs. A vacant table sat by the fireplace, so I took it. I watched the flames mingle with one another, swaying and curling in an intricate dance of heat and light. The restless energy of the fire matched my own.

I took a long swig of my water, and when I lowered the tankard, I found a stranger sitting in front of me, blocking my view of the fire. I lowered my eyes in hopes to conceal them while I searched for another place to sit. It was rude of her to just sit without asking, but to keep my identity hidden, I wasn't going to argue with her about it.

"No, please. Stay. I only ask for a moment of your time…Dragonheir."

I froze and slid my gaze to hers. I couldn't make out the features of the woman except that she had dark hair that peeked out from her black hood and rested below her shoulders. Because of how much she was covered—her sleeves were also long and black—I couldn't tell if she was a Dragonborn or a human. Her hood dropped so low over her head that it almost sat on the bridge of her nose. I lowered my head slightly to ensure she couldn't get a full view of my eyes. Under the table, I tugged at the cuffs of my sleeves so that only my fingertips were visible.

"Who are you?" I whispered.

"That information is not important."

"I disagree."

"Just know that I am a friend."

"No friend would leave me in a vulnerable position such as this. And a friend would at least tell me her name."

"Listen, please," she begged. "You must be careful in the city."

"If you're talking about the cultists, they're already looking for me."

"The cultists are not your enemy," she said, and I could feel the shock written on my face. I didn't speak for fear of giving my emotions away.

"That's the Dragoncouncil," she continued. "And despite his welcoming reputation, King Tellus is a businessman. He will try to find you, take you, and ransom you off. He knows how badly Anwir wants you."

"I know Dragonmaster Anwir wants me. I have a prophecy to fulfill which you're probably going to tell me you know all about."

She didn't speak, but instead, she shifted in her seat and leaned in, keeping her head low so that I couldn't see her eyes. Her voice dropped barely above a whisper. "Anwir cannot be trusted." It didn't escape me that she referred to the Dragonmaster by his name only. No title, just the name. It meant this stranger had a relationship with the priest. "They have a different agenda that doesn't favor the humans, only Dragonborn," she finished.

I tried to sense any signs of deception, but I couldn't.

I leaned back but still kept my face lowered. "Really? So, what's this hidden agenda the council has? Because the way I see it, they're the ones wanting to bring peace and balance to the six kingdoms."

The stranger laughed quietly but then pursed her lips, thinking. "I wouldn't say the Dragoncouncil is all bad. But they are heavily influenced by Anwir. Anwir believes that only the Chaos Dragongod Amram—the third Chaos Dragon—should rule over the six kingdoms. They intend to resurrect Amram from his grave. With Amram alive, the Dragongod can then resurrect the Dragons that fought alongside him during the War of Three. He had thousands of Dragons on his side. To resurrect his army would be the end of days for humans."

I stared blankly at her to not give away the shock that sprinted through my mind.

"That's not what you were told," she guessed.

I took a breath and sighed, feigning annoyance. "I'll be leaving now. Thanks for the warning." I stood to leave, my cheeks now hot from embarrassment because of the anger and resentment that bubbled inside of me.

"Wait!" She grabbed my arm and waited until I—against my better judgment—sat back down. She lifted her hands, grabbed her hood, and pulled it back. The most startling eyes I'd ever seen stared back at me.

They were pure white with heavy black lashes sweeping over them.

I concealed my surprise by studying the rest of her appearance. She had an oval-shaped face, and her beautiful light olive skin radiated against her silky white hair that was tucked behind her ears. I could see her beautiful white scales on the sides of her head. She was a Dragonheir, and her Elemental Dragongod was Endrit, the Dragongod of Light. She was a Lightenion. Calian's words came back like a subtle warning.

"You're…," I whispered.

"I am." She leaned back, not caring to hide anything about herself anymore.

"I'm going to assume you were told that Ragnar was the Chaos Dragon to betray Nimerah." She didn't pose it as a question, so I didn't see the need to respond. "Ah, so I assume correctly. Well, that is not true. It was the Dragongod Amram. Ragnar sacrificed himself for Nimerah. Ragnar and Nimerah loved each other."

"The War of Three started because of a love feud?" I asked. I couldn't believe it.

"Don't all wars start because of love? Love for someone? Love for power? Love for one's self?"

She had a point.

"It's time for a history lesson," she answered. She leaned in toward the middle of the table and motioned for me to do the same. I didn't refuse. I placed my arms on the table and leaned in. My scales peeked out from beneath my sleeves, but I didn't care. What was the point? She knew who I was. And she'd shown me her true self. She'd given some semblance of trust. It was my turn to do the same.

"Ragnar insisted nothing come of their love for the sake of maintaining a balance of power. He knew Amram was not to be trusted. But somehow Amram discovered it and became angry. He thought Ragnar was controlling Nimerah to gain her power—Ragnar was her general, after all. So Amram reasoned it was his duty to kill Ragnar to save Nimerah. Scholars say Amram was secretly in love with Nimerah which was his true motivation for the assassination, not that he thought Ragnar was trying to steal power. Regardless, Amram didn't anticipate Nimerah coming to Ragnar's aid. Ragnar ended up sacrificing himself for Nimerah. With that sacrifice, she gained Ragnar's power. Amram became furious, accusing Nimerah of devising the plan to trick Ragnar into loving her so that she could steal his power. In his mind, Nimerah betrayed them both. He tried to do what he thought would hurt her: eliminate humanity. He built an army and began to slaughter the humans. Nimerah built hers, and eventually, Amram was killed. It is said that Nimerah was also killed—that it took her entire life force to take down Amram. She'd already used most of her Dragonmagic to save humanity, so she was depleted once she and Amram met on the battlefield. But we know the truth, don't we?"

I blinked several times, digesting all of the information I'd just heard. It was nothing like the history I'd learned. My blood boiled beneath my skin.

"Anwir wants Amram resurrected so that he can finish what Amram started. Eliminate all of humanity. Except

Amram can only be resurrected by the blood of a Chaos Dragon. Chaos blood runs through your veins which is why Anwir has sought you out. What Anwir doesn't know is that you are not the only Daughter of Chaos."

I stood abruptly, ignoring the looks of the other patrons within the room. "That's not possible," I declared.

She tilted her head and looked at me curiously. "I find it interesting that Nimerah has not yet given her blessing. I suggest you figure out how to get her blessing soon before Anwir figures out there's a second Daughter of Chaos. Your very life could depend on it."

With false conviction, I stood my ground. "I'll do my best," I insisted. "Now, are you going to tell me who this second Daughter of Chaos is?"

She opened her mouth and started to speak when the door to the inn opened and slammed against the wall, causing the windows to rattle. I pulled my hood back down over my eyes and wriggled my sleeves until they were back over my hands. I turned to the front door to see what had caused the surrounding conversations to stop. A tall, muscular man walked through the room toward Oren.

"I need to leave," she said suddenly. "I cannot be found here."

"I can help you," I said without looking back. I got no response, so I turned back to her. "Just tell me your name."

She was gone.

Although I wasn't that tired, I needed to rest some for the Partition. I left the common room and withdrew back upstairs. Once in the room, I made sure Calian was sleeping before I dressed in the thin nightshirt that he'd packed for me. I sat in the chair next to the dying fire and watched Calian in his peaceful slumber. If Anwir was the bad guy, then the council was too. And that meant so was Calian. I bit down on my lower lip. There was no way the council and Calian were the villains here. Right? All of the questions plagued my thoughts until I finally drifted to sleep.

CHAPTER

THIRTEEN

When I woke the next morning, Calian was lounging in the chair by the fireplace eating a small piece of bread, and I was lying on the bed with one arm outstretched under my head and the other bent over my forehead. I could feel the crusty dried-up drool at the corners of my mouth and the pool of fresh drool under my cheek. Humiliation crept into my chest, up my neck, and warmed my cheeks. Stupid drool.

I stretched my arms, arched my back, and gave an embarrassing groan while my bones cracked and popped. I then wiped my mouth with the back of my arm while Calian stared at me, probably repulsed by my sleeping habits. Well, he could get over them. I never pretended to be a lady.

"Seems like a hearty breakfast," I said with a yawn.

"Humph," was his response. He jerked his head to a plate sitting by the bed. Resting on the plate was a variety of meats, cheese, and bread. Two tankards sat on either side of the plate. I scooted myself over. I reached over to grab some fruit, but I paused. The side of the bed smelled like him. It was the same campfire smell I had inhaled the first time he'd carried me in his arms—which had been an unusual number of times. I caught him staring at me and realized I probably looked stupid just lying there, so I tried to recover from my stupor and grabbed the closest thing to me which was the tankard. I sat completely up and took a deep swig.

Pfft!

What is this?" I asked after spitting out the tankard's contents.

"Wine," Calian answered casually. "I just asked for breakfast to be brought up, and that came with it." A faint smile tugged at his lips, and his eyes had a slight twinkle to them. I felt my heart flip, so I bit my lip as a distraction. Too hard because I tasted blood. He seemed to notice and found it amusing, to say the least. He leaned forward, his elbows on his knees, and asked, "Is it not to your liking?"

"It's not what I expected," I replied. I licked my lips to get rid of any trace of blood and took another swig of the wine. I let it sit in my mouth for a moment before forcing it down with a deafening gulp.

"Better?"

"M-hmm," I lied.

"Good. We need to get moving. The Partition will take place soon."

He stood and walked to the bed, tossed me a bag, and swung the other across his back. As I watched him, I recalled the conversation with the white-eyed stranger. Should I mention it to Calian? Should I keep it to myself? I argued back and forth within my mind until I'd had enough. I needed to know something—*anything*—that would ease my mind.

He leaned down to grab more food from the plate when I asked, "How well do you know the council?"

"That seems like a loaded question," he answered without hesitation. "Is that what you were doing last night? Trying to figure out my secrets." His tone was playful. That was a good sign. It had to be a good sign. It meant my question didn't knock him off balance. It meant he didn't have to stop and search for a lie.

"It's just that I've heard rumors about them. That they're hiding something. And my understanding is that they're a large part of your past, yet you've never given me any solid details about you or them, so I was just wondering."

"All right." He sat on the bed and swallowed the remaining bites of food. "When I was younger, I was living in the City of Vukan. To be specific, I lived on the streets as a thief. A very skilled thief," he added.

"Noted," I said.

"My mother and father were gone. They were victims of the plague, so I only had myself to rely on to survive. One day I happened to be conning a shopkeeper when a man walked in the door, wrapped an arm around me, and led me out of the shop. Gods, I thought I was done for." Calian bent his head and chuckled to himself. Then his voice softened. "He didn't scold me or judge me. He walked me to the nearby inn and that was that. I participated in my own private Partition when I reached the City of Nimerah."

"Sounds fortuitous. Who was he?"

"His name was—and still is—Dragonmaster Anwir. He's the highest ranking Dragonpriest in the six kingdoms and head of the Dragoncouncil, hence the name

Dragonmaster. He saw potential in me, so he took me off the streets and raised me. The members of the Dragoncouncil ended up being my family, helping me learn how to wield my Dragonmagic. I owe them my life." The affection in his voice was apparent: he loved Dragonmaster Anwir. I remained silent and kept the conversation with the stranger to myself.

"Calian?" I shifted my weight nervously.

"Yeah?"

"Is it possible for the council to be the bad guy here?" I held my breath.

"No." Unsure of what to do next, I clenched my teeth and waited for the follow-up question. "Why do you ask?" There it was.

"Oh…I…um…I," I stammered. I needed a lie and fast. "I overheard someone talking about the council last night. They did not sound too happy with it. Just made me wonder since I don't really know much about them aside from what every person is told growing up."

Calian's brows tightened together in contemplation. "Well, in a world of Dragonborn and human tension, the Dragoncouncil can't please everyone." Although his answer wasn't as reassuring as I'd hoped, it wasn't all that bad. It gave me some hope that maybe he wasn't lying to me. Because if the stranger was telling the truth, then Calian wasn't. Or he was led to believe false information by the council—the council that was essentially his family.

Calian hopped off the bed, his feet making a loud thud when they hit the wooden floor. "Come on. I'll go make sure everything is straight with the innkeeper, and you can get dressed."

There was no use wallowing in despair, at least not in front of him, so I slid off the bed, grabbed the bag he'd given me, and waited for him to leave. After he'd closed the door, I discarded my nightshirt in the bag and dressed quickly. I grabbed my bow and quiver of arrows from their resting place and pulled my hood down as far as I could.

I descended the stairs one last time and stood beside Calian who was still talking to the innkeeper and his wife. While they finished up business, Willow tugged on the ends of my cloak.

"Dragonheir," she whispered. I patted her head, and she responded with a mischievous smile. I knew that smile. Willow was a strong-willed girl who pushed boundaries. Strong-willed girls grew up to be women who changed the world. At least, that's what my mother always said about me.

We left the inn and made our way to the center of the Market Quarter where the Partition would take place. I marveled at how alive the market was. Merchant carts and tents were placed sporadically throughout the market, and doors to the established shops were wide open, inviting shoppers to enter at will. We passed an apothecary, and I wavered at its entrance. The rich smells of spices, herbs, and flowers filled my nostrils. My chest tightened, and tears stung my eyes from the images of my mother and father that formed vividly in my head. I could see their smiles, hear their laughter, and feel their warm embraces. It was all I could do to not walk inside. But I didn't. I took a couple of steps back and slowly turned, picking up my pace so that I was once again in step with Calian.

At the Market Quarter's heart was a large fountain of a tree with the Earth Dragongoddess Dhara curled around its trunk. Streams of water shot up from various branches and arced outward, crisscrossing in mid-air. The water streams were various shades of green and the arcs were at varying heights. It was a beautiful homage to the goddess.

Just beyond the lavish fountain was a small stage with Dhara's picturesque castle standing behind it. At the center of the stage was an altar, and sitting atop it was an emerald pedestal dish adorned with embossed leaves. Beside the dish was an elaborate dagger, the hilt the same emerald glass as the dish. A priestess stood at a podium next to the altar, hunched over an outspread tome with her eyes closed. She moved her hands over the tome gracefully as if trying to extract an incantation from its pages. Her lips moved swiftly yet patiently throughout her recitation. Upon finishing, she opened her eyes and brought both hands to her heart. She then lifted her eyes and hands to the sky, her arms stretched out above her.

A large group of young men and women, all of whom had reached their eighteenth birthdays, were congregated on the left side of the stage just before a small set of wooden stairs. Some spoke enthusiastically to each other; some stared in silence past the stage at the castle beyond; some cried, sobbing and whimpering into their hands. I couldn't quite make out how I was feeling. Jealousy taunted me, reminding me that the Partition was stolen from me. Never mind that I hadn't believed I was a Dragonborn.

"Jealous?" Calian asked, and I snapped back into reality.

"Of course not," I lied.

Calian smirked. "Of course not," he repeated. He didn't believe me. *I* didn't believe me. He walked two steps and stood directly behind my left shoulder. Grabbing my right shoulder, Calian leaned around my left and pointed across my body at the top of a towering shop roof. "See there?" He asked.

I didn't. Why? Because I was too busy noticing how close he was. His scent filled my lungs, and his touch was electric. Our eyes met, and we each took a deep breath. I wondered what it would be like to kiss him. I'd never kissed anyone before. Would I even be good at it? I really needed to think of something else, so I slowly looked to where his finger pointed. Directly on the shop's roof was a hooded figure, a bow at his or her back.

"And there," Calian said quietly and turned me to a shop directly on the other side of the market. Another hooded figure stood with a bow on its roof. "And there and there." He continued to point around the market at various locations where hooded figures stood. All of them were wearing dark green tabards with chainmail underneath for protection. Across the tabard was a tree with Dhara wrapped around it, her head looking directly out. These were Dharian guards.

"Are they all necessary?"

"They're here to keep the peace. Riots have broken out before during a Partition. And there will be one today."

"How do you know?"

"Because we're going to start it."

"We're what?" I took a step back from him, and my body instantly cooled from the lack of warmth between us. Calian stood up straight and pretended to dust off the dirt from his shirt.

"One of those candidates is the Dragonheir we need."

"But we won't know who until the activation starts."

"Which is the problem," Calian pointed out. His eyes moved back and forth, examining the stage and the rest of the area. "Once the heir participates in the activation process, we must get to him or her before the guards do."

"How will the guards know? Won't the heir's blood just show as a regular Dragonborn?"

"Dragonheir blood is more potent than just Dragonborn blood. It will call to the Dragongoddess Dhara. Being that this is not a Chaos Dragon, it's safe to say the Dragonheir will connect with the Dragongoddess immediately and be affected in some way. A shift in the wind, the sun shines brighter, something. Just watch each candidate as their blood spills into the basin. You'll be able to tell."

"And if I can't?" I asked.

"Even if you don't first notice a change in expression or posture of the heir, that's not the tell-all."

"And what's the tell-all?" He pointed to his eyes, and they flashed red. I picked up what he was saying. Their eyes would change colors or glow. He started walking to the side of the stage that was opposite the gathering participants. I followed behind him.

"The shop over there is the rendezvous point." Calian pointed to a shop that stood behind the stage to the left. "Behind it is a hidden entrance within a hollowed-out tree," he continued. "It goes to the underground tunnel system that runs from the palace deeper into the Arden Forest. We will travel back to the river we crossed to get here. That is where we will meet once you or I have the heir. Don't wait outside. Just get there and hide in the tunnel." I started turning my head to see what he was talking about, but I stopped when he vehemently whispered, "Don't look!" I snapped my head back to face the stage. "You'll draw attention to yourself. Everyone else is looking at the stage. Keep your eyes forward.

Remember those guards I pointed out to you earlier? You give yourself away, and you're their target. They would absolutely love to get their hands on you. You know…for *ransom*?" I felt my face flush. He knew.

"You heard?" I squeaked.

"I'm not an idiot, Emera. I wouldn't let you go anywhere in the City of Dhara by yourself. Even if it was just to the common room of an inn."

"Because I always need protection?" I hissed.

"Because I must get you back to the Dragoncouncil safe and ready for what comes next," he snapped. We were back to duty above all else. I rolled my eyes. He added, "*Senna* may have tried to convince you otherwise, but you'd be best off not trusting her."

"Senna?"

"The woman you were speaking to last night."

"You spied on me?!"

"I needed to make sure you weren't going to level the building," he said, laughing.

I made a fist and punched his shoulder. He only laughed louder. Strangers turned their heads to see what was causing all the commotion.

"Who's drawing unnecessary attention to us, now?" I whispered.

He placed his hand on his chest to gather his composure. "We knew each other—if you can really say that. She was the daughter of a diplomat, and they came to the Kingdom of Vukan once. I happened to steal from her father. I'm not proud of it."

"You were young. You were starving and alone. No one would blame you."

The corners of his mouth curled slightly. "Anyway, she caught me, but she didn't turn me in."

Hearing Calian's words eased my anxiety about it all. I could finally concentrate again. "I'm sorry," I whispered.

"You have nothing to be sorry for. Senna is very convincing. She almost convinced me."

"She told you the same thing?"

"Her father was always jealous of Anwir," he answered. We stood in silence for a while, watching and listening to the crowd around us. He finally broke the silence. "Let's put that past us and focus on what we need to do. The Partition is starting." He jerked his chin toward the priestess who was now standing in the center of the stage addressing the crowd—the crowd that had tripled in size. Human and Dragonborn onlookers stood shoulder to shoulder as the young men and women lined up for their turn. No one argued and no one pushed. No one said nasty things to each other.

The priestess finished her welcoming speech by giving thanks to Dhara and placed herself by the altar. She picked up the dagger and recited the activation enchantment. She motioned for the first participant to step forward. A young man walked toward her confidently, his chest pushed out. He held his wrist out over the dish, and the priestess made a small cut with the dagger. He didn't even watch but smiled heroically as droplets of red blood hit the ceremonial basin. Instantly, green scales formed on his skin, starting at his temples and moving down to his hands. He closed his eyes, took a breath, and opened them revealing the same brown eyes he'd had before. He seemed shocked and disappointed even as the crowd cheered. The new Dragonborn was ushered off the stage. He was not the Dragonheir no matter how much he'd wanted to be. I guessed in Dhara that the tales of Dragonheirs were not just bedtime stories. *Unless it was just a bedtime story to me,* I thought. It made sense. My parents didn't want me to know who I was, but they needed me to know the basics for when the time came, so why not pass it off as a bedtime story? Another pain of betrayal fell into the pit of my stomach.

Calian snapped me out of my stupor. "You stay here. Once the Dragonheir begins to reveal himself…"

"Or herself," I remarked, cutting him off.

"Or herself," he repeated, "I will shoot out a few random fireballs into the crowd." I glared at him. "Don't worry, I won't hit anyone," he insisted. "Once the riot begins, and everyone is distracted, you grab the heir and head toward the shop. Again, don't wait for me above ground. Get into the tunnel. And Emera…" He paused and his eyes flared to life. "If I'm not there in a reasonable amount of time, then leave. Head out of the tunnels into the forest. Call for Zari and go back to the camp."

The second participant was already walking off the stage. Not a Dragonborn.

"I can't leave you here," I hissed.

"You will if you have to. But let's hope it doesn't get to that."

"What if I have to fight?" I regretted the question the moment it left my mouth. "Right. I fight." Time to be brave, Em.

"And don't hold back," he said and disappeared into the crowd. I stood still. I reminded myself that I couldn't let my feelings interfere with what was at stake. I needed to get the heir to the tunnel. The third participant, a young woman with warm beige skin, walked across the stage. Her light voluminous curls—darker toward her head but almost white as they reached her shoulders—bounced with every step she took. Tiny braids were woven by her face making her every bit the warrior. She had a strong, yet feminine jawline and full lips, but what made her absolutely captivating was her confidence. She walked with conviction as she crossed the stage, and she looked straight ahead. Our eyes met. I didn't know how I knew, but I did.

She was the Dragonheir of Dhara.

I did the only thing I could think of next. I carefully drew my hood back a little to expose my eyes more to her. To my surprise, she let out a visible sigh of relief. The silent communication told me she knew who I was. I slowly swept my eyes over the crowd hoping to locate Calian while I maneuvered my way through the onlookers. If I could somehow alert him that the Dragonheir knew I was there to help, then this whole thing could go more smoothly. But I couldn't find him anywhere, so I watched the heir's wrist be cut and her blood spill into the dish. Calian was right. New energy swirled around me and up to the stage. The leaves on all the surrounding trees began to rustle loudly as a growing wind rushed through them. Whispers and mumbles erupted from the already stirring crowd. Everyone was looking around in confusion, but I knew what was going on. And that's when the Dragon appeared in the sky.

CHAPTER

FOURTEEN

It was chaos. And not the magic kind. Once the Dragonheir's eyes glowed green and her scales appeared, a few people from the crowd threw off their cloaks and revealed themselves as cultists. This caught the guards' attention—which meant they wouldn't be looking for me, so it was a nice distraction. The next thing I knew, arrows were shooting down from the shop rooftops and past my head. I held up my arm in front of my head and imagined an invisible shield protecting me. Men, women, and children were screaming. Everyone panicked and ran for cover, shoving me away from the stage.

The Dragon above was large with black scales and jagged edges. It flew from over the palace and landed on top of the Arden Inn. Its sharp claws dug into the roof causing part of the inn to cave in on itself. A large blast of fire shot from the Dragon's mouth, setting several roofs aflame and killing the guards on top. I held in my horror at the sight. Then I thought of the innkeeper, Oren, his wife, Lily, and Willow. The inn's structure was breaking down under the weight of the Dragon. I had to get the beast off. Then those in the inn could get out to safety. With my left arm, I reached for my arrow that was fastened to the quiver strapped on my back, and with my right, I pulled out an arrow. I aimed the arrow for the Dragon's head, and with a steadying breath, I let it fly. The Dragon leaped into the air so that the arrow punctured its leg instead of its head. I didn't know Dragons could move that fast. Regardless of how impressed I was, I backed away, turned, and ran.

I fought my way through the stampede of humans and Dragonborn, calling to my magic to form a shield of air out in front of me, and it worked. Anyone who ran into my shield ricocheted back. Finally, there was a break in the crowd, and I sped back to the side of the stage. The Dragonheir was gone, and in her place, was a cultist. How was this cultist larger than the one in Medora? What did these guys eat?

Our eyes met, and he knew instantly who I was. "Any chance you'll just leave me alone?" I joked.

The man just stared at me.

"Guess not," I mumbled. Without hesitation, I shot an arrow at him. He dropped to the ground, but not before the arrow pierced his arm. He groaned in pain, but it didn't stop him from pulling the arrow out. I hastily refastened my bow to my back and threw my hands out. Powerful gusts of air expelled from my hands to push me up on the stage. Although I was sick of the relentless practice during our trip here, I was thankful that Calian pushed me. I had better control of my magic. I mean, I just flew on the stage. I felt my chest flutter when the thought popped into my head that I couldn't wait to tell Calian.

The cultist, on the other hand, didn't seem to care. Once my feet hit the stage, he came running. He leaped for me, so I slid underneath his legs and turned in time to freeze the water from my palms and propelled sharp icicles at him. My icicles hit him square in the chest and through the heart. The cultist's body twitched furiously as he clawed at the ice to try and pull it from his chest. His eyes went wide with terror, realizing he couldn't save himself. Light vacated his eyes, and he fell backward off the stage onto the ground.

I'd killed a man. And at the end of his life, he was…*scared*.

I shook the image from my mind and looked back up at the Dragon. It had risen off the inn and was circling above. It looked for something.

Or someone, I realized.

I needed to get off the stage. I glanced around the area for Calian. My breath caught in my chest when I spotted him. He stood face-to-face with a Dharian guard who also happened to be a Dragonborn. Calian's flames were at his side, ready to be unleashed. From the guard's hands sprouted vines with sharp thorns. The guard shot the vines toward Calian who threw a fireball at it. It only deterred the vine for a moment. It shook off any flames that had scorched it and wrapped itself around Calian's ankles and his wrists. The guard pulled the vines back, and Calian went with them. He fell flat on his back, and I could hear him cough from the force of the ground. I had to think of something. The Dragonheir needed me, but so did Calian.

A light tug pulled my body toward him so abruptly that I almost tripped over my own feet. I ran toward him when a deafening roar filled the marketplace, and the Dragon came into view. It spotted Calian and dove downward at him. I jumped from the stage and ran toward Calian, weaving in and out the fighting going on around me. The remaining cultists, several citizens, and Dharian guards were all engaged in fighting. The ground was covered with the dead. I ran through blood, torn limbs, and those begging for mercy. I gritted my teeth and clenched my fists, hurtling toward Calian. His hands were still burning as he tried to free his ankles from the vines that dug into his skin. I kneeled quickly beside him, gripping the vines as the guard continued to drag Calian to him.

"Let me help you!" I yelled. I closed my eyes and sent a silent prayer to Dhara, requesting her help.

"What are you doing?" he snapped.

"Saving your butt," I spat. "Let me concentrate!" With my hands hovering over the vines, I continued to pray that Dhara would loosen them. "Please let me help these people," I pleaded. I slowly opened my eyes to see the vines moving, steadily untangling themselves. Calian sat there, either impressed or dumbfounded. Probably both.

"You're welcome, by the way."

"Thanks," he said and started to work on loosening the vines faster.

The Dragon landed, shaking the ground. I stood slowly and turned. It sauntered toward me, its eyes black as night and hungry. I placed myself between the Dragon and Calian. What did it want with him?

What a stupid question, Emera. It clearly wants to kill him. Well, that wasn't going to happen. I set my jaw and grounded my feet. In an act of complete ignorance, I waved at it.

"Hello! What you're doing is completely unnecessary!" I yelled. The Dragon angled its head. Could it understand me? A low grumble vibrated the Dragon's throat, and as it reached the Dragon's mouth, smoke exited along with it. I could swear it laughed as it moved closer and closer.

Out of the corner of my eye, I saw that the guard had stopped pulling once he saw the Dragon. Good. I could save Calian time. The vines had stopped dragging against the ground as well, and Calian appeared to be close to freeing himself from their entrapment. Maybe if I distracted the Dragon long enough, Calian could free himself and get to safety.

I needed to figure out what I was doing. I managed to calm my mind briefly enough to connect with the life force of the vines, and they released themselves from

Calian's ankles and slithered back. I raised my arms to my sides, the vines rising with them. Then I thrust out my hands, commanding the vines to wrap around the Dragon, which they did. Well, they tried anyway. They did their best, and tightened, leaving the Dragon captured for a moment. A brief moment. But they were no match for the Dragon's strength. The Dragon's wings ripped through the vines and the force threw me back across the market. I landed on my back with a resounding thud, the air knocked out of my chest. I coughed before I sat up, gasping for air. I was too late. The Dragon was circling Calian and with it, a whirlwind of black smoke. The smoke continued to swirl around them both until it was so thick, I couldn't see Calian.

I jumped back to my feet and ran toward them both. With my hands thrust outward, I called to my magic and caused the wind to blow the smoke away. I was just in time. The smoke cleared, revealing the Dragon standing above Calian about to make a final blow.

"Hey, you! You big ugly lizard!" I shouted. The Dragon looked up from Calian, who was lying still on the ground, and glared at me with what appeared to be pure hatred. It opened its mouth, and I saw the stirring of fire emerging from its throat.

I thrust my palms out and blasted the strongest wind I could at the Dragon the same time it unleashed its strong inferno. We stood there, a power of wills. My air magic held just as strong. The Dragon stopped once it realized its fire couldn't overpower my wind and lifted itself into the air.

Calian, having regained consciousness, grabbed my hand without a word, and pulled me toward him. "You were incredible." He bent down and lit a quick flame from his fingertip. Through gritted teeth, he sealed the gashes shut on his ankle. We ran back toward the last spot we'd both seen the Dragonheir.

"You seem to be okay," I pointed out to Calian.

"The ankle is stiff," he said with a subtle limp. "It hurts like Dragonhell, but I'll be fine."

"So, if you haven't noticed, there's a Dragon here."

"Oh, I definitely noticed," he said. "We need to find the Dragonheir so we can get back to camp and figure out how that Dragon exists."

"Let's do it!" I said enthusiastically. I felt energized, so I playfully shoved his shoulder. He stopped in his tracks and looked at his shoulder. Then he looked at me. My cheeks warmed with embarrassment.

"I'm sorry," I said. "It just seemed like the right thing to do. You know? Teamwork?"

He reached his arm out and pushed me back lightly. Then he took off toward the stage. I slowed down and watched him because he didn't limp. Didn't he limp earlier? He was tough, so he probably just ran through the pain. Typical Calian.

We were closer to the stage now after having dodged flames from the Dragon and arrows, blades, boulders, gusts of leaves, and other forms of magic from the cultists and Dragonborns. But there was no sign of the Dragonheir. Calian pointed to the back of the stage, a sign that I was to meet him back there. We separated, and he went left while I went right. I rounded the corner of the stage when suddenly a hand grabbed me from below and pulled me to the ground just in time to dodge a flying blade that would have struck me square in the head. Behind me, a cultist lay sprawled on the ground, a pool of blood at his side from the blade that was embedded in his chest. A guard was in front of me, having thrown the blade. He motioned to my arms. A sleeve had ripped, exposing my scales.

"Well, isn't this interesting?" the guard said with delight. "The king will be pleased when I return two

Dragonheirs." He motioned toward the person who'd tripped me. The Dragonheir of Dhara was crouched by my side. Her eyes glowed green, and her hands were spread out, ready for a fight.

A smile crept up the sides of my lips. "You can try," I said, more confident than ever. The Dragonheir smiled as well, and I caught onto her excitement. She was willing to fight beside me.

The guard reached for his bow, but I was too fast for him. I sprang to my feet, raised my palms, and projected fire into his eyes. The guard threw himself on his knees while his hands acted as a shield.

"My eyes! Oh, my gods, my eyes!" he screamed in a panic-filled rage. "Dragonwhore!"

The Dragonheir of Dhara stood quickly. In one smooth swoop, she lifted her palms. Roots erupted from the ground and wrapped the guard where he stood.

"That was mercy," came a gruff voice from behind him. I watched as the hilt of a sword connected with the back of the guard's head. The guard slumped to the ground revealing Calian behind him holding the blade.

I placed my hands on my hips. "Was that necessary?" I scolded him. "I think blinding him did the trick."

Calian shrugged. "Would you rather I have killed him?" He had me there. "Besides, he called you something unpleasant, and I'm a firm believer that no one speaks like that to a lady."

"I would think you'd know by now that I'm no lady," I teased. "Where'd you get the blade?"

"There are many dead cultists and guards around if you haven't noticed."

"I was too distracted by the guard trying to kidnap me."

The Dragon's roar thundered through the sky.

We all looked upward and found the Dragon flying above us. Its sleek black scales were almost iridescent in the sun. It narrowed in on us and hovered overhead, tilting its head to one side looking like it was trying to figure us out.

"What's it doing?" I whispered.

"I don't know," Calian answered. "This is the first time I've encountered one."

"First time for everything, I guess," I mumbled.

The Dragon lowered its head, and its nostrils flared. I could have imagined it, but it looked like it was smiling at me. But not in a friendly way. No, the smile was menacing. Then it spoke to me, and everything around me slowed.

Daughter of Nimerah, I've been looking for you. Its voice was light and airy like a distant memory.

You know who I am. It's only fair that I should know who you are, I responded. The Dragon chuckled. A Dragon chuckled! How was that possible?

I am no fool, it answered.

Neither am I, I assured it. The Dragon chuckled again. I don't think I'd ever get used to the sound.

Perhaps, but you are still inexperienced. And if the Dragon laughing wasn't surprising enough, this time it winked at me.

The fighting behind us picked back up, and the Dragon opened its jaws, flames erupting from its mouth. All three of us jumped out of the way just before fire lit up the stage. I looked back and saw the Dragonheir waving me under the stage.

"Calian! Go under!"

"Good thinking," he said.

I sat beneath the stage and breathed, and I placed my hand over my heart to steady its furious beating. The Dragon kept circling the stage shooting flames on all sides.

"Thank…you…" Calian got out between gulps of air.

"You're welcome," she replied. "I figure it's time to regroup before we face it head-on."

I looked down and pinched the bridge of my nose. "Not sure that's wise," I argued. I needed to think. How would we get out of this situation alive?

"That Dragon is killing everyone. If I had any control over my new Dragonmagic, I'd be out there!"

Calian scooted closer. "Slow down. We need to think about our next move before we just go out and get ourselves killed."

The Dragonheir narrowed her eyes, but she sat back and didn't argue further.

"I'm Calian Westbow, Dragonheir of Vukan. This is Emera Edevane, Dragonheir of Nimerah. We need to get you out of here," he said. "We've got to get to the tunnels and out of the city."

"That sounds fantastic," the Dragonheir agreed, her eyes locked on mine. "But how do we do that?"

"Let me see if I can help," I told her. My eyelids dropped quickly, and I held them there in concentration. My arms lifted from my sides with my palms facing up, but this time I didn't just call to my water element, I called to all of my magic and let it flow throughout my body. I felt the cool rush of tranquility pass through me. The tranquility then shifted to buzzing energy. I held tight onto that energy and let it pulse within every fiber of my being.

The air shifted and everything became still and silent.

I opened my eyes.

"Her eyes," the Dragonheir whispered.

"They'll do that," and the awe in Calian's voice fueled my magic. "Each time she passes a Trial." His voice was somewhat distant, indicating he spoke more to himself. Maybe trying to figure out why the Trials weren't as complex as he'd thought. Because they sure didn't seem that complicated to me.

In my mind, I pictured dark clouds rolling in, bringing with them darkness that limited everyone's sight. A violent wind howled, lightning cracked, and thunder rumbled so loud no one could think. But that wasn't enough. This time, my earth magic begged for release, so I placed my hands on the ground and brought forth a strong tremble from below. I heard merchant carts and goods topple over with ease as the earthquake shook the ground. More flashes of bright lightning streaked across the sky. A bolt hit a large tree branch with a resounding crash, and the branch split open. Roots shot up toward the sky, splitting the stones they erupted from. I took another deep breath and opened my eyes.

"Holy Dragongods," I heard the Dragonheir say in unmistakable wonder.

A smile of victory tugged at my lips. The Dragongoddess Dhara found me worthy of her blessings.

Calian started to crawl toward me, but he stopped. "What's your name?" he asked the Dragonheir.

"Avani," she answered.

"Avani," he repeated. She affirmed with a nod. He shifted closer to me and leaned in, "Your eyes are green now," he told me.

My heart flipped in my chest. He scooted away and cautiously looked out from under the stage. Still focusing my mind on the storm and earthquake I'd produced, I followed Calian and Avani out into the surging storm. I took a second to glance at my hands, marveling at the green scales that now appeared mixed in with my silver and blue scales. The earthquake stopped at my will, but the storm raged on. We were met with destruction.

The fighting had finally ceased. The guards, cultists, and Dragonborns were either lying dead on the ground or running for cover from the lightning that now crashed around them. I looked to the sky and saw the Dragon above us doing its best to maintain flight, but it wavered as the wind pushed it back and forth. I met its gaze and smiled. Anger sparked in its eyes, and it roared as it shakily lifted higher into the sky and flew off. Pleased with myself, I steadied my thoughts, and the thunderstorm ceased. With no one—more like nothing—in our path, we were finally able to run to the back of the shop Calian had pointed out earlier. As he'd said, a tall, wide tree stood planted just beside the back wall of the shop. Calian pushed on the weathered wood, and a hidden door creaked open. He jumped into a hole located within a large tree trunk.

Avani followed, and then I jumped down the hole and landed in a small puddle beside her. Calian laughed at my misfortune, so I threw him a sour look. "Let's go," he said. "We need to get out of the city."

"Wait a moment," I said and turned to Avani. "How are you feeling?"

"Em, we don't have time for this." He ran his fingers through his hair—his tell that he was frustrated. He then leaned against the tunnel wall and folded his arms in front of him. Ah…this was more than just frustration. This was his classic *I'm annoyed* stance. I glared at him. A smile pulled at his lips, and he raised his hands in defense.

"Fine. You ladies chit-chat, and I'll scout ahead. We wouldn't want to come across a hostile cultist with a newly activated Dragonheir." Our eyes locked for a moment, and there it was. The pull from earlier. The want—no, the need—to stay close to him. I took a silent breath and turned to Avani. Even though I didn't hear him leave, Calian was gone.

"You are leaving behind the life you've always known. You are leaving your family…"

Avani interrupted me. "I don't have a family anymore," she stated bluntly. She was trying to hide it, but she was in pain. "My family was murdered."

I knew the shock was plain as day on my face. "Oh. I…Well…I'm sorry." I didn't know what else to say. I had just met her.

"I think they were following me," she said. "The cultists, I mean. They knew somehow that I was a Dragonheir. My mother and father were Dragonborns, so it was only natural that I would be as well. My parents were lesser Dragonborns, though."

"You don't have to continue," I said gently, but she did so anyway.

"I came home from my lessons to find my parents hanging from a tree in front of our home. If I hadn't taken the path through the willow trees, they would have seen me coming up the path. That decision saved me. I can only assume the cultists were waiting inside. I didn't stay to find out. I just ran."

I didn't know Avani at all, but she was strong. Like I pretended to be.

"I am so sorry," I whispered.

We stayed there until Calian came back. He looked from me to Avani and back. "What did you do?" he demanded.

"Nothing." I barked at him.

Calian frowned, his eyebrows closing in on themselves. "Well, now that you ladies are done, let's move. The way is clear. We will keep walking until we come out further into the forest." He turned from us, but he wasn't as cautious this time when he walked down the tunnel with Avani and me following him. After a while, he stopped and faced me. "You need to call your horse," he stated.

"My horse?" I asked suspiciously, tilting my head to the side. "I've never heard you refer to Zari as my horse."

Calian looked startled. "Huh. You're right...It must be because of my encounter with the Dragon. I remember being knocked out for a moment while we were in the smoke. I won't lie. Some things were a bit hazy when I came to. Apparently, some things still are." He closed his eyes and shook his head in an attempt to clear the fog within his mind.

"We need to get you to camp then," I said.

He nodded. "Tell Zari we're under the stables. She needs to head back east to the river we crossed and wait there until we arrive. If we haven't arrived in a couple of days, tell her to go back to camp. Fin isn't a Dragonborn, but he's not dumb. If the horses go back to camp without us, he'll know something is wrong."

I quieted my thoughts and searched for the thread that connected my mind to Zari's. *Zari, my girl. Are you there?*

My queen! I have been worried.

I am all right, Zari. We managed to escape through the city's tunnels. You and Dhruv need to head back to the river we crossed when chased by the wolves. Wait for us there. We have the new Dragonheir.

As you say, my Kahina.

"Done," I said. "Now, can we please get out of the tunnel? The stench is awful."

CHAPTER

FIFTEEN

"Zari, am I glad to see you!" I yelled when I finally laid eyes on my beautiful horse. We'd exited the tunnel precisely where Calian said we would and made the trek to the river. It was an uneventful journey filled with absolute silence. No one spoke. Avani didn't because she was still processing; Calian didn't because of gods knows what; I didn't because the other two were awfully quiet, and I didn't want to intrude on their self-reflecting. When we stopped to eat or drink or rest, we made light conversation to help Avani adjust. Many moments of awkward silence were painful. But still, I practiced controlling my magic here and there, conjuring each element I possessed. However, the focus was mainly on helping Avani—who honestly was a complete natural and didn't need much help at all. Because her parents had been Dragonborn, she already knew the ins and outs of her magic.

Now I stood by Zari's side, shaded by thick trees with an abundance of branches and leaves.

I am glad to see you, too, Kahina. And it is wonderful to see that you have been blessed by Dhara. She smiled—as much as a horse could smile—and I was overcome with happiness. I ran my hand over her long neck and hugged her.

I held my hands up for her to see my new scales. Zari whinnied in delight. *I hope the stables treated you well before all havoc broke loose*, I communicated to her.

The boy, Holt, was so kind. He gave me extra treats and brushed my mane thoroughly.

That is good to hear. Did you see the Dragon?

I did.

Have you ever seen one before?

Dragons have not been around since the War of Three, my Kahina.

I broke my mental connection with Zari and bit my lip while I contemplated Zari's words. Senna told me that for Dragons to be raised from the dead, my blood was needed to resurrect Ragnar who would raise his dead army. My blood hadn't been used for any such ritual that I was aware of, so how did that Dragon come into existence? Surely Rehema would know. I'd ask her when we returned to camp.

Let's go, Zari. I patted her rump and hopped on her back. Avani had no horse, so it meant she was either riding with me or Calian. It seemed obvious who she'd ride with. Dhruv was a much bigger horse. As much as I loved Zari—interesting that I already felt such a strong connection with her—she was not built to carry a lot of weight. She was insanely fast. Dhruv, however, was the largest horse I'd ever seen. He was pure muscle meaning he could carry a lot. It made sense that Avani would ride with Calian.

And that didn't sit well with me.

Zari sensed my hesitation. *Is everything all right, my Kahina?*

Not exactly, I answered. I shifted my weight and watched Calian feed Dhruv the remaining apples we'd found on the trek to the river.

Is there anything I can do to help? Zari offered.

How would you feel if you took Avani to the camp? I responded sheepishly.

Zari knew. I didn't know how she knew, but she did. And I didn't know how I knew that she knew, but I did. Gods, my thoughts were giving me a headache. I rubbed my temple to ease the dizziness.

If that is what you wish, I will gladly take her, Zari replied.

Thank you, Zari. I swung my leg over and hopped off of Zari. Avani was sitting on a large rock, with both of her legs out straight in front of her. Her arms held her up with her chest elevated to the sky, and her chin tilted upward.

"You look comfortable," I mentioned and sat beside her.

"I'd sunbathe on the roof of my house. I'd sit up there all day just soaking in the warmth. It's soothing."

"I don't doubt that. Although, I'm not sure how I feel about sitting on the roof of a house," I grinned. "Look, we're about to make the ride back to camp. I'd like to offer Zari to you. She's quick and gentle."

"Ah," she said and nodded her head and chuckled softly. "So, you two do have a thing going on."

"Excuse me?"

"Don't worry. I had no plans to intervene."

"We're not…" I insisted. I did not like where this conversation was going. I began to twist my hair.

"Not yet," she interrupted.

"You can ride with him if you'd like." The words tumbled out awkwardly before I could stop them. I immediately regretted saying them.

"That's ok. I'll take Zari. She's a beautiful horse. I haven't seen one like her in a long time." She smiled and brought herself to her feet. I exhaled softly once she walked over and boosted herself up on Zari.

Calian was finished feeding Dhruv when I walked up to him. "I'm riding with you," I said and put my foot in the holster.

"Wait," he said, and I paused, stopping for him to tell me to ride Zari. She was my horse after all. "I need to get on first," he said.

"I can ride behind you."

"Absolutely not."

I hopped off Dhruv, and Calian took my place. He held out his hand for me, and I gently placed mine in it. I mounted the horse and leaned into Calian. His warmth was comforting, and I breathed in his familiar scent. The spark of energy I usually felt between us wasn't there, but I didn't care. I was right where I wanted to be.

Well, until a roar reverberated from above, causing the birds to scatter from the trees. The Dragon found us.

The air sizzled with a potent mix of anticipation and fear. The dominant creature, its scales shimmering in the afternoon sun, towered above us, casting an ominous shadow. Calian, Avani, and I braced ourselves, ready to challenge it.

"Space yourselves out!" Calian commanded. Avani and I ran in opposite directions, forming a triangle between the three of us. With magic at the ready, Calian conjured flames, Avani brought forth swirls of sand and dust, and I formed spheres of electrical energy. My fingers crackled, but I welcomed the feeling. Bring on the Dragon.

With another deafening roar, it swooped beneath the canopy of trees, crashing through branches and splitting the trunks before flying back into the sky. There was no question that this Dragon would be difficult to defeat. It soared back around and descended on Avani, spewing scorching flames toward her. Avani, with what little time she had, flung sand and dust into the Dragon's eyes. It roared again, but this time the roar was more like a shriek. The dust had hurt it.

The Dragon ascended back into the sky, shaking its head. It flew back around, looking angrier than before. Avani had done an excellent job of irritating it.

With its first target out of the way, the Dragon plummeted downward toward Calian. It lashed out toward him with its razor-sharp claws, swiping at his body. Calian dodged with ease, somersaulting out of the way and back onto his feet. Flames erupted from his outstretched hands, whipping back and forth with an intensity that matched his determination to bring down the Dragon. He hurled fireballs toward its head, but he missed.

This would be more difficult than I thought because Calian never missed.

The Dragon landed, shaking the ground. With a whip of its tail, the Dragon sent Calian careening backward until he slammed into the trunk of a tree. His head slumped forward.

"No!" I screamed.

I ran toward the Dragon and silently prayed to the Dragongod Vukan, hoping he'd grant me access to his fire magic—whatever amount he deemed worthy.

The Dragon landed, and I almost fell over. In a surge of energy, I regained my balance and thrust my hands outward. Fire exploded from the Dragon's mouth, but it was met with my own.

The Dragongod Vukan had heard my prayer.

Blazing fire blasted from my palms, meeting the Dragon's and stopping it. We stood there in a battle of determination, neither of us willing to budge. I knew I'd run out of energy before it did, so I envisioned the essence of the fire—its warmth, its intensity, and its power—like a volcano. My magic responded, and the fire from within me became tendrils of flame, extending from my core, down my arms, and out of my palms like geysers of molten heat. It forced back the Dragon's magic slowly until it lifted itself back into the air.

You're getting stronger, it said.

Strong enough to beat you, I replied. It was a lie. But I needed to appear confident.

Not yet.

"Then why don't you just kill me now!" I screamed.

Because that would be too easy. And it's not part of the plan.

As it flew back over the trees, it turned its head and our eyes met once more. *Thanks for the distraction*, it said.

CHAPTER

SIXTEEN

The Dragon's words repeated over and over in my head. *Part of the plan. Thanks for the distraction.* We would see it again. I hoped I was strong enough to defeat it once and for all.

"I'm sorry I failed you," Avani said. She'd been mostly lost in her thoughts as she rode Zari back to camp.

Calian sighed from behind me. "You can stop apologizing now. You should be proud of yourself. You are a new Dragonheir, yet you stood and fought bravely against a Dragon. If anyone should feel ashamed, it should be me."

"You were knocked out cold," I pointed out. "What were you supposed to do?"

"Protect you," he said.

"Didn't look like she needed protecting," Avani observed. I might have blushed. Just a smidge.

"No more blame. We need to focus on what lies ahead," I said.

I was more than right.

From a distance, we saw darkness hovering over the camp. My senses heightened and anxiety took over. My pulse quickened, and my breathing became ragged.

"What is that?" Calian asked. He leaned over my shoulder to see better.

Dhruv took off in a full sprint. Nearing the entrance, the thick black smoke filled the sky like ink spilling on a blank blue page causing my heart to sink into the pit of my stomach. Flames were everywhere, and there was nothing but destruction. We raced through the open gate, and I immediately coughed when the smoke filled my lungs. It also stung my eyes so much that tears seeped from them, spilling onto my cheeks. I reached for my newfound magic and envisioned a protective shield around us and thrust it out as far as I could, hoping it would provide relief for Avani and Zari. Dhruv and Zari carried us through relentless smoke and violent flames. From every direction came shouting and crying for help. Soldiers screamed in pain and horses were running wild.

For a brief moment, I let my empathic abilities take over. The mixture of emotions from everyone within the camp hit me in the gut, and I doubled over, gasping for air. Then I heard shrieks of, "Dragon! Dragon!"

"Emera?" Calian said behind me.

"I'm okay," I managed to choke out. "It's just the soldiers. They're in pain, and they're scared. I can *feel* it!"

"You need to try to focus," Calian said. His voice sounded distant. I was being pulled under a rolling wave of suffering.

I gasped for air, "Easier said than done." I groaned from the pain I felt from the soldiers. It weighed down my bones like a large boulder of dense obsidian rock. I started to slip from consciousness. My head rolled back.

"No, you don't," he warned. He pressed into me, and I could feel the heat from his chest pouring into my back and throughout my body, filling my soul. The warmth was comforting, a relief I desperately needed, and it brought me back to the present.

Then we heard the roar again. It was my least favorite sound now. It boomed overhead, and cries of pure terror erupted throughout the camp. Soldiers ran in every direction, doing their best to navigate through fire and debris.

"The Dragon from Dhara," Calian guessed. I had to agree with him. It was the only thing that made sense.

"I need to help them. I need you to stop."

"Not a chance."

"Please, Calian. I can do this," I pleaded. I hated to beg, but I needed him to listen because the soldiers needed me. I twisted in the saddle to see him. Another punch to my gut came when I saw the emotion in his eyes: fear. Pure, unadulterated fear. I reached up and touched his cheek. He tore his gaze from the camp and finally looked at me. "I can do this," I repeated firmly. Without a word, Dhruv stopped.

"This is no time to be foolish, Emera," he barked. I ignored his tone. He was furious, and above all else, he was scared.

"Calian Westbow, you don't have to protect me all the time. Leave me here, and I'll try to take care of the flames. If you see Morwen, tell her to find me. I might need her assistance. Please."

He blinked slowly, giving in. "I need to find Fin," he said.

"Go. I'll be alright." Our eyes met. He brought his hand to my cheek and nodded. I leaned into his palm, savoring the unspoken bond between us.

"What about me?" Avani asked, breaking our moment.

"Follow Calian. Get to safety."

"I'm not going to hide. I can fight," she insisted.

Calian didn't wait for me to respond. He leveled with Avani. "Right now, there's too much smoke and her shield that she has around you…" he jerked his head in my direction, "…is failing. You need to get to higher ground which can be done further into camp. We're headed up the path. Zari will stay close to Dhruv." Dhruv took off running. Before Avani could protest—because I could tell she was determined to stay—Zari ran after Dhruv.

With both of them gone, I focused my shield on me. I wasn't sure what to do. Should I call another storm? Should I try to lift the darkness? Should I attend to the injured first? Regardless of the confidence I had been gaining, I felt a wave of anxiety rush through me. In all honesty, conjuring up a thunderstorm to distract the Dragon in Dhara was nothing compared to this. Most of the destruction had been focused on the market, and the citizens of Dhara had mostly vacated. I didn't care if the guards and cultists died. If that made me a bad person, then I didn't care about that either. This was different. If I didn't do something here, all of these soldiers—and possibly my friends—would die.

Get it together, Emera. One problem at a time. The flames need to be extinguished.

I took a deep breath, clapped my hands together, and tried to shake the anxiety out of my body. Trying to force water from my hands was not going to do much, so my only other option was just rain. I needed to focus my magic on water alone and not the thunder and lightning that usually came with it. I dropped my hands to my side and faced my palms outward. Drawing in as much of my magic as I could without losing my protective shield, I gathered all of my elemental magic and raised my hands to the sky, gathered the energy there, and called for a torrential downpour.

But before I could bring down the rain, everything around me went still. Only a cool breeze remained, causing the flames to whip their fiery tales back and forth, forming a circle around me. I was at its center. I spun myself around and forward again, straining to hear anything, but only the crackling of the fire spoke to me. I could no longer hear the voices of soldiers or the collapsing of tents. I looked around and saw a slender figure in all black walking through the flames toward me. The figure had to be a Dragonborn. Only a magical barrier could prevent one's skin from burning to a crisp when walking through the flames as the figure did. It sauntered through slowly and stepped over a log—no, that was a body. It was now in the ring of fire with me, but it was no longer a shadow in the flames but a woman with tanned skin and raven black hair thrashing around her. Her dark purple eyes that were once hazel twinkled and when our eyes met, her lips curved into the graceful smile I had never forgotten. I stared in shock.

"Dwyn?" I called out. My heart leaped with joy. I didn't know how she found me, but she had. I couldn't believe it.

"Did you miss me?" Dwyn asked innocently. My longest friend's graceful smile widened into a wicked, wolf-like grin.

Something was wrong.

"Wh-wh-what are you doing here, Dwyn?" I stammered. She threw back her head and cackled. It was crude and soulless.

"That's not my name, Emera. My name is Valda, daughter of the Dragongod Amram."

I couldn't say anything. I just stood there, speechless.

"Good gods, Emera!" She shouted to the sky. "You're not the only daughter of a Chaos Dragon." Her words almost knocked me over, but I planted my feet and stood my ground. Senna was right.

"Day in and day out I had to listen to you go on and on about Dragonborn this and human that. What I find immensely satisfying is that you hated us Dragonborns so much, and yet here you are…a Dragonborn!" She laughed again. "But not just a Dragonborn though," she continued, "You're the daughter of a traitor." Her eyes flashed with contempt; a fiery wrath simmered behind them.

"You were my best friend," I seethed.

"Anyone can pretend, Emera," she snapped. "You should be used to that. The priest—who didn't have a clue who I was, by the way—pretended to know what he was doing. He was a blubbering idiot." Her smirk sickened me. She enjoyed every part of this.

"And your parents." She groaned in disgust. "Gods, I hated them. They were so *perfect*, and everything they lived for was all about you. Emera the intelligent blah, blah, blah. Emera the brave blah, blah, blah. Emera the strong blah, blah, blah. Spare me! You were none of those things. You just put on a facade for everyone to think you were. But you and I," she pointed at me, then to her, and finally to the temple of her head, "You and I know differently. You're nothing like that. You're ignorant, you're scared, and you're weak." She started to walk around the circle, but I stayed in place at its center.

I could feel a blazing heat within my core demanding release. "I'm so sorry for the inconvenience of my parents' love for me," I bit out.

"Apology accepted," she taunted. "Isn't it refreshing having an honest conversation for once? I'm sure you don't get a lot of those hanging around *Captain Westbow*."

I just stared at her, my hands sweating from the heat radiating beneath my skin. Sparks of resentment tingled beneath my skin with unrestrained ferocity. I had nothing to say. And if I did, I probably couldn't get it out. My throat burned as it continued to push lump after lump down. I willed the flames to fizzle out and called to my water magic once more. Valda noticed my internal struggle and smirked.

I need to keep her talking, get my water magic back, and soak the camp.

"Ah, Captain Calian Westbow. Now there's a specimen not too many girls get to see every day. Lucky you, right?" She was mocking me.

I refused to back down. "Just get on with it, Valda!"

"All right, all right," she said and chuckled. "Patience is a virtue—or so they say."

I looked her straight in the eyes to where I could see her soul. I thrust my arms above my head, filled my body with all the magic I could muster and called for the rain once more. I gave Valda a ruthless smile, and I brought my arms down. The clouds split and rain poured to the ground, washing away all the flames. Once the flames were out, a wind that was silent and cold blew throughout the camp. I stood, my hair drenched and rain dripping from my nose, but I didn't care. The rain ceased, and I clenched my teeth together. I begged my soul for my magic once more. In the blink of an eye, darkness fell upon the camp.

"I like this new Emera. Less talk, more action. You're much easier to talk to this way. Is Calian easy to talk to? Do you even do any talking?" She howled at her own joke, and I winced. "Naw. You're not like that are you, Emera? You're so good and true. I bet talking is the only thing you do. That man does have an opinion about everything. Unless it's about himself. Then he's all..." and she pursed her lips together. She brought her fingers to her lips and mimicked locking them. "Do you want to know his secret?"

It took everything to say anything to her. "I'm sure whatever it is, you'll rub it in my face." Did she see that I was doing my best to hold in the pain? I couldn't keep it in much longer. Walls attempted to form a barrier around my breaking heart, but they were cracked.

"Captain Westbow is..."

A horse neighed, and we both turned. Dhruv came to a halt between us. "I'm what?" Calian snarled. Fin rode behind him on Zari, and he immediately slid off, his bow and arrow at the ready. He aimed the arrow directly at Valda. The lump in my throat was back. I was thankful to see Calian. I was also relieved to see that Fin was okay.

"Fintan, how's the Dragonmate? I heard she put up quite the fight. Feisty thing, that one." She winked at Fin whose shoulders went rigid.

"Give it up. You're cornered." If Calian hadn't spoken, Fin would have shot her. I was sure of it.

"Hmm," she contemplated and turned to me. "It seems that way, doesn't it? But do you really think you three can match me?" She raised one arm toward Fin who raised in the air, level with her arm. "A magic-less human?" She waved her arm, and Fin's body was thrown into a pile of smoking logs. Valda raised her arm again. "A hot-headed Dragonheir?" In the same motion, she magically threw Calian off of Dhruv into a horse trough. She then turned her evil glare at me. "And a Dragongoddess *without* chaos magic?" I held my breath, waiting to be flung across the space. But I stayed where I was. "Unlikely," she said savagely.

She looked me dead in the eyes, but I didn't waver. I wouldn't give her the satisfaction of being the coward she accused me of being. "Look, Em, it's been great catching up with you. Just like old times, am I right?" She winked.

A noise came from our right, and we both turned to see Calian limping back toward us. "Oh, Captain. Ever the brooding hero," she crooned. She sauntered up to him, leaned in, and placed her cheek next to his. She whispered something I couldn't hear. Calian did not move, nor did his expression change. She backed away from him, lifted her arms, and circled them in front of her, gathering her chaos magic. Purple smoke began to form around her like a swirling tornado. It grew taller and taller until a dark tail that was the deepest purple I'd ever seen—almost black depending on how one looked at it—swung out and slammed into my stomach. I cried in pain, and my breath was knocked out of my chest. I felt the instant shattering of rib bones where the Dragon's—no, Valda's—tail hit me. I hurled back into the air and landed on my back in a deep mud puddle. I looked down at my chest to see my clothes torn and large gashes across my stomach. Tears ran down my face as Valda, now in Dragon form, loomed overhead.

This is what true Dragonpower looks like, Emera. Consider this a final warning. Get in my way, and I'll end you. She lifted into the air and hovered for a moment. I tried to get up, but she flapped her magnificent wings with such force that I fell back over. The crunch of my ribs was sickening when I connected with the ground a second time—only this time my stomach hit first. I just laid there, and the dam keeping my tears from spilling finally broke. I began sobbing uncontrollably. Despite the pain from my injured body—my rib cage felt like I'd been stabbed multiple times—the shattering of my heart was worse. Broken shards filled my chest, puncturing holes into my soul.

The Dwyn I knew was a lie. She was Valda, and she hated me. For years she was my closest friend. I confided in her, cried to her, laughed with her. And it was all a lie! I pounded my fists into the dirt like a child and screamed.

Calian was at my side, and he placed his hand on my back. "Are you okay?" he asked.

"No!" I yelled into the ground. "I. Am. Not. Okay!" On the last word, the camp plunged into complete darkness.

"She's definitely not okay," Fin said. I turned my head just in time to hear him stumble over a log.

"Shut it, Fin!" Calian growled.

"Sorry. It's just how I deal with it," Fin mumbled.

"She was my friend," I said between my gasps for air. "She was my closest friend. She meant everything to me."

"I know," Calian whispered. "Come on, let's get you out of the mud."

"I can't move," I moaned. "My ribs are broken."

"You can move. And I'm sure you don't want to hear this, but your ribs will heal. It will take some rest, but they will."

I lowered my voice. "I don't know if I want them to." I knew it sounded absurd, but if it weren't for my broken ribs, I would be numb inside, void of any emotion and feeling.

"Yes, you do," Calian insisted, his voice soft, and I wished I could see his face. But even though I couldn't see him, I could feel him. I gingerly braced my palms on the ground and pushed up from the ground. Pain seared my body, moving from my chest all around my midsection. I clenched my jaw and forced myself to a sitting position. Calian leaned over, took my arms, and pulled me up. I smothered my face into his neck and cried. I felt his hand cradling the back of my head which was still soaked from the mud and muck.

"It's so dark. Everything outside and inside is so dark." Tears continued to fall.

"I know," he whispered.

"You need to tell her," Fin said. Calian didn't respond. "Cal, you *need* to tell her," Fin repeated firmly. I broke away from Calian's neck.

"Tell me what?"

"Morwen's gone," he answered softly.

"*Taken*," Fin added angrily.

"And…" Calian's voice trailed off.

"And?" I whispered.

"And Rehema is dead."

CHAPTER SEVENTEEN

I laid on a cot in the spot that was once the magnificent sanctuary of worship. It was now in tatters on the ground. The statue of Nimerah in her Dragon form was charred, and there were no banners to be found. The strong stench of smoke still penetrated the camp no matter how well the rain had washed out the fire. I stood and placed my feet on the cold, ashen ground and looked out to the rest of the camp, but I couldn't see much save for whatever was positioned near a torch. Several were placed throughout the camp to provide lights along the intertwining paths. I glanced down when I stepped on something soft. Fresh clothes lay on the ground. I picked them up and turned them over. They were clean and almost an exact replica of what I had been wearing, including tight pants, a hooded tunic with long arms and a corset. But instead of black, they were deep purple. The leather corset was fashioned to look like scales. How fitting.

I discarded my previous attire and surveyed the camp more closely. Valda had truly done what she sought to do. She destroyed the camp and my spirit. I cautiously walked to the statue of Nimerah and picked it up from the rest of the damage. I slowly turned it over and over in my hands. The gut-wrenching scene from the ruin before me was enough to tear me open and rip my heart out. I felt cold and empty.

"How are you feeling?" Calian asked gently behind me. He held a torch that illuminated his ruggedly handsome features. He looked tired but clean. His previous clothes were replaced by fresh black trousers and a black tunic—opposite of his usual white.

"Broken," was all I managed to respond with. I turned and faced him. He opened his mouth to say more, but I held up my hand. "Where is she?"

It was Fin who answered, coming up behind the path. I didn't see him until he finally stood next to Calian. "Under the willow tree beside the pond to the east. She and Morwen would walk there and pray sometimes. She found the spot to be peaceful—or so Morwen told me."

He stood frozen in place clad in black leather, daggers, and his bow and quiver.

"She can't be moved?"

"There's no chance we could transport her body safely to the City of Nimerah," he replied sullenly. I sighed more heavily this time. Rehema would have wanted to be buried in the City of Nimerah within the Tomb of the Dragonelders—the highest honor amongst priests and priestesses. Because of me, it wasn't possible. I should have been here.

The only sliver of peace that I had with her death was knowing that she had passed through the Dragonsoul Plane of Existence and was now among the dead in the afterlife. She had made it to DragonEmpyrean.

"And Morwen? Any idea where she's been taken?"

With his head still hanging, Calian answered, "We originally thought your friend was working for the cultists. But the more we think of past events, we don't think that's true. And before you even think about it, no. I do not know Valda. I've never met her."

I faced Calian head-on. "She knew your name," I pointed out. He flinched. "What did she whisper to you?" I demanded.

Calian took a step back. "Are you accusing me of something?"

"What did she whisper to you," I repeated.

Calian stepped closer and leaned in. "That we couldn't beat her," he growled.

It didn't make sense. She could have said that out loud. Why did she feel the need to whisper in Calian's ear?

Fin intervened with his voice of reason. "More than likely, she's been following you ever since you left Medora. She could have infiltrated the camp and picked up information on all of us." Fin had a point, and I hated it. I wanted to kick and scream like a child. I wanted to throw myself on the ground and cry because the sickening truth was that everything was my fault.

Everyone remained silent until Avani walked into the light with a soldier beside her. They both looked disheveled and tired, which was just another thing to add to my list of annoyances. I was the exact opposite of them. My Dragonmother must have healed my wounds while I'd slept because I awoke to clean my clothes, hair, and skin. I wasn't even hungry or thirsty.

"All of the seriously wounded have been treated, Captain," the soldier told Calian.

Avani spoke up. "Most will make a full recovery, but there are some that even I cannot fully heal with my medicinal herbs. They will need stronger Dragonmagic." I could feel her gaze shift to me: the strongest, most powerful Dragonheir among them. I could tell what she was thinking. Surely, I would be the one to heal them. How could I? I glanced back down at the statue that I had forgotten was still in my hands.

Realizing I wasn't going to say anything, Avani spoke directly to Calian. "What's wrong?"

Fin snapped, "What's *wrong* is that someone very close to her turned out to be…"

"An enemy," I finished for him, my voice barely a whisper. I tore my eyes away from my mother's statue and looked at the people around me. I took a deep breath, let it swirl in my lungs, and released it. "And that enemy has killed someone that I loved and respected." I continued my walk through the wreckage of the sanctuary.

"I'm sorry," Avani directed to me. I ignored her.

The soldier with Avani cleared his throat. "There's more, sir," he stammered.

"What is it?" Calian sighed.

"This is Jimmu," Avani interrupted. "He was a member of a traveling party on their way back from the City of Nimerah with supplies. They were ambushed on their way back. He claims a large Dragon stopped them."

"Sir, there were cultists with the Dragon. They had Dragonheir Erjon and Dragonheir...er...Princess Morwen with them. I managed to get away so that I could tell you." Jimmu puffed out his chest proudly.

I really needed some space to process everything, so I passed right through our small crowd and began my descent into the main part of camp. Tears stung my eyes while I witnessed the burned and injured soldiers trying to piece their lives back together. More torches were placed strategically to get what little supplies were left onto two wagons.

A woman drew my attention. She coughed violently on her cot and her body convulsed in response. With my hand, I managed to call forth a flame. My torch in a sea of darkness. I knelt by her side and with my free hand, I gently caressed her palm, a comforting action my mother used to do to me when I felt ill. Her eyelids fluttered then opened, revealing a beautiful blue, the color of the clearest ocean. I recognized her then. She was the same woman who comforted me after the storm I'd created.

"Daughter of Nimerah," she gasped and grabbed my hand. I squeezed her hand to comfort her.

"Shh. You need rest," I said gently. She nodded and closed her eyes once more, but she wasn't at peace. Her body still shook from her injuries. I released her hand and looked past her at the rows of cots with soldiers lying in agony. I had to do something, but so far all I seemed to be able to do was create thunderstorms. Still, I couldn't leave until I'd attempted to right the wrong that I had brought upon them.

"You did not deserve this. You were here to protect me. And what did I do? I brought destruction. I brought pain. I brought darkness." I sobbed, and I stood. With a wave of my hand, my torch vanished. A few hiccups escaped my lips as I brought my hands to my chest and clasped them together in a silent prayer to all the gods and goddesses.

"Please," I whispered. "I will give all of my magic for them to live."

A surge of magic swelled within me, so I grabbed hold and gathered it into my hands. My entangled fingers began to glow brighter and brighter like a star in the dead of night. I opened my fists and twisted them, my palms now facing out. With a focused mind, I guided the light in front of me and pushed it to all of the injured soldiers, manifesting any healing magic that I possessed. I swept my arms horizontally in front of my body, attempting to blanket the soldiers with my light magic so that I could bring them restoration and rejuvenation. I continued to do so until all the magic had weaved its way to each of the injured, washing away pain and all afflictions. The coughing and cries of pain had ceased.

The only heavy breathing I could hear at that moment was my own. I felt sluggish and dizzy. The world began spinning until muscular arms swooped me up and held me close. The sight of Calian broke me, and I flung my arms around his neck. He carried me as I cried, fully mourning the loss of my home, my greatest friend, the camp, Rehema, and ultimately, my innocence.

"Please take me to her," I begged. Without a word, he carried me to Rehema's resting place. The soldiers had lined the path with small torches, guiding anyone who needed solace to her. The mound of fresh dirt protruding from the ground and an array of candles marked the exact spot where her body was buried.

Calian sat me down next to the tree. "Soldiers were able to save some candles from the sanctuary. They thought it would be a nice tribute to her."

"No one will know she's here," I whimpered.

"We'll know," he said, taking my face in his hands. "And that's enough. She believed in you Emera. From the moment she received word that your powers had activated, and I was to retrieve you, she believed in you. She understood the dangers of it all. She was prepared for an honorable death. And that is exactly what she got."

I contemplated asking Calian if he knew how she'd died, but it was none of my business. It was Rehema's, and hers alone. I took Calian's hand because I needed to feel comforted. We walked to the edge of the pond. I sat down, but Calian stood behind me. He said nothing, so comforting me must be out of the question. His lack of empathy seemed out of place. Sure, he was a bit gruff, but he'd softened so much since we'd met.

He looked back and forth, surveying the area to make sure no other cultists were lurking about. I focused my attention on the still water. We said nothing for a few minutes.

"When do we move out?"

"Tomorrow. Final preparations are being made. Soldiers will carry what they can, and we'll load up as much as we can on the two remaining wagons. It's not much, but hopefully, it will be enough."

"Where are we going?"

"The City of Nimerah to the Dragoncouncil. It's time you meet Anwir."

"I haven't completed my Trials though." I hung my head in defeat and closed my heavy eyes. Some prophesied Dragonheir I turned out to be.

"Not all, but most. This may not help, but you've been blessed by Endrit. Your eyes, they're pure white, which is frightening if I'm being honest. Your hands now have white scales, too. Blue, silver, green, red, and now white."

"That's not enough," I said, shaking my head.

"You are enough," he whispered. And with that, I rested my head on his shoulder and drifted to sleep.

*　　*　　*

I awoke with a groan. The pain from my ribs was almost non-existent, but the ache in my heart was still there. I had no intention of getting up. I would rather just lie on my cot and sleep away the pain. All I felt like doing was sleeping.

"Emera." I sat up instantly, ignoring the slight protest from my ribs. I looked toward the sound of my mother's caressing voice. I found her sitting across from me in the tent. She was on Calian's side; the barrier he'd put up days ago was gone.

"How?" I managed to squeak.

She raised her hand. "I am not who you think I am," she responded. She stood and walked to my cot. She angled her neck, tilted her head down, and swept her eyes over my face, studying it. It was like she'd never seen me before.

"Mother," I drew out, "What are you doing?" She angled her neck to the other side and continued her evaluation of my face. I didn't make a sound because deep down I had no inclination to embrace this woman. There was no warmth in her eyes. She didn't radiate love and understanding. She looked everything like my mother, but the woman before me was not her.

"It is time." She abruptly turned her back to me and walked toward the opening of the tent. Where was Calian? Did he know a stranger with my mother's face was in my tent?

"To do what?" I asked.

"What you were born to do," the woman said over her shoulder. This was ridiculous. My patience was wearing thin.

"If you don't tell me who you are, I'll raise hell in this tent. I'm tired of the cryptic statements. Who are you?" My words hit their target because she whirled on me, her eyes now glowing a vibrant violet. This was my mother, but not the one that raised me.

"You are my daughter. I am your mother. That is enough." Was she serious? She began walking out of the tent, so apparently, she was serious.

"You're going to have to give me a little more than that," I argued, rising to my feet and following her out. I stopped in my tracks once I stepped outside of the tent. I expected to see the camp in ruins. I expected to see tents destroyed, grass burned, and injured soldiers lying on cots and blankets. But the picturesque world before me was nothing like the image I had formed in my mind. This world was devastatingly beautiful. The grass was a vivid green with flowers from all the kingdoms in full bloom. A slight breeze played with my hair and sang lullabies in hushed tones. In the distance was a mountain range with white-capped snow tops. The sky above was painted as if the dawn and sunset were one, like the painter used only the finest blue, orange, gold, and pink paints. The sky transitioned into the night where stars twinkled overhead in various constellations. The view was breathtaking.

We were definitely not in the camp.

"This is where you've been all this time." It was a statement, not a question. Still, she answered as if I'd asked.

"This is where my spirit is, but my body is elsewhere," Nimerah answered. At least she was being less cryptic this time. "This is the Dragonsoul Plane of Existence. You would not be here if you were not a Dragonborn."

"I'm dead?" I asked, horrified.

"No. I pulled your spirit here so that I can tell you that it's time." She stopped and stared at the moon—one of the moons as there were two in the sky—and a smile spread over her lips. It was the first time I'd seen any hint of compassion. I stood beside her and looked at the moon, too.

"Is Rehema here?"

"She has already passed through. She is now forever at peace wandering the hills of DragonEmpyrean." She paused. After a moment of silence, she added, "She doesn't blame you."

"I don't know what you mean," I lied.

"Daughter, lying to yourself is never the answer."

"It's all my fault. I don't know what I'm supposed to do, who I'm supposed to trust…" She held her hand up again, and I stopped speaking. She then waved her hand over her face, and she transformed. No longer was a copy of my mother standing beside me, but a beautiful woman with long, wavy red hair. It was like looking into a mirror of the future. The only difference was that her eyes were still the same startling violet she'd had earlier. "I take it this is your true form."

"When I'm not in my natural Dragon form, yes."

"I see where my hair comes from," I said. She stood silent. "Why did you choose my mother's form?"

"I figured it would be the most comforting. I didn't want you to be frightened when you woke up."

"Can you help me?" I whispered in desperation. I couldn't tell if she was thinking about what she would say next, or if she was just ignoring me. "Nimerah…*Mother*…please," I pleaded. "I have so many questions." That got her attention. She looked into my face, and in a brief moment of clarity, I knew her. I knew her voice, her face, her soul. It was a satisfying sensation. Like the feeling one gets when they figure out the answer to a complex riddle. "I do know you," I said with awe and admiration.

She smiled a true, deep smile that reached the corners of her eyes. "I've been with you this whole time, my daughter. I watched your first steps, I heard your first words, and I felt your first spark of Dragonmagic. I have guided you as you navigated this world. You are my daughter, Nykemera.”

“Nykemera?”

“Your given name. A little too conspicuous for a human name, so your parents shortened it to Emera.” She lifted her palm and rested it against my cheek. “It suits you.”

After a brief moment, she spoke again. “They did an incredible job in raising you. I chose wisely, it seems.” She truly admired my parents. I felt it.

Tears already filled my eyes. “I miss them. So much.”

“Of course, you do,” she said gently and wiped away a tear that had fallen down my cheek.

I placed my hand on top of hers and held it there. I closed my eyes and drank in the love and compassion I could feel from her. Although the hurt that I felt from the absence of my parents still remained—I imagined it would never go away—the tears began to dry.

“Please help me,” I pleaded again.

She dropped her hand and motioned for me to walk with her. “Come,” she said. We walked down the path that led to what looked like a glistening lake. Standing next to a fallen tree by the riverbank was another woman with stark white skin, dark black hair, and onyx eyes that somehow twinkled like stars in the night.

The woman turned to face us as we approached. She took my hands in hers and they were surprisingly warm.

"Emera, I am Tamasvi," she said. Her voice was soft and gentle.

"The Dragongoddess of Darkness," I murmured.

"Yes. My dear, I can feel your coldness. Your numbness. Your emptiness. You have spiraled into your own darkness, but do not let it be your enemy. It is your refuge. Let the darkness heal you. Let it be your safety, your security. Through your darkness, your Dragonsoul will be revived." Tamasvi motioned for me to sit on the large fallen trunk as she did.

"I've just always thought that one's darkness was a frightening place filled with their inner monsters," I admitted.

Tamasvi shook her head and laughed. "Goodness, no. It is where we find solitude. We learn from it. In your darkness, you will truly learn who you are."

At that moment, my Dragonmother sat on the other side of me. I instinctively rested my head on her shoulder. She made no indication that the gesture was unwanted.

It was an uncanny feeling knowing my life had changed so much in such a short period of time. I had gone from sitting in an apothecary to sitting between two goddesses.

"Learn who I truly am," I whispered, and both she and Tamasvi nodded.

In the distance, we heard the rustling of leaves, yet there was no breeze. Nimerah angled her head slightly, trying to determine the origin of the sound and Tamasvi stood. Nimerah shook her head as if trying to remember what she was saying. "You are on the correct path, my dear. It may seem harsh and violent, but you are exactly where you need to be. But be careful, for you will encounter many false people."

"False people? Valda? Or someone else?" I asked hastily.

A flock of birds retreated from their trees in a panic. Just then a dark shadow appeared on the other side of the lake beneath the trees. Nimerah's eyes glowed the most vibrant purple I'd ever seen, and she stood quickly next to Tamasvi who was now looking left then right.

"We are not alone," Tamasvi whispered in alarm. "I will see to the noise at once." She stood before me. "You are worthy," she told me. "Believe it." And with that, she placed both of her hands over her heart and nodded. Then she turned and vanished.

I looked at my Dragonmother. "I thought this was a safe place."

"Under normal circumstances, it is. But something is wrong. I must send you back."

"I don't want to go. I want to know you," I cried. "I need you!" Tears pooled in my eyes then poured over my cheeks. "You're dead," I blurted. "Please tell me you'll bring me back here. I've only just met you."

She shook her head and winked at me. "I am not dead. I have been asleep for many, many years. I am waiting for you, and you *will* find me."

"Where?" I asked.

She took my hands and brought me into a lasting embrace. The Dragongoddess of Chaos that essentially built the world—and who was my mother—was hugging me.

"Go home, Emera," Nimerah said hastily. She lifted two of her fingers and pressed them to my forehead. "Go *home*, my daughter of Chaos."

*　　*　　*

The sun greeted the camp with its golden rays piercing through the canopy of trees and was a welcome sight to the soldiers who had been longing to be freed from the darkness. It poked its head above the tree line, creating a burst of activity. The horses—well, what remained of them—were ready. The wagons were packed, and some soldiers paced in anticipation while others rested for the journey ahead. Calian and Fin had decided—while I was vising with the goddesses, so I had no input—that the whole camp would split into two parties and depart at different times. Calian and Avani would ride out first with Avani disguised as me. If any cultists or Valda were to intercept, they'd attack the first group. If that happened, the second group, including Fin and me, would take a different route to the city. I hated the plan. I hated Calian for leaving me. I hated that Fin was essentially babysitting me. I hated that Avani was going to be my decoy. I hated that Rehema wasn't coming with us. I hated it all.

Avani approached carrying two large, mostly likely heavy, crates while I strapped my bow on Zari's back. "First of all, your eyes are black. Did you know that, yet? They're really terrifying, honestly. You look like a demon."

Tamasvi had blessed me after our encounter. I soundlessly thanked the goddess and looked at my hands, discovering that black scales had joined the others. I had them all. All six Elemental Dragongods and Dragongoddesses had blessed me. But my Dragonmother had not. It seemed my triumph was short-lived. A heavy ache gnawed on my insides. Tamasvi believed in me. Why didn't Nimerah?

"Second of all," Avani continued, "are you sure you're okay riding in the back with Fin instead of with Calian? Because that was not my idea. In fact, I was against it. Calian should be back there with you."

"Avani, the answer is still yes," I assured her. I was the most powerful of us three, so it made sense for me to ride alongside Fin who was not a Dragonborn. I wanted to ensure the saddle wouldn't slip when I mounted Zari, so I gave one last tug to make sure the cinch was tight.

Does that hurt? I asked Zari.

No, my Kahina. It's just fine, she replied.

I looked at Avani. "What I'm not okay with is you being my decoy. That is going too far. I don't think you should put yourself in that kind of risk," I said.

"Don't worry about me, Emera. I'm stronger than I look," she replied.

"Of that, I have no doubt." I paused. "Why are you doing it? You had every right to tell Calian no. I personally think he needs to hear that word more often."

"My parents believed in the prophecy. They believed in a better future. My parents may not have been the socialites of Dhara, but they were kind to everyone—and I mean everyone—they met. That is a world they believed in. It is a world I will fight for. If that means protecting you at all costs to get it, then that's what I will do." All I could do was nod, and Avani nodded in return. She then left to make sure her wagon was ready.

Zari, I have something I need to take care of. I'll be back soon.

Take your time. I will not leave without you.

I smiled and hugged her neck. I found Calian and Fin getting the small group of scouts ready to ride ahead of us, so I took advantage of it and quietly slipped away to Rehema's grave with the statue of my Dragonmother in my hands. I stopped at the pond first and did my best to clean the statue. Spots were still tarnished, but it was better than when I'd found it in the wreckage. I dropped to my knees and placed it at the end of the dirt pile as a headstone.

"I know it's not much, but I thought you'd like to have it." The tears were coming, but I pushed them back. "I'm so sorry, Rehema. I'm sorry for all of this. Had I known about Valda, I would never have left you. Because I could have protected you. You would know what I'm talking about had you seen me in Dhara. Rehema, I did it. I was able to control my power." I had fooled myself into thinking I could keep the tears at bay. The newly formed lumps in my throat burned like hell.

A hand rested gently on my shoulder and gave it a light squeeze. The scent of an autumn campfire filled my nostrils and stirred within my lungs. I faced Calian with tears streaming down my face. He raised a hand and wiped the tears gently with his thumb. With his other hand, he tucked fallen strands of my hair behind my ear. I craved the familiar shock of electricity I'd grown accustomed to feeling when we were close. His hands moved around my waist, drawing me into his warmth.

I wrapped my arms around Calian's neck and pulled him in closer. With a sense of urgency and an insatiable hunger, I pressed my lips against his. At first, he flinched in surprise, but then his shoulders sagged slightly, and his shock dissipated. His hands hastened and found their way to my hair, twisting and turning the strands at the base of my neck. He deepened our kiss, parting my mouth and claiming me.

After a few seconds, he pulled back, his chest rising and falling slowly. A devilish smirk parted his lips. I smiled, but it didn't reach my eyes because as tender as the moment was…

There was no spark.

The electric energy I'd felt before hadn't been there. Something was lacking between us. Had the Dragon taken more of him than we'd both thought?

I nodded, and we walked hand-in-hand back into the camp. All I could do was watch as he mounted Dhruv, gave Fin a final nod, and rode off into the morning sun.

CHAPTER

EIGHTEEN

The mid-day sky was calm but dreary. A heavy blanket of gray clouds stretched across the sky, casting a somber atmosphere on the second group of soldiers. Shortly after Calian left with the first group, the sun bid farewell and disappeared behind ominous clouds. Everything seemed dull and lifeless. The moisture from the air seeped within my bones, creating an oppressive weight inside my limbs. I sat on a log eating stew by a campfire Jimmu the soldier had crafted. Jimmu looked pleased that he'd started it with little effort, but he was a Dragonborn of Vukan, so it wasn't that impressive. I kept my face neutral while he puffed out his chest, but I failed to keep my eyes from rolling. Fin threw his head back and howled with laughter.

"You weren't supposed to see that," I grinned.

"You might want to try to be more inconspicuous next time," he suggested and chuckled.

Gods, I missed his laugh. I missed laughter in general. "You seem to be in good spirits," I pointed out.

"I choose not to wallow in self-pity." He took a bite and with a mouthful of leftover deer and cabbage stew, he pointed his spoon at me. "You should try it sometime."

I threw my hand to my heart like an arrow had been shot there. "Ouch!" I cried. I took a breath and threw him a faint smile. "Doesn't seem like there's much to smile about is all."

"Maybe to you."

"Well, considering we're abruptly leaving a camp that was decimated by a Dragon that turned out to be a woman who was once my best friend but is actually my sworn enemy," I paused and leaned toward him, "I feel that my distress is warranted."

Fin looked up from his stew. "Did you practice that?" he asked. "You practiced that, didn't you?"

I ignored the smug look on his face. "Let's also not forget that she killed our friend and aided in the kidnapping of Erjon and Morwen who is your mate, which I didn't even think was real, by the way."

"It's real, and I haven't forgotten," Fin remarked between bites.

"Good," I said.

Fin positioned himself so that he was facing me. "We need to stay calm so that we can thoroughly assess the situation and plan our next move. If we give into our fears, we are destined to make mistakes. Mistakes get people hurt." He repositioned himself and continued eating.

I looked down at my stew. Lately, it seemed I was never hungry. I leaned down and sat the bowl on the ground. I'd deal with it later. "You're right. I just…Are you okay?" I asked, looking back at him. It seemed like a stupid question, but I went with it.

"I'm okay. I'll be better once Morwen is back. When she's safe."

"I have a good feeling that Morwen can take care of herself."

"Your feeling would be correct," he said.

"I still can't believe you're *together*," I admitted. "No offense."

"None taken. We don't look like a pair, that's for sure," he mused. "She's unbelievably stunning, and I'm not. But looks don't matter. She's my Dragonmate for life. Seems unfortunate for her considering I'm just a human with a regular human lifespan. I guess the Dragongods have a sense of humor after all. Very fitting for a jokester like me." His tone was void of any humor. Fin had thought about this. Dragonborns lived longer than humans, so Fin would die well before Morwen. I wondered if there was anything I could do. Or that my Dragonmother could do.

"How did you know?" I asked, trying to shift the conversation.

"That we were Dragonmates? When these showed up." He opened his shirt, and tattooed on top of his heart was a tiny set of beautiful blue wings. "Once these showed up, I did some research. Once the mating bond has been connected, a pair of wings in the color of the dominant element appears—in our case, blue for water. Each set of wings is different for every pair of Dragonmates. If one of the Dragonmates dies, the wings disappear. Mine are still here, so Morwen is still alive."

"They're beautiful."

"I'm lucky. It's rare for a human to be mated to a Dragonborn."

"I'm assuming that the bond presents itself rather quickly after you've found your mate," I said softly. I was more so talking to myself than Fin, but he still replied.

"Not necessarily, Emera." I looked at him, and I rolled my eyes at the lopsided grin on his face. I couldn't hide anything from Fin. He patted my leg and stood. "Come on. It's time," he said.

I stood and crossed to Zari. I lifted myself and gazed out into the sky beyond us. It was foolish to try to see Calian and the first group, but I looked anyway. There wasn't a trace of them on the horizon.

"Time to head out!" Fin yelled. He mounted his horse and trotted up beside Zari and me. I took one last look back at what was left of our camp. With a deep breath, I urged Zari forward, and we began our journey to the Eternal City, the City of Nimerah.

*　　*　　*

I was told the journey would take several days and nights for the soldiers to march. It turned out that the City of Nimerah was slightly farther south than the City of Dhara which meant we'd be venturing further into the Arden Forest. Our path took us next to the river Calian and I had crossed over, but this time, we would follow the river as it flowed south.

It was our sixth night in the forest. So far, the journey had been uneventful, and there had yet to be any word from the first group, so we took it as a good sign that they were doing fine. I rolled out my blanket under a tall oak tree while Zari grazed on the grass next to the river. I tried to focus on what lay ahead of us in the City of Nimerah, but all my mind kept going back to was the kiss. I touched my lips and recalled the memory. Calian's mouth on mine, his hands in my hair, and…the lack of a connection. The lack of heat. The lack of that electric feeling I'd been hoping for. What did that say?

I looked to my left, then my right. Once it was clear that no one was around, I pulled back the collar of my shirt and peered down at the skin above my heart. There was nothing different about it; it was still a blank canvas ready for its masterpiece. I envisioned elaborate wings of purple because a Chaos Dragonheir would surely be dominant over an elemental. I lightly traced an outline of imaginary wings until a cough interrupted my solitude. I yelped when I glanced up to find Jimmu standing above me.

"Good gods, Jimmu. You scared me," I placed my head on my chest to steady my breathing. A few deep breaths soothed my racing heart. The magic that had awakened was more difficult to ease. Even after I'd called to my water element to calm me, my magic continued to pulse under the surface of my skin. Did it sense that something was amiss?

Jimmu kept a straight face as he presented a sword from his back. I raised my eyes from the sword to his face. It contorted into a look of a predator ready to kill its prey. Pure evil glinted in his eyes. He lifted the sword over his head and thrust it down in an attempt to plunge it into my chest. I rolled out of the way just in time. The sword plunged into the ground with so much force, the ground shook.

"What the hell, Jimmu?" I screamed. I pushed myself off the ground and turned to keep Jimmu in my line of sight. I glanced briefly beyond Jimmu's shoulder to see Fin running from across the encampment, jumping over fires and soldiers who were sleeping. I must have woken him because he stumbled a little, fumbling with his bow.

My eyes slid to Jimmu once more. He was still working to free his sword. I reached down deep for my empathic magic so that I could gain an understanding of what Jimmu was feeling. He felt…soulless. He was a walking, breathing corpse.

"Fin, wait," I said. I held up my hand to stop Fin—who had just reached Zari with a nocked arrow—from moving any further. He halted without hesitation. He trusted me.

Jimmu finally pulled his sword free from the ground and stalked over to me. I held both hands up to signal that I didn't want to hurt him. "Jimmu, please. I know we don't know each other well, but you don't want to do this. I could kill you. That sword is no match for me." I could imagine the wheels turning in Fin's head. "No jokes, Fin!"

"Wouldn't think of it," he shouted back.

Zari snorted in response.

I waited for a reply from Jimmu, but he made no indication that he wanted to talk. He held the sword firmly with both hands and moved into an attack position. "Jimmu, please. Let's figure out what has happened to you. You are not yourself." He continued to glare in silence.

It's the amulet, my Kahina. My eyes darted to Zari, and she nodded. Yes, my horse nodded. I glimpsed the amulet Jimmy was currently wearing. It was just like the one my father had given me. It hung on a braided chain of the same golden metal, and a pear-shaped gem was embedded at its center. Unlike mine, however, this one was glowing. Was it controlling him?

"That's a beautiful amulet, Jimmu," I said.

"Won't be that pretty with blood all over it," Fin yelled.

"Shut it, Fin!" I barked.

"You sound like Cal," he laughed.

I ignored him. "Jimmu, hand me the amulet," I said sternly. No response. "Fine. I'll take it myself." No more playing nice. I pushed a gust of wind toward him. I expected Jimmu to go flying backward with the amount of force I threw at him.

But he didn't.

He stumbled backward a few steps, but he still stood. My jaw dropped. "How?" I whispered. I gathered more magic and shot an ice ball at Jimmu, but once it hit him, it evaporated. He lowered his eyes to where the ice ball hit and then raised them back up at me. With a loud grunt, he charged toward me, enraged by my failed attempt to kill him. I shuffled my feet backward, and he swung the sword. I jumped back, pulling my stomach inward. The sword barely missed me. I hastily took a few more steps back but was stopped by a tree. I raised my arm, and with all my power, I froze it right when he brought the sword down. It connected with my skin and stopped. It was wedged in my arm. I glanced at Fin and nodded.

A few seconds later, Jimmu staggered back, his eyes wide. Blood seeped from his lips and down his chin. He coughed a few times before clawing at his neck where Fin's two arrows protruded out. I side-stepped, and Jammu's body connected with the tree then slumped to the ground. Fin stood still; his expression cold. He'd saved my life.

"You're going to tell Calian, aren't you?" I asked when Fin approached me.

"A corpse-like Dragonborn who couldn't be killed by magic? Absolutely!"

"All-powerful, and I can't even save myself," I mumbled.

He wrapped one arm around my shoulder. "Even the most powerful Dragongods needed help. It's what we're here for. So…About that?" He pointed to my arm. I'd forgotten that the sword was still stuck in it.

"I got this," I said. "It might hurt a bit, but I'll heal," I joked. I thawed my arm just enough to loosen the blade. Fin grabbed hold of both and pulled the sword out. Blood gushed down my arm, and I doubled over in pain. Okay, so it hurt a lot. The light from my healing magic shined and soothed the pain then closed the gash. I rotated my arm. "Good as new," I said.

"Show-off," Fin mumbled.

"You have no room to talk."

He bent down and rolled Jimmu over. Jimmu's neck was bent awkwardly from the way he'd hit the ground, and his eyes were open wide. None of that bothered Fin. He took the amulet, pulled it free, and inspected it in his hand. It no longer glowed red, but instead, radiated vibrant purple. "Here," he said, holding it out.

I hesitated but eventually took the amulet. The glowing stopped immediately. "What did I do?" I looked at Fin. "What did I do?" I repeated vehemently. I grabbed Fin's hand and thrust the amulet into his palm. As soon Fin took hold of the amulet, it began to glow again. It was a deep purple, the color of chaos.

"What does this mean?" he asked.

"I don't know," I answered. "I don't even know what it is. I have one just like it, but it doesn't glow."

He held it up to his face and inspected it. "I know what it is but not why it glows."

"What is it?" I asked.

"It's a Chaos Amulet," he answered. "There are three in existence."

"That's what my father said when I left my home. We were in a hurry, so he didn't tell me much else about them. Just to keep it close and that I'd know when it was time to give it to someone."

"One was created for each Chaos Dragon. That's all I know."

"Jimmu was immune to my magic," I mused. "I wonder if you'd be too if you put it on."

He didn't get the hint this time.

"Maybe you should put it on?" I suggested.

He knitted his brows together and hung the amulet in front of his face. "And if you're wrong?" he asked slowly.

"Then I'll take you out before you cause irreparable damage." I gave him an exaggerated wink.

"It's immune to Dragonmagic," he pointed out.

"I have my bow and arrows," I replied.

He turned the amulet over in his hands, but before he could put it on, we were interrupted by a noise in the distance. I cast a beam of light from my palms and squinted my eyes. Dhruv galloping down a hill, riding toward us. But Calian wasn't on him.

"Something's wrong," I breathed. It was the fastest I'd ever seen Dhruv run.

The soldier riding Dhruv sounded out of breath when he reached us. "Sir, Captain Westbow needs you. The Dragoncouncil is under attack," he exclaimed between breaths.

With his eyebrows knitted together in confusion, Fin glanced at me and then back to the soldier. "Me?" he asked. "Not her?"

"It's the Waterion Military. They're convinced the Dragoncouncil is responsible for the disappearance of Princess Morwen. They've taken Captain Westbow and the rest of the council hostage. The captain believes only you can convince them otherwise."

"Because Morwen's your mate," I guessed. "Take Zari, she's fast."

Fin shook his head. "Absolutely not. She's your horse."

"That's an order."

"You're pulling rank now?"

"I am. Now go!"

He didn't waste time arguing. He jumped up on Zari.

I whispered to her, "Run like the wind."

And she did.

CHAPTER
NINETEEN

I thought Zari flew like the wind, but I was wrong.

Zari was the wind.

In an instant, Fin and Zari were gone. The soldier immediately gave Dhruv to me and took command of the second group. Dhruv took off and did his best to keep up with Zari, but he just couldn't. She was too fast. Dhruv never stopped, though. We raced through the rest of the forest and exited the southern part of it in half the time it would have normally taken.

Once out of the forest, night had transitioned into day, and the City of Nimerah eventually came into view. The city's pristine outer walls were in plain view. Words couldn't describe them. They were majestic as they glistened like diamonds in the late afternoon sun.

We rode the horses to a large drawbridge that was already open. However, the interior gate to the city was closed beyond it. Two men on horseback were stationed outside the city gate wearing what looked to be uniforms of the Waterion Military. But what really grabbed my curiosity was that aside from those two soldiers, there was no other sign of a military presence. The land was beautiful, lush, and green…but empty. There was no military camp. There were no tents, no horses, and no other soldiers maintaining a presence outside of the city.

"What's going on Dhruv?" I asked. He shook his head. It seemed he was just as confused.

I directed Dhruv to slow down to a trot because intuition told me to be cautious. We neared the city's drawbridge, but we stopped when the two soldiers on horseback rode out to meet us. The first soldier wore a scowl on his face. The other looked indifferent.

"I'm here to see Captain Westbow," I announced as they came closer.

"Of course, you are," the first soldier said. Ah! So, he was the one in charge. His finely groomed mustache, deep blue scales, and I'm-better-than-you sneer reeked of arrogance. I guessed he was a captain or a soldier of higher rank. The second soldier remained quiet, assessing the situation. Dark glasses covered his eyes. I'd heard of those things. They were crafted to block out the sun. I'd just never seen a pair before.

"Then lead me to him."

"Or what?" Sneering Soldier asked. Silent Soldier stayed quiet, but probably because he looked bored.

I let sparks come to life at my fingertips. Sneering Soldier grinned so much, it overwhelmed his face. Silent Soldier didn't flinch. Instead, he tucked his hair behind his ear which exposed his black scales where blue should have been. He was a Dragonborn of the Kingdom of Darkness serving in the Waterion Military. It wasn't unheard of for citizens of different kingdoms to serve in another kingdom's military, but it wasn't common.

Focus, Em. I could think more about Silent Soldier another time. Right now, I needed to establish that I wasn't afraid of them and that I, in fact, had the upper hand.

"You think that scares me, princess?" Sneering Soldier asked in regard to the sparks crackling at my fingertips.

"Goddess," I corrected. "And it should. I could destroy this place."

Silent Soldier finally spoke up. "Let's just remain calm here," he said lazily. A strand of hair fell onto his face, and he blew it back. It was straight and curled slightly where it rested on his shoulders. He had pale skin that was lighter than my own. I'd heard that Dragonborns from the Kingdom of Darkness had the palest of skins and the darkest of eyes—Dragonheir or not. They were nicknamed the Dragondemons, and they were not to be trusted. I personally felt that the goddess Tamasvi was misunderstood. I'd have to talk to my Dragonmother about it.

I reached down low and pulled from my earth element. With my palms facing downward at my sides, I pulled energy from the ground which began to quiver beneath the horses' feet. Dhruv stood silently, still looking bored and unphased by the small earthquake I was causing. Sneering Soldier's horse, however, went berserk and almost threw him off. He pulled on the reins to make sure it stayed put, but the horse struggled to maintain its composure. Silent Soldier just shook his head. Maybe Sneering Soldier wasn't the one in charge.

"You'll do well to keep that Dragonmagic in check, *princess*," Sneering Soldier snapped. I wondered if he had any other facial expressions.

I held his gaze. "Take me to Captain Westbow, and I won't cause any problems. I am not your enemy unless I need to be." The breeze picked up and blew through my hair for a dramatic effect. It worked because Sneering Soldier jerked his chin over his shoulder, motioning for me to follow him. Silent Soldier remained…silent.

I kept my head held high as Dhruv followed the two soldiers. We crossed over the drawbridge and the inner gate opened. I expected to see dozens of soldiers maintaining order.

But there were none.

The city was still. The beautiful shops made of the smoothest deep purple stone were vacant. The streets were empty. Homes in shades of gray, silver, and white with black rooftops were uninhabited. The numerous flowers of varying shades of purple and violet looked lonely. The only sound I could make out was a slight whistling from the light breeze. It was as if the town were occupied by ghosts. A chill climbed up my spine.

"Where is everyone?" I asked. I tried to keep my face impassive because deep down, I was worried about the entirety of the situation. I found it hard to believe that King Elderbrook would just take Calian prisoner without cause. I found it hard to believe that the city would be void of life. I found it hard to believe that the council would just succumb to a military presence without some sort of resistance. What I didn't find hard to believe was that this all could be a trap for me.

"Hiding," Silent Soldier replied. I didn't believe him.

I continued to look left and right, into dark alleys and down streets searching for any sign of life. We approached the Tomb of the Dragonelders, and my breath hitched in my throat as we passed by its tall towers and a large courtyard. Although it held the skeletal remains of the faithful priests and priestesses, it seemed welcoming, designed as a warm reception for any traveler that wished to honor those that served. A lump formed in my throat. Rehema should be in there. The lump burned, but I forced a slight wave of water magic to help me gulp it down. I could not afford to get emotional right now. Rehema wouldn't want that. She'd want me focused. She'd want me ready for every possible scenario.

We finally arrived at the Temple of the Dragoncouncil. It stood at the very center of the city. If my studies were accurate—I was more unsure of than ever—the city was built around the Temple, not the other way around. The Temple was constructed of glistening white stone. A bridge suspended over a small pond led to a large opening of the main building. White trees of differing heights with sparkling leaves surrounded the temple, and numerous plots of lush foliage and Twilight Orchids lined the exterior walls. It was mountainous in size compared to everything else. We stopped just before the bridge, and I gaped like a fool. Its immaculate condition was breathtaking. There was no other way to describe its intricate design.

Silent Soldier slid off his horse which I took as a hint that horses were not allowed to cross over. We had to continue on foot.

Silent Soldier offered me his hand to help me get down. Two scenarios played in my head briefly if I took his hand. I could take it and look weak like a little girl who needed help, or I could take it and look like I trusted him. I chose the latter for diplomatic purposes.

"Thank you," I said. He didn't answer. He just nodded curtly and grabbed Dhruv's reins. I attempted to keep my voice firm yet calm. "Where are you taking him?" I asked.

"To the stables. Your other horse is there as well." He looked at me, and there was a dire seriousness in his eyes. "The stables are located just outside the city gate near the northern guard tower." Why he was offering me that information, I couldn't say. He shifted his weight when he noticed Sneering Soldier looking at him distrustfully. "Please don't worry. Your horses are in great hands." He led Dhruv away from me, and I watched them go until they were out of sight. The soldier never looked back.

Sneering Soldier walked around his horse and glared at me. Using his finger, he motioned for me to follow him like I was a child. My temper flared. Sneering Soldier made me want to throw all my power at him just to wipe the sneer off of his face. Instead, all I could do was clench my fists at my side. My skin stung from my nails digging into my palms.

Sneering Soldier abruptly turned his back on me and headed toward the entrance of the Temple. We crossed over the bridge, and I paused momentarily to take in the scenery. It was absolutely stunning. I felt at peace, and I couldn't help but notice the slight feeling of being connected to it all as I walked to the edge of the bridge and peered down into the crystal-clear water of the pond beneath it. My reflection startled me. I looked older than I had before my Trials. My hair was disheveled, and my eyes were dark as coals. Avani was right. I did look like a Dragondemon.

The soldier cleared his throat, indicating his annoyance at my lack of haste. I picked up my pace and joined him under the entrance's archway. I ignored his snicker because now that I was up close to the walls, I saw that chiseled into the stone were scales. The entire temple was covered in them. I chose to admire the hard work put into the temple instead of setting the soldier on fire. The thought had crossed my mind.

The double doors each contained a carving of my Dragonmother. Two soldiers stood on either side of the double-door entrance, and they moved quickly to open them for Sneering Soldier. Their expressions didn't change as I walked by, but I could sense distrust and hatred. It didn't make sense. None of it made sense. I lived in the Kingdom of Water my entire life. I was blessed by Anahita first. I was only there to speak with the king; I had no intention of harming him anyway.

The doors slammed behind me, and I jumped. The soldier laughed at me, shaking his head. I lifted my hand slightly. I could do it, but I didn't bring lightning crashing down on his head. Instead, I took deep breaths and followed him into a large hallway. Statues of the Elemental Dragons aligned the walls leading into a large sanctuary. They stood, looking regal yet cold. Each statue was painted the color of its element.

Once inside the sanctuary, I widened my eyes in wonder. It was like I had stepped into a fantasy. Trees and pools of water with flowing streams and fountains greeted my soul. Each side of the sanctuary contained one door. I took a mental note of each in case I needed an escape route. Sneering Soldier walked toward the center of the sanctuary where the largest statue of any god or goddess I'd ever seen. It was Nimerah, perched on a boulder. Surrounding her were small fountains shooting water in varying arcs into a small pool. I felt a tad uncomfortable gazing at her Dragonform since I knew her personally in her human form. I smiled, knowing that I was probably the only person still alive that had seen her like that. It was a secret I'd hold close to my heart.

Sneering Soldier walked right past my Dragonmother, not even taking a second to avert his eyes to her towering figure. "Traitor," he muttered. I ground my teeth together, trying to maintain control of my emotions. But that guy was really testing me. Up until now, I'd been focused on obtaining the blessings needed to obtain my magic. Now that I had my magic—well, most of it—it was starting to set in that some people would look down on me for my power. Naive? Sure.

I continued to follow him as he rounded behind the statue up and the wide stairs leading to more double doors. He stopped just outside of them and beckoned me to go inside. "After you," he said with a lazy grin.

"Need me to make sure it's safe, huh?" I teased. He didn't like that much because he shoved me into the double doors. I felt a pain in my back where the door handles had jabbed into my back. He stalked up to me, quickly raised his hand, and backhanded me across the cheek. My head snapped left, and I winced.

"You mean like you kept your Priestess safe?" he taunted. How did he know about Rehema?

I touched my cheekbone, finding the spot he'd hit tender and warm. I pulled my hand back and saw blood on my fingers. "Excuse me?" I growled. Valda was responsible for the death of Rehema.

"She had some fight in her, but not enough."

"You're quite bold for someone with very little power," I seethed. Keeping my eyes locked on his, I lifted my hand and placed my palm gently on the wound. Magic surfaced to my palm and healed the cut.

He just shrugged, looking annoyed. He straightened and planted another smirk on his face.

That was it. I'd had it. I closed my eyes slowly and reopened them, my temper flaring. He just stood there, pleased with himself while I let my air magic fester within me. I wanted nothing to do with *creating* air.

I wanted to take it.

I could feel my eyes glowing, the heat from concentration surging behind them. The smirk quickly faded from the soldier's face. His eyes widened, his mouth opened, and he began to cough. He brought his hands to his neck and clawed at it while gasping for air. A distant voice, subtle yet firm, whispered in my ear, "My daughter. This isn't you."

My Dragonmother was right. I exhaled and dropped my magic. The soldier fell to his knees and bent over, wheezing and laughing. I thought I'd feel satisfied, but instead, I felt ashamed. My anger faded, and I stepped over him, leaving him on the floor laughing.

I opened the double doors and found myself standing in a small foyer of sorts. Lavish chairs and a fireplace gave the room an inviting feeling. There were two doors on each side with the names of each council member's name on the outside. These were the council member's private chambers. Beyond the foyer was another door with the name that read Dragonmaster Anwir. I walked through the foyer and stood outside the door. Confusion swept through me as I listened to voices talking and laughing. Two voices I made out, and my breath caught in my chest. I hastily opened the door to find who I figured to be Dragonmaster Anwir talking animatedly.

He was talking to Calian and Valda.

CHAPTER TWENTY

I couldn't move. I couldn't speak. I couldn't breathe. What the *hell* was Calian doing with Valda?

"There she is!" The older man—my father's age—rose from his chair and dashed to the door. His white hair was clean and crisp beside his emerald scales, and his short black and gray-peppered beard gave him an air of authority. His robe, a deep purple, was not the usual color violet that represented Nimerah. Silver and gold stitching formed the outlines of numerous Dragonheads that were certainly not that of my Dragonmother's.

He grabbed both of my upper arms and held me tight, looking me up and down in a slow, inappropriate manner as if he hungered for physical contact. I cringed beneath his gaze and tried to wriggle free, but he held tight. I connected with my magic, and before I could blast him across the room, he lowered his arms, trailing his hands down mine in a slow caress. It was all I could do not to spill the contents of my stomach.

Who did this man think he was?

As his hands reached mine, he eased his grip, and I shook him off. Calian now stood beside him, smirking. His lack of interference with what his so-called *father* had just done angered me. Even Valda looked disgusted, yet she remained where she stood, leaning against a bookcase and picking at her fingernails.

"She doesn't have Nimerah's blessing yet, Anwir. As I said, she's useless to the cause," Calian remarked.

Did Calian just call me *useless*?

"I wouldn't say that," Anwir replied. He angled his head to the right, inspecting me again. His green eyes flared with amusement when he noticed my scales. "Look at those colors," he purred. "So exquisite." He grabbed my hand and turned it over, rubbing his thumb along each color of scale. I could hear the gulp he took to stifle a moan. I yanked my hand away from him and slapped his cheek.

"Don't touch me again," I said through clenched teeth. Calian moved to detain me, but Anwir held his hand up.

"Quite the feisty one," he chuckled. He leaned in, his lips resting just below my ear. "I appreciate that." He straightened and faced Calian. "Leave her be…for now," he ordered.

Calian backed away. His lips pursed together with annoyance. "We don't need her. We should just lock her up…or kill her. Just like her traitor of a mother did to Amram." Tears welled within my eyes. What was wrong with him? Surely, he was under some sort of spell or hex by Valda. Calian wouldn't do this. My mother wasn't a traitor. He knew that.

Valda clicked her tongue. "Aw, you're going to make her cry." I had no retort because she was right. I could feel the dam about to break. I ignored her and focused my attention back to Calian. I needed answers.

"How could you?" I hissed.

He stepped closer to me. I reached to him with my empathic magic, and all I could feel was anger.

"Your mother was a traitor to all Dragonborn. She deserves to die with all of her precious humans." His words punctured my heart like a viper, its venom filtering through my body. I staggered backward until I hit the wooden door I'd just entered.

"But you…and me…We're…" I said, my voice now shaking. Was it from anger? Was it from sadness? Was it from shock? It was probably a mixture of all three. However, anger was leading the force.

"We're nothing," he said without hesitation. There was no kindness in his voice.

"I thought I knew you," I whispered, and my body began to tremble.

"Knew me?" He threw his head back and laughed. When he lowered his chin to face me, his eyes were bright red. "You don't know me at all." He took a couple of steps away from me and red smoke poured from his hands and swallowed him. Anwir leaned on a nearby desk looking pleased. Valda rolled her eyes in boredom.

As the smoke thickened, I couldn't see Calian's face anymore, but I could make out the outline of his body. His frame was narrower, his shoulders were less broad, and his height had shrunk a little. When the smoke cleared, a different man stood before me. His dark hair fell past his shoulders. He had strong black eyebrows over his sharp red eyes, and his nose was longer and more slender than before. His chin was pointier, elongating his face with high cheekbones. This man was a shapeshifter, and that meant…

"Emera, let me introduce you to Elio: Dragonheir of Vukan," Anwir announced, his words filled with pride. He placed a shoulder on Cal—Elio's—shoulder.

I just stared at the stranger before me where the Calian I had known once stood and let the deception set in. Fury imploded within my body while agony clawed at my heart.

"And the real Calian Westbow?" I asked.

"Disposed of," Valda snickered. I felt my face fall, and my heart fell with it. My knees buckled, and I stumbled, bracing myself with the corner of the table. Valda shrieked with laughter.

"Was it you the whole time?" I asked.

Elio sighed. "Unfortunately, no. Although, that would have been a lot of fun."

"It was tricky to find the perfect time to make the switch, I'll admit," Anwir said with a slight wave of his hand.

I met Elio's eyes and glared. "So, when?"

Valda grinned, showing her teeth like a wolf. "Dhara," she answered.

The memory flooded my brain. The cave. Calian went ahead. Alone. That was the switch. It all made sense now. The real reason he'd referred to Zari as my horse. The real reason he'd left me at the camp when Valda showed up. The real reason there was no electric feeling between us. And my Calian was dead.

"It was perfect, really," Elio mused. "You and Avani having your little chat gave me the perfect opportunity to make the switch and communicate the position of the camp to Valda." He pressed his hands together like a prayer and leaned toward me. "Thank you for that."

The piercing ache from Calian's death ignited a fierce blaze of fury beneath my skin. I was about to explode. I would kill them all.

"And Fin? Avani? Erjon? Morwen?" My voice kept getting louder and louder with each name I spoke.

Anwir shot Valda a look before she could respond. "Very much alive," Anwir assured me. Valda rolled her eyes. She had probably wanted to kill them, but Anwir left them alive.

"Where?"

"You'll see them soon enough," Anwir replied. Elio's eyes flashed. He didn't like that answer.

Valda shifted her weight and waved her hand casually, ready to change the subject. "I agree with Elio. Can we please just get rid of her now?" My magic flared in response, but I held my ground, keeping the rage harnessed. Okay, so neither Elio nor Valda liked Anwir's response.

"Why would you do this?" I demanded.

"Emera, please sit," Anwir said and motioned to an empty chair in front of his large, dark oak desk. I hesitated but knowing Valda wanted to kill me made me think I should play along. I could do that. I raised my chin slightly to show no fear —it was really to make them think I had no fear.

I took a step forward toward the seat. Anwir moved his hand to the small of my back, but stopped after he caught the daggers my eyes were shooting at him. He held both hands up in surrender, and I sat cautiously.

"Let me make this clear to you, Emera. You've been lied to your entire life."

Wow. You don't say, I thought.

I kept my voice even. "How so?" I asked.

Anwir took a sip of whatever liquid filled his golden goblet that sat on his desk. "What do you know of the War of Three?" he asked.

"To make what I'm assuming would be a lengthy history lesson short, Nimerah and Amram were at peace with the humans and Ragnar decided to betray them in their attempt to bring balance and prosperity to the six kingdoms. Does that sum it up?" I hoped my lie was convincing. I didn't dare acknowledge that I knew the truth.

Anwir laughed. "My dear girl. You have been brainwashed."

I scoffed and folded my arms. "I doubt that."

His smile faded, and his eyes turned icy. "Your mother was a traitor to all the Dragonborns." I fought to cage my anger.

"She preferred her precious humans to her kind. The Dragonborns were dying, and she did nothing." Valda snarled from across the room. The temperature in the room rose as she stalked toward me. She bent down, leaning into me as her hands rested on the arms of the chair that I sat in. "My father was the only one willing to fight for all Dragons and the Dragonborn. She and her stupid General interfered. They were traitors."

I cocked my head to the side, "Hmm…" I drawled. "That's an interesting theory, Valda. I've got a better one." I leaned forward and lowered my voice. "Maybe the war started because your arrogant, power-hungry father couldn't handle the fact that my mother rejected him."

I stood to my feet just as she lunged forward. Her arms swooped in an attempt to grab me, but I was too quick.

Before Valda could manipulate her magic to keep me contained within the room, I opened the door, ran out, and slammed it behind me. I took off back where I'd come from, keeping my arm extended behind me and forcing my air magic to keep pressure on the door. It would only give me a moment, but it would have to do. The magic was strong and enabled me to keep them in Anwir's chambers long enough to enter the great hall and close those doors behind me. There was no sight of Sneering Soldier who must have gone about his other duties somewhere else within the temple. With my water magic, I froze the frame of the doors. It wouldn't stay shut, but hopefully, it would give me a minute to escape.

I twisted and turned, frantically looking for any way to block the doors, but I couldn't find anything heavy enough. Anything except my Dragonmother's statue. I paused and looked at her. She looked so calm, so serene. Then I recalled what she'd said when she'd pulled me into the Dragonplane.

"You knew, Mother," I cried angrily. "You knew! And you didn't tell me!"

She had warned me that people were deceiving me, yet she didn't tell me who. And here I stood, embarrassed that

I'd fallen in love with a man who wasn't who he had claimed to be.

I picked up a vase with intricate swirls of violet flowers and scales. I screamed and chucked the vase at the statue. It connected with its head, shattering upon impact. In my previous life, I would have fallen to my knees and cried. I would have let my emotions control me. But not this time. Not this Emera.

The doors behind swung open, banging against the walls. Valda entered the hall first looking like she was enjoying this game of cat and mouse.

"Emera," she sang. She was followed by Elio who looked distant and unfeeling. Anwir strolled in next, his expression undisturbed. I had to get out.

"You have nowhere to run," Valda pointed out.

"You're so thoughtful," I said. Her smile only widened as she stepped forward, her arms rising to blast whatever magic she had at me. Elio took a fighting stance, flames growing from his palms. Anwir stood still and silent.

"Valda, my dear. We want her alive," Anwir said.

I threw out water so cold that it formed a protective ice shield in front of me. I hoped it was strong enough to hold so that I could get to a tree or some other obstacle to hide behind. Then I could formulate a plan of attack. Valda was the main target, then Elio, and then Anwir. He was an Earthean Dragonpriest, so he had some power, but he would be weaker than the other two.

Valda released fire magic so potent, it melted my shield. My mind went blank. There was no way my magic could compare to hers. No way I could win this fight. The door was twenty feet away, and I had no options.

"I never said I was going to kill her," she told Anwir. "That doesn't mean I can't have a little fun." She held out her hands and I rose slowly off the ground. I struggled to keep my feet connected to the floor, but it was no use. She held me there and laughed while I kicked and swung my legs. I attempted to bring magic to my arms, but it was no use. She held them at the sides of my body with her power. Again, it was much stronger than mine.

"Keep fighting it, Emera," she purred. "I'm thoroughly enjoying this."

A loud crash broke her concentration, and I fell to the floor on the pieces of the broken vase I'd thrown at the statue. Pain seared my palms and blood trickled down my arm and onto the floor from the glass still stuck in my skin. Ignoring the pain, I glanced in the direction of the crash and saw numerous broken vases. All three of them knelt on the floor with vase fragments all around their feet. Anwir had his arm draped over his face to protect him; blood ran down Elio's arms from multiple cuts; Valda was picking shards out of her hair, not a scratch on her. I used the brief moment to stand and dart behind a tree. It was small, so it didn't quite provide the coverage I needed, but it was better than nothing.

I looked around frantically, assessing the area to locate a way out. By divine luck, I noticed a tapestry on the left wall was askew, and behind that tapestry was a hidden door. I threw a quick glance back to Valda who now searched the area for me—Elio and Anwir were now arguing as they cleaned themselves up. Valda slowly paced back and forth before heading in the opposite direction of the sanctuary from me. She disappeared behind my Dragonmother's statue which, thankfully, was large enough to block me from her sight. I sprinted toward the door, conjuring darkness from my hands, and made the room go dark. I forced all of my magic into it, to hold it in place.

"Emera. You know that won't hide you," Valda taunted. "I can just snap my fingers, and it will be gone. It's no use."

Just keep talking, I thought. I opened the door, snuck in, and grabbed the tapestry, pulling it into place before I closed the door. The darkness vanished just as the last sliver of my view of the sanctuary disappeared. There was no lock, so I did the only thing I could think of: I called fire magic to my hands and melted the door hinges then froze them. Hopefully, the door wouldn't open easily when they found it which would give me enough time to get out.

Satisfied with what I'd done, I turned and evaluated my new location. It was the opposite of the beautiful sanctuary I'd come from. There were no sconces or torches. Just complete darkness. I held up my hand and created a beam of light so that I could see my surroundings. It was a dark hallway, filled with dust and mold. Not too many people would have been allowed in here. The air was stale, slightly chilled, and smelled of dense must.

But I didn't have time to complain. I took off running but stopped when the hallway floor dropped off. Before me was a descending staircase. I thrust the beam of light down, but I still couldn't see the bottom.

This must go deep underground, I thought. *Why would they have anything like this?*

Well, time to find out because I obviously didn't have any other choice but to go down. I took a step downward.

I kept going down and down until I reached the hard stone floor at the bottom. Another wooden door stood before me; the sound of light whistling emitted from the tiny crack beneath the door. With a deep inhale, I opened it and entered a large room that was musky, cold, and damp. Several torches were attached to the wall, illuminating the room enough that I quit casting my beam of light. Small holding cells shut off from the room with metal doors made of bars on each side of the room. The bars extended from the ceiling to the floor.

I widened my eyes in surprise. "A dungeon?" I asked aloud.

"That would be correct," came a male voice, and a man turned the corner of a cell and stepped into view, a sword in his hand. I mentally prepared myself for another fight. I raised my hands with sparks rolling off my fingers, ready to defend myself.

"I was hoping I'd see you alive," Silent Soldier said.

"I am not sure I can say the same about you," I replied coolly.

He took a step toward me. I responded by immediately taking a step back.

"I am not your enemy," he said. He held his hands up, but the blade was still in his hand. I looked up at it, and I let air flow from my hands to create a force of wind if I needed to knock it out of his hands. He saw the magic and lifted his gaze to where I was looking. Realization set it in, and he dropped the sword. It clanged loudly on the stone floor, echoing throughout the room.

"You caused the explosion," I said.

"I did. I hoped it gave you the time you needed."

I eased my magic back. "Who are you?" I asked, eyeing him cautiously.

"I'm a friend of Senna," he replied. My thoughts drifted back to that night in the City of Dhara at the inn. Senna had called herself a friend. I had been skeptical, but what if she had sent this soldier—or whatever he was— to help me?

"What I meant was, what is your name?"

He cleared his throat. "I'm Kedron: Dragonheir of Tamasvi. I'm here to help you." He discarded his glasses, fell to one knee, and bent his head. It was supposed to be a serious moment, but I laughed.

"Get up. You look silly."

He smiled, and it was then that I took in his face and saw that his eyes were black like mine.

"So, what kind of temple is this?" I asked.

"The kind that tortures those who don't believe in the elimination of humankind," said a husky voice from within one of the cells. I whipped my head in the voice's direction.

My gods! How many people are in this dungeon?

I looked back to Kedron and flipped my thumb at the darkened cell.

"Who's in there?" I asked. We both leaned closer and peered into the cell.

A figure stumbled into the light, revealing a man in tattered clothing, his head hung low. He limped closer and clung to the bars to keep himself upright. Then he looked up and our eyes connected. Relief flooded my body.

The man was Calian.

CHAPTER TWENTY-ONE

Or at least, the man looked like him.

Flames ignited within my palms instantly. This had to be another deception, and I didn't think I'd be able to take it. The Calian Westbow I knew was supposed to be dead. Wasn't that what Valda had said? Come to think of it, she had said Calian was *disposed of*, not that he was *dead*. I had just assumed.

I confronted the man in the cell. Was this him? Did I have my Calian back? His features were the same except for his bruised skin which indicated he'd been beaten severely. His coloring was sallow, and his lack of muscle showed how boney he was from being starved and possibly sick. My heart fell.

"Calian? Cal?" I asked. My voice trembled with every syllable. I waited with bated breath for his reply.

He gripped the bars serving as his cage and leaned in. He angled his head and searched my face for any recognition of who I was. "Emera?" he breathed.

"Yes," I said and paused before adding, "How can I be sure it's really you?"

"You can't," he replied tersely. "It sounds like you don't know a shapeshifter from a succubus, so I figure you can't be sure of anything." A slow grin spread across his face. Yes, it was him.

I moved closer until I was right in front of him. "I don't think you're in any position to be rude," I pointed out. "Seems like you need my help."

He leveled his gaze and hunched closer. Our bodies were so close to touching, my heart began beating rapidly.

"It would seem," he admitted.

Acting on impulse, I reached through the bars, pulled him closer, and pressed my lips to his. His body went rigid from shock, but then he relaxed. Time stopped for just the tiniest of moments while we savored the moment. He was alive! My heart flipped in my chest. The electric spark I'd grown accustomed to when we were close was back. But now it was nothing like how I'd felt before. It was a jarring sensation. A sudden surge of energy jolted me, disrupting my senses and leaving me stunned. I let go of the bars and stumbled backward. He must have felt it too because he gripped the bars even tighter to keep from falling.

"How long have you been down here?" I asked between deep breaths, fighting to gain my composure.

"I don't think this is the right time," Kedron interrupted. "We need to get out of here."

An explosion from above rattled the doors. Valda had figured out where I'd hidden.

"Stand back," I ordered Calian. He did as I said without arguing. I'd remember that for later. Fin would love it.

I flexed my fingers. But before I could do anything, Kedron placed a hand on my shoulder. "I've got this," he said.

I lowered my hands. "Okay," I responded skeptically.

I watched him take a deep breath and close his eyes. He opened his eyes, and in a heartbeat, he vanished. Kedron no longer stood beside me. I jerked my eyes back and forth, trying to locate him in the room. Calian cleared his throat. Kedron was in the cell.

"That was incredible!" I exclaimed. "How did you do that?"

"I can teleport," Kedron said.

"Oh, right," I said, embarrassed. "Tamasvi's secondary power."

Kedron held out his hand out to Calin, who hesitated, but eventually acquiesced. In the blink of an eye, Kedron and Calian weren't standing in the cell anymore. They were beside me. Calian lost his balance, almost falling to the ground, but Kedron wrapped his arms around Calian's waste to provide support. Calian was too weak to run.

"I was your distraction," I claimed.

"Excuse me?" Kedron asked.

"No, it's okay. You needed a distraction to get him out. I was it. Everyone was so focused on me that no one was down here."

Kedron blushed then shrugged. "I was going to come back for you."

Calian groaned. That's when I noticed his hand on his stomach. When he pulled it away, blood stained his hand and saturated his torn shirt. "This wound just won't seem to heal."

Valda, Elio, and Anwir were closing in. They were moving at a rapid pace to intercept us.

"I'll find my way to you and heal you, but we need to get you out now."

Kedron's face sobered. "The rendezvous point is the stables. But I can't transport more than one person."

I gave him a reassuring smile. "It's okay. I'll hold my own. Get him out of here."

"You can do it, you know," Kedron said.

"Do what?"

"Teleport."

"But I've never done it."

"No time like the present to learn." The footsteps were getting closer and closer. We were running out of time. Kedron knew it, too. "There are two ways you can do it," he continued hastily. "The first way is to see the place you want to be. Close your eyes, see it, and let go. Use your Dragonmagic to guide you there."

I couldn't hide my nerves. "Sounds so easy," I joked.

"However, you must have been there before for it to work."

Definitely not easy. I'd never seen the stables.

"And the second way?"

"See who it is you want to be with," he said. Okay, so think of Calian.

"But what if something happens to you when you get there?"

"I didn't say you had to see a person." He grinned, the corners of his mouth almost reaching his eyes.

Zari.

I nodded an unspoken farewell. Kedron teleported with Calian seconds before the door flung open with Valda standing in the entryway.

"Well, well, well. What have we here?" she crooned, stepping into the light.

Elio entered after her. He looked around, but nothing would have looked out of the ordinary to him. The door to Calian's cell was still closed, making it appear he was still locked in. "It looks like you're trapped, Em," Elio chuckled.

"Let's just calm down, everyone. Emera, darling, you are in no danger with us," Anwir said, finally stepping into the room.

"Could have fooled me," I replied flatly. In my head, I began to form an image of Zari. I missed her. I needed her. "As fun as this has all been for, well, no one, I'm going to have to take off."

"You can't fly without Nimerah's blessing, you idiot," Valda snapped.

"Who said anything about flying?" I asked her. She angled her head to the side, trying to figure out my game. When it dawned on her, she lunged for me. But she was too late.

I'd already closed my eyes and propelled myself into nothingness.

*　　*　　*

My eyes cracked open one at a time to the sensation of something whipping my face. I had teleported directly behind Zari, facing a part of her I didn't care to see. Her tail continued flinging back and forth, scratching my face. My appearance startled her because she raised her leg to kick. I dodged out of the way just in time and leaped into a pile of hay.

I'm so sorry, my Kahina.

Don't be! I pulled myself up and began picking hay out of my hair. I dusted my clothes off before wrapping my arms around Zari's neck in a huge embrace. *I'm so relieved to see you! Where's Dhruv? Please tell me he's here.*

He's here.

Good. Are you ready to leave? I don't know where we're going, but any place is better than here. I will fill you in on all the details, but we need to get out of here quickly.

Kedron, leading a horse, appeared beside Zari and me. "You made it!" he said joyfully.

"I did just as you said. Where is he?"

Kedron pointed beyond me. I turned, and Calian was standing there. I ran to him and threw my arms around him.

We stayed there in our embrace until the electric feeling was back. Then, his hands found their way into my hair. They entwined themselves in my thick red strands and stayed there, keeping me nestled close to him. He dipped down and his mouth slowly claimed mine. His full, warm lips gradually opened my own and his warmth poured into me. I leaned into him, taking full advantage of the moment. A low rumble came from his throat, and he pulled me closer.

Kedron cleared his throat. "Ahem."

Calian and I pulled away from each other, but I kept ahold of his hand and let my healing magic flow within me. White light flowed from my hand into his and to the rest of his body. Calian seemed to glow while his wounds healed, his coloring returned to normal, and his form filled out. I let go of his hand and stepped back. I gazed up at him.

Now he truly looked like himself.

"Thanks," he breathed. He lifted his arms and inspected his hands. He then felt his neck and face, making sure everything was back to normal. Finally, he ran his hand through his thick hair. The slight curl I loved so much was there now. "I finally feel better," he sighed.

"Good," I said. I started to walk away, but something small caught the corner of my eye. I glimpsed down to where a small hole in Calian's shirt exposed his heart.

"What's wrong?" he asked. He looked down and began to wipe his shirt with his hand. "I'll find better clothing once we leave," he insisted.

"It's not that," I whispered. I grabbed the collar of his shirt and pulled it down. There, right above his heart was a pair of vibrant purple Dragonwings. My breath caught in my throat.

Calian reached for the collar of my shirt and gently pulled it down revealing…nothing.

I placed my hand over the spot where a matching set of wings should have been. I lifted my gaze to his and found disappointment. He was disappointed.

I gulped loudly. If not me, then who. The wings were purple.

"Valda?"

Calian couldn't answer because a rumbling shook the ground.

"Yes. She's coming," Kedron said.

I let my hand slide from Calian's chest and hurried back to Zari.

Let's get out of here, I said to Zari when I got back to her.

Yes, please.

I placed my foot in the stirrup and swung my leg over Zari. I didn't have to give her any commands. She just turned and raced after the two men who'd already taken off.

CHAPTER TWENTY-TWO

We rode out of town and back north into the forest. The sun started to bid farewell just as the moon said hello. The evening sky transformed into a tapestry of dark blue and black. We followed Kedron who seemed to have a destination planned out. We maintained a fast pace since it was only a matter of time before Valda would realize we were out of the city and flew after us in her Dragon form.

We changed direction, heading west after we crossed the river. We traveled day and night and didn't stop until we'd finally reached the edge of the forest just outside the Kingdom of Air. The Arian Mountain Range loomed in the distance, its snow-capped mountains and lustrous evergreen trees were a sight for sore, tired eyes. A light breeze chilled my skin as the temperature dropped from the humidity that inhabited the inner part of the forest. I welcomed the breeze's caress and dipped my head back to enjoy the brief reprieve. I hoped we were traveling to the City of Ilmari and to an inn. I dreamed of a soft bed with a plump pillow and warm blanket and longed for a night's rest. No. What I truly dreamed of was a cot in a tent that was divided in two. A tent that was located in a camp surrounded by joy and laughter.

The sudden thought of the camp caused my chest to ache and my heart to feel heavy. So much had happened since I had strolled through the camp's gate that fateful day. I had already lived an eternity since then.

Zari came to a sudden halt, and I almost propelled forward. Looking ahead, I saw Calian had stopped as well, which prompted Kedron's stallion to also slow to a stop. Calian was looking toward the mountains at a black figure swirling around. Kedron looked up, searching for what Calian was looking at.

Valda.

Rage burned within me.

"What do we do?" I asked.

"As long as we stay within the tree line, she won't see us. We need to get to the cave," Calian answered. I didn't have a clue what cave he meant, but I appreciated that he was calm and collected in a moment like this. He turned Dhruv north and headed for what I figured was the entrance to the cave he mentioned.

Zari trotted up alongside Kedron's steed. I looked at Kedron. "The cave?"

"There are people in there we must protect," he answered.

"And that would be?"

"The remaining citizens of Nimerah."

"So, they are safe?"

"We've been working day and night to get them to the City of Ilmari. Queen Eteri is an ally to our mission of stopping Anwir. It helped that Anwir was so occupied with training and bringing you to the city at full power, that he forgot about his citizens, so we were able to move them out gradually. It took a lot of teleporting, but we were able to get most of them here. Some remained hidden in their homes in the hope that this would all go away.

"That is very honorable, Kedron," I said.

He shrugged and tried to hide his smile, but he failed. Then he straightened in his saddle. "All was going well within the forest, but they weren't used to surviving outside of the luxuries they'd been given, so we set up a small settlement within one of the caverns just on the forest's edge. We proceeded to guide a group at a time into the Kingdom of Air where Queen Eteri had soldiers meet us. The harsh terrain of the mountains is dangerous, and a large group would have caused avalanches or attracted large predators, so a group of soldiers helped them travel up to the City of Ilmari. We have one last group to move. Senna is there now with the remaining Dragonheirs."

"The remaining Dragonheirs?" I asked in disbelief. Was he serious?

"Yes. I've been teleporting them here one at a time while the Dragoncouncil was occupied with you." No words could ever describe the admiration I now had for Kedron. I was forever in his debt.

Calian called to us from over his shoulder and beckoned us over to a large group of trees. Through the trees was a large, weathered rock wall with an opening just wide enough for our horses to pass through.

We entered into its dark and dreary mouth. The light faded gradually into nothing but thick darkness. The horses stopped abruptly, refusing to venture any further. I held my hand, but I couldn't even make out its shape. I conjured a beam of light to guide our way.

Calian held up his hand. "We must stop here. The horses will not be able to go further. Soon the floor will drop, and we'll have to climb down to get to the inner chamber."

The cave's atmosphere was thick and moist, making it somewhat difficult to breathe. I could feel the air stick to my lungs when I inhaled deeply. Before us stood towering columns and pools of water. Jagged rocks sculpted by time sat on the cold, dank floor of the cave as well as protruded out from the walls that were adorned with rough textures and layers of sediment.

He was right about the horses needing to stop. The further back we went, the shorter the ceiling of the cave got to the point where I hunched over to keep from hitting my head. The silence was penetrated by our breathing and the soft echoes of our footsteps. I was forced to use my free hand to hold the wall so that I wouldn't slip and fall when walking downward into the depths of the cave. My light flickered from my lack of concentration.

"How much further?" I asked.

"Almost there," Kedron responded. Several steps more and the path widened, the ceiling heightened, and the slope evened out. We'd reached a large chamber where numerous lanterns sat on rocks or hung to the walls. Approximately twenty people sat on the cavern floor or laid on bedrolls. Others chatted near a large campfire that illuminated most of the chamber, and an animal I couldn't make out roasted above it. I eased my way into the crowd but gasped loudly.

"What is it?" Calian asked. He crouched defensively and looked around.

"Some of them…They're…"

"Cultists," Kedron finished.

A woman drew closer to me. "I told you the cultists were not the enemy," she said. She pushed her hood back, revealing her face. It was Senna.

"Yes, you did," I admitted. I swore her eyes glowed brighter.

"You've been taught to fear them from the Dragoncouncil. The very council that wants to erase humanity from the six kingdoms. We do not want to see that happen," she explained.

"But they still tried to kill me."

"My people were instructed to obtain or kill Calian Westbow, a member of the Dragoncouncil who was tasked to train you. They failed…obviously." It could have been my imagination, but her eyes glowed brighter. I guessed she was not accustomed to failure of any kind. "And now we know that he is not the enemy either," she finished.

A voice beyond Senna spoke. "It's true, Emera." Senna stepped aside revealing Morwen. Fin stood next to her, and beyond him, Erjon and Avani engaged in conversation. Once they noticed who Morwen spoke to, they rose from their seats and rushed over. Well, Avani rushed over. Erjon meandered.

Morwen hugged me, and her chin hung over my shoulder as she wept. "I thought you were dead," she cried.

"I thought you were dead!"

"I think we all thought we all were dead," Fin chimed in. Morwen let go of me, and he swooped in, lifting me up into the air and twirling me around. "It's so good to see you're here, Em." He lowered me to the cave floor. Erjon had now joined our little reunion.

"All the Dragonheirs are here," he said. "Well, *almost* all." None of us had to be mind readers to know he talked about Elio. Heat rose into my cheeks. Just the thought of Elio caused flames to ignite from my fingers. Not only that, but the temperature in the room lifted to an unbearable warmth.

"Calm down, Em," Fin said. He lowered his head in shame, "He fooled us all." After a quiet moment, he lifted his eyes to Calian. Everyone else followed his gaze. Calian just shrugged, the first movement he'd made since we'd entered the chamber.

"Anwir is an excellent teacher," he said.

"That is no excuse for my ignorance," Fin responded. I could see the lump forming in his throat. "I'm so sorry, my friend," he choked. He walked quickly to Calian, and they embraced. It was a heartfelt moment. I might have teared up, but I was still spitting mad from the mention of Elio's name. Stupid Elio.

"You must be hungry," Erjon interrupted, and Fin let go of Calian. "Please, eat." Was he actually being nice to me? He waved his hand out and bowed slightly, motioning toward the campfire. Citizens of the City of Nimerah were eating from small bowls around it. My stomach grumbled.

I picked up the first piece of freshly cooked meat just in time to face Morwen standing beside me. "I supposed it's your turn to tell me what happened to you," I said between bites of meat. I thought about asking her about the meat, but I decided against it. I didn't want to know what I was ingesting.

"No one was prepared for a Dragon, Em. Everyone did the best they could. Even Rehema…" her voice caught in her throat. She took a deep breath and forced herself to continue. "Even Rehema fought valiantly. I was with her at the end, and I held her hand as she took her final breath. She was smiling."

It gave me a sense of peace knowing that Morwen guided Rehema into the Dragonplane of Existence. I sat my bowl down and placed my hand on Morwen's knee. "She is at peace now," I assured her. "My Dragonmother saw to it." She laid her hand on mine and rested her head on my shoulder. It was what she needed to hear, so hopefully, I had eased her mind. I glanced at Fin who stood by the fire, warming his hands.

"Avani and I were taken as prisoners at the gate," he said, his back to us.

"I was taken just after I left you and Elio at the mountains," Erjon added, grabbing his bowl of meat he'd placed on a nearby rock. A scowl sat on his face. He'd been bested, and he didn't like it.

"What about the soldiers from the camp?"

Pain reflected in Morwen's eyes. "We discovered later that most of them were killed."

They'd died for me. Someone they barely knew.

Erjon interjected, "Some did survive. Those who did have already moved ahead." A small comfort. I would speak with them when we got to the Kingdom of Air."

"And we owe our rescue to those two," Morwen said, pointing at Senna and Kedron who now stood toward the opening of the chamber. I stood from my boulder and walked to them. Their heads bowed together as they conversed, probably planning their next move. Whispers from the other people in the chamber filled the air as I passed them. They all hunched into each other, trying to speak so that I wouldn't hear them. It was impossible with my Dragonheir hearing, but I didn't tell them that.

"Daughter of Chaos."

"Daughter of Nimerah."

"Our Savior."

I flinched at the last word: Savior. I was no savior. Still no chaos blessing for this Dragonheir.

I ignored their comments. "Thank you," I told Senna and Kedron when I reached them. "I don't know what I can ever do to repay you for what you've done here."

Senna took my hand. They were soft, yet cool to the touch. "We only ask that you help us stop Anwir. We all have friends and family that are human. They deserve to live just as much as we all do."

"Agreed," Kedron said, nodding.

"I'll do whatever I can," I assured them.

"That's all we ask," Senna replied.

*   *   *

The ascension to the mouth of the cave was still pitch black regardless of it being morning. I wanted to check on Zari while the others stirred and prepared for the day. She and Dhruv had ventured out into the forest with the other horses the previous night, and I wanted to make sure she was okay. After feeding her an apple and letting her know how everyone was doing—she was so relieved that Morwen was safe—I stepped into the early morning air. It was crisp and clean with no trace of humidity yet. I stood there, breathing in the forest's scent of pine and dirt. The earthy fragrance was soothing.

But not for long.

Footsteps crunched the fallen leaves and twigs on the ground. I crouched low near a tree, making myself less visible. The footsteps became more audible the closer they got to me. I held my breath and peeked around the tree and saw Calian looking into the sky beside a mammoth of a tree, his arms stretched into the air to loosen his muscles. Panic consumed me, and I froze. Was this really Calian? Or was this Elio? Hadn't I seen Calian talking to Fin when I slipped out to visit Zari?

I shook my head, dislodging my paranoia.

I sized up the man before me to see any tell-tale signs that he was actually Elio. After a few minutes, he flexed his hands, interlocking his fingers and stretching them outward. He extended his arms in front of him, and I watched fire slowly come to life in his hands. He twisted and turned his hands, letting the fire dance between his fingers. Then he held the fire and let it burn higher and higher until it reached the top of the tallest tree. My mouth gaped open at the sheer power he had. His flames when I first met him were wondrous to behold, but this was something else.

"Spying on me?"

I looked up to see Calian towering over me. I stood and wiped the newly formed sweat from my palms onto my pants.

"I didn't know someone else was out here with me. I was just trying to be cautious. Besides, I wasn't sure if you were…well, you."

"Ah," he said and nodded. "That's fair."

I pointed to his hands. "First time using magic in a while, huh?"

"That noticeable?"

"Took a minute for it to gather momentum."

He looked down at his hands and studied them for a minute. "They poisoned me in the cell. I couldn't use any Dragonmagic while I was there," he said softly, his voice barely a whisper. His face wore the remnants of pain and sorrow.

"Calian, I've been wondering. If Elio is the Dragonheir of Vukan…Then what are you?"

"I don't know," he admitted.

A sense of awkwardness stifled the air. "I'm sorry," I finally told him.

"You have nothing to be sorry for. I let down my guard." He straightened his back and his chest rose. "It won't happen again." The finality of his words strengthened my confidence. This was a man beaten, starved, and drugged by the person he had once called father. If anyone was going to see the downfall of Anwir, it was Calian. Revenge was a bittersweet poison.

I turned to walk away and leave him with his thoughts.

"Wait," he said. I hesitated and turned to face him.

"Yes?"

"I was Anwir's pride and joy. He sighed and leaned against a neighboring tree, crossing his arms. "He trained me to fulfill the prophecy because he said it was my duty. He even made me a captain, and I ate it all up. He saved me from a life on the streets, so in my mind, I owed him my life. I went along with everything he and the Dragoncouncil told me. I trained. I learned all there was to know about our history, and I perfected my Dragonmagic. I sought to fulfill the prophecy…well, his interpretation of the prophecy."

I could hear the hurt in his tone, and it killed me. I wanted nothing more than to run to him and hold him, but I remained where I stood.

"According to Anwir, the only way to bring peace and balance to the kingdoms is to resurrect Amram and eliminate all the humans. Amram believed humans to be inferior creatures that should never have existed. He only tolerated them because Nimerah loved them so much, and Amram loved Nimerah. Deep down, Amram believed the only way for Dragons and Dragonborns to prosper was to exterminate them. He grew his army tenfold and had his daughter lead it. The humans would have been exterminated if it weren't for Nimerah."

"Valda was his General," I whispered.

Calian nodded. "Anwir didn't know about Valda at the beginning. The plan was to get you to believe in his cause and carry it out. I was his method of doing that. Once he saw that I was second-guessing what he wanted to accomplish, he searched for other means to carry out his plan. That's when he met Valda. Then she found Elio, who already hated me from our past, and convinced him to do what I could not." By this time, Calian paced back and forth.

"He doesn't need me, does he?"

"No. The ritual requires the blood of *any* son or daughter of a Chaos Dragon. It doesn't have to be you." He looked at me with sorrow in his eyes. I knew that look. He'd set out to protect me, not even knowing who I was, but he'd failed."

"Anwir will stop at nothing until he has the blood of the six Dragonheirs. He thinks Amram will finally bring an age of prosperity to Dragonborn. But only the strong Dragonborn are worthy enough to live. He believes lesser

Dragonborn—meaning those without formidable Dragonmagic—should be moved into servitude." Air blew into my mouth which gaped open in shock.

Calian didn't finish his thought because a figure stepped out behind the large trees.

"Surprise," Elio said.

I hurled a force of wind so strong that it threw him back into the tree behind him. His back hit the tree with such pressure it nearly knocked him out cold. He fell to the ground face first and coughed profusely. Out of the corner of my eyes, I saw Calian's expression morph from shock to awe to hate. Elio's coughing became laughter as he got to his hands and knees.

He threw a palm up just as I readied myself with an icicle. "Wait!" he said.

Calian stepped forward. "I don't think so," he said. He threw a large fireball the size of Elio's head. Elio rolled out the way as the fire slammed into the tree. The bark sizzled from the hole now in the middle of the tree trunk.

"I know what you're thinking," Elio wheezed. He was still breathless from hitting the tree.

I called to my earth magic. Vines sprouted from the forest floor and wrapped Elio into a cocoon of thorns. He thrashed about, trying to free himself from their grip, but it only made matters worse. Thorns cut into his clothes and skin. Blood began to drip from his body to the vines. He yelped in pain as the vines suspended him into the air. I walked closer and positioned myself right at eye level.

"I don't think you do," I snarled.

Elio's eyes widened, and he looked to Calian for help. "Please," he begged Calian. "You'll want to hear what I have to say."

"Don't look at him!" I snapped. "He can't help you. I'm the one in control here. Anything you have to say goes through me." I commanded the vines to lower him to the ground and released his neck.

His voice was now hoarse when he said, "She's coming."

"Excuse me?" Calian said.

Elio took another breath, "Valda knows you're here. She's coming."

Screams erupted from the cave.

"Correction. She's here," Elio whispered. It was probably stupid of me, but I let him go from the vines. The screams from the cave grew louder. Elio staggered back into the forest and ran before I could ask why he came to warn us.

There was no time to think. Calian and I raced back to the cave. The horses were running out along with several people.

Zari!

I'm here, Kahina. Zari came trotting up beside me. I placed my forehead on hers.

Good. Please stay with those people.

Calian was already entering the cave when Zari galloped away, Dhruv close behind her. I ran after Calian, but stopped to help the remaining people exit and escape. "Head to the Kingdom of Air!" I shouted. "Don't look back! Just run!" Many nodded as they held their loved ones and ran to the edge of the forest. I turned my attention back to the cave where I could hear fighting. Valda was in there with the other Dragonheirs. I had to get to them. It was me she wanted, not them.

A sense of urgency kicked in, and I stopped at nothing until I got to the chamber. Valda was backed into a wall, the other Dragonheirs spread out in an arc before her.

Morwen blasted Valda with a geyser of water, but she just threw up flames that evaporated Morwen's water.

Erjon attempted to lift Valda from the floor with his wind, but she countered with wind so strong, everyone was propelled backward. I heard Avani's scream of pain as she fell at an angle on her arm. Valda winked at me and snapped her fingers. We instantly found ourselves outside the cave. She'd teleported us all at once.

"There," she said. "That's better. It was just too dark and drab in that awful cave." She brushed her hands together. "Now, it's time for some fun."

"No," I said.

"No?" she asked. She tilted her head to the side, trying to decipher my motives.

"You want me, not them. Let them leave unharmed, and I'll go with you."

She clicked her tongue. "Emera, darling. You're so naive. I'm not here for you…or them." I didn't understand what she meant. "We have everything we need to resurrect my father. In fact, Anwir is performing the ritual right now. I'm just here to clean up…Loose ends and all." She threw her hands out and a blast of chaos magic erupted from her toward us all. I threw myself in front of the blast, hoping to save as many of my friends as possible.

"No!" I heard Morwen scream. She kept screaming until suddenly, she was silent.

I opened my eyes and found myself hovering above the ground. I wasn't dead, which came as a surprise to me.

"How?" Valda growled.

I took a breath and mentally prepared myself for another blow, letting peace and tranquility release within me. I threw up a wall of magic. Valda sent a strong wave of magic, but it couldn't penetrate my shield.

"No! You cannot be stronger than me!" Valda screeched. With pure evil in her eyes, she pulled her arms into her core, gathering more chaos magic.

I placed my hands on my chest and let them rest there. The tranquility morphed into a build-up of energy that seized my magic and hastily took over my body. The old me would have panicked, but the new me didn't. I thought of my father and his warm laughter that always made me feel safe. I thought of my mother and her kind spirit that always made me feel special. I felt stronger and ready to take control of my destiny.

Hovering there for a little while, my magic unleashed itself a little bit at a time. Violet chaos magic sprouted from my core and wrapped around me like silk ribbons.

Rehema's voice whispered in my ear, "I have every bit of faith in you," she said, and a sense of peace filled my core. I relaxed, and the ribbons grew longer and longer, curling around me and then shooting into the sky where they burst, creating a powerful wave that rattled the trees and shook the ground. Everyone below me fought to remain standing.

Still wrapped in a cocoon of chaos, I slowly lowered to the ground. My feet connected to the floor one foot at a time and rested there softly. I opened my eyes and exhaled, feeling a sensation of being reborn. The cloud of chaos magic that surrounded me gradually evaporated. That's when I saw her standing before me. Did the other see her as well? No. They were frozen in place, expressions of wonder set on their faces. Valda dropped her arm, looking bewildered. She hadn't expected this.

"For you, my daughter of Chaos. For your unwavering strength and willingness to sacrifice yourself for those you love," a new voice said. Nimerah, my Dragonmother, had blessed me.

I threw out my arms, launching a force of chaos magic so strong it knocked Valda back into the cave. She flew backward, screaming until her body met the jagged rocks. A piercing pain-filled shriek echoed throughout the cave. I stalked inside with violet spheres of chaos energy hovering above my palms, expecting to see her getting up to her feet and healing injuries.

But I was wrong.

I found her writhing in agony, her body impaled on a sharp, slender rock that jutted out from the cavern floor. She no longer screamed but made gurgling noises from the blood that spilled from her mouth.

"You think this over?" She spit blood. "It has just begun."

I didn't say anything. I just backed away, watching her thrash her arms in an attempt to free herself. She tried to change her form, but the rock through her stomach and loss of blood made it impossible. I looked at her one last time. Our eyes met, and she knew. They widened, and for the first time since I'd known who she was, there was fear in them.

I turned and walked a few paces outside of the cave then faced it one last time. I brought my arms up and let the chaos magic fill my core and spread to every fiber of my being. The ground rumbled and the cave began to tremble. I dropped my arms, and the cave crashed in on itself. I pivoted away and walked back to the gaping expressions of those I'd just saved.

*　　*　　*

"Have I told you how much I'm jealous of your eyes?" Avani asked.

"Only like a thousand times," I chuckled.

"They're beautiful, Emera," Morwen added.

I held the mirror to my face for another minute and absorbed my eyes of chaos. The dark pupils stood in stark contrast against the deep purple of my irises. Specks of silver twinkled throughout the mixture of dark purple, lilac, and blue. They twinkled in the reflection, and I felt more at one with my magic. I placed the mirror on a nearby table and spread my arms and legs out on the beautiful gray velvet settee of Queen Eteri's formal sitting room. Beautiful tapestries of gray and silver depicted mountain rangers, starry skies, and swirls of wind and clouds. Soft furniture with gray velvet upholstery was strategically placed around the room so that all visitors had a view of the queen. Avani, Senna, Morwen, and I were lounging, enjoying fruit, meats, cheeses, and wine. We didn't know where the men had gone off to, and we didn't care.

The Kingdom of Air rested within the mountains, its palace extending high into the clouds. I looked out the window to see the evening sky through the wisps of the moving clouds. The sun was below the mountaintops, and the first signs of night had come to blanket the world with its stars. I cherished the sight and the moment with the women in the room. I might not have known them for long, but the light, airy feeling in my heart told me we were destined to stay connected for the rest of our lives. The only one missing was Rehema.

A quiet knocking on the door tore my attention to the front of the room. Calian rushed in with Fin following closely. My good mood faltered a fraction because I still wasn't quite used to Calian being himself again, and his sudden appearances made me restless sometimes. I couldn't shake the memories of my time with Elio.

"We have news of a Dragon attack," Fin exclaimed. He was out of breath, so he placed his hands on his knees and bent over to recover his breathing.

I sat up and looked at Calian.

"Dragongod Amram has been resurrected," he said. "The City of Nimerah has fallen."

The room fell into a dead silence. They all looked at me.

"We need to find Nimerah," Senna said. It was the logical next step, but no one knew where she was. I shook my head. I had to tell them I didn't know.

Before I spoke, Calian grabbed my hand and brought it to his lips.

"We will find her," he whispered, and he pressed his lips tenderly to the back of my hand; the first intimate touch we shared since seeing his Dragonmate wings.

That touch must have been what I needed because the memory of Nimerah's last words to me resurfaced.

Go home, Emera. Go home, my daughter of Chaos.

"I know where she is," I said, my voice barely a whisper.

"And where would that be?" Calian asked.

I looked at Morwen.

"Home."

ABOUT THE AUTHOR

From an early age, Sarah Edgerton had an active imagination, creating stories, make-believe worlds, and songs. Now, she is using that creativity to share stories with others.

Sarah currently lives in Kansas with her husband, Michael, and their two children, Dexter and Penelope. The family has a dog named Hugo and a cat named Ari. When not pursuing her writing career, Sarah teaches at her local middle school.

Sarah considers herself to be a geek. She loves Star Trek, The Mandalorian, and Marvel. If she is not reading or writing, she is watching movies and television shows, traveling, training for half marathons, or shopping.

For more information, including new book announcements, please go to www.sarahedgerton.com.

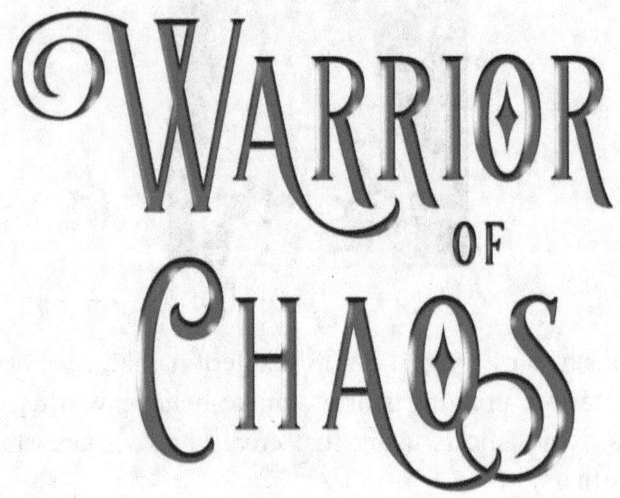
WARRIOR
OF
CHAOS

9 7989886 03603